IRIS

Also by Jean Marsh

THE HOUSE OF ELIOTT
FIENNDERS KEEPERS

JEAN MARSH

IRIS

ST. MARTIN'S PRESS
NEW YORK

 For information,
address St. Martin's Press, 175 Fifth Avenue,
New York, N.Y. 10010.

www.stmartins.com

ISBN 0-312-26182-9

First published in Great Britain by Macmillan,
an imprint of Macmillan Publishers Ltd

First U.S. Edition: July 2000

10 9 8 7 6 5 4 3 2 1

Part One

1952

Chapter One

'Don't mind if I do.' He copied her accent, exaggerating it. Most of the people at the table shrieked with laughter.

'Shrieked' was the right word, Iris thought, but what was so blooming funny?

'Don't mind if I do! Delicious. You ought to be on the radio, *ITMA*, isn't it? Funny girl, it isn't given to many to be attractive *and* amusing.'

She wriggled in her chair uneasily. What he said, the man, was what her mother called a back-handed compliment, she knew, but what was so funny? 'Don't mind if I do' was a polite and proper thing to say and just a bit saucy if you said it a bit knowing like.

The man pinched her cheek, grinning. 'What's the other one? You know, from the same show, the old char says it. "Can I do you now, sir?" '

One of the other men – he was old too, at least forty – tried to put on a cockney accent. 'Aren't they marvellous, all those sayings. Real life, you know, everybody's got a char like that, a cleaner who "does", and what would we do without them, eh?'

'Oh, do stop, Charlie. You'll be calling them the salt of the earth next.'

That was the rather frightening woman, very black hair, very blue eyes, not nice blue though. Not really dressed up but the black suit fitted her all over and, although her neckline was dull – just pearls and only one string – it all worked somehow and made the other women look too planned and uncomfortable.

Now she knew what they were going on about, the old char character in *ITMA*. She knew it was a mistake, another mistake, like 'pleased to meet you'. She was going to try and keep her trap shut till she got the hang of everything. And where was her champagne then? The man who'd imitated her had said, 'Would you like a glass of champagne?' and she would.

'As I said,' she piped up. 'Champagne? Don't mind if I do.' This time she overdid the accent, mimicking her Auntie June, and pushed her glass forward. There was a little titter but they had all gone on to something else.

The man on her left whispered, 'That, Miss Winston, is your wine glass. Burgundy, to be exact.'

The way he looked at her she knew he'd twigged. She could tell he knew all about her.

He signalled the waiter to bring a glass and champagne 'for Madam'. He seemed to find her funny to look at. He was smiling. Quite nice, but too much, that smile.

'So, Iris Winston, when did you come out? Or are you too young? Young women behave in such an extraordinary way today. They go out before they come out.'

She listened to this, interested. It was like a foreign language, what with their toff voices and everything. 'When did I come out? About half past eight. Why?'

'Not very funny, Nick, and not very kind. Take no notice of him, Iris, and drink your champagne. Happy New Year.' The woman raised her glass.

Iris raised hers then waited. The woman started drinking and didn't seem to want to clink glasses so that was probably 'not done' too.

What a most wonderful, wonderful evening; warm, nice, pretty restaurant and all she was learning. It was like stuff in olden days that young ladies would learn in Switzerland, and books and women's magazines. She'd read all about it. And the elocution teacher at school, she'd known. Finishing off school. Those who went, though, were already ladies so it was a bit of a waste. If you were posh, you must know it all, anyway. Maybe the woman was nice really and just *looked* hard and grown-up. Not much older than herself probably, though certain to be twenty or more.

She took a small sip of the champagne and then a bigger one. 'I like it. This is really nice, lovely.'

'Do you prefer it to Bollinger?'

'Stop it, Nick. Just stop it. You are a bitch, we all know that. It isn't necessary to advertise the fact.'

Iris drank again, shutting her eyes and smiling. 'If he's teasing, don't worry, I don't mind.' She finished her glass and lightly hit his arm. 'Anyhow, I don't know what he's talking about because I've never had champagne before. Yes, please.' She nodded to the waiter hovering discreetly within her eyeline with the bottle.

The woman had turned her attention to the man on her right, and was looking away from them.

'What's her name, please?' Iris indicated with an elaborate gesture. 'She's nice.'

'Betty. Betty Bailey, although she prefers to be known as Bébé.'

'Baby? Good God!'

'No, not Baby, Bébé – BB – see?'

'No, I don't. What is it and tell me slow. Baby? or BBC? I don't get it. Are you having me on again?'

'Ssh. I can't, she's too near. Tell you later. But you are Iris and I am Nicholas.'

'How do you do,' she said carefully with pride. No 'pleased to meet you'!!

'Who did you come with, Iris?'

'No one really.'

'Ah . . . I see. Then who are you going home with?'

'How do I know? Depends, doesn't it?'

'On what?'

She wondered why he looked worried. 'If anyone lives near Kilburn.'

'You live in Kilburn?'

'Yes. So it's either that or there's a bus stops outside Lyons in the Strand at half past one. Well, five and twenty to two actually but safer to say half past.'

'Oh yes. Much safer.' He was laughing at her again, but so what. 'You know I've got a feeling . . .' he looked around the table, 'that nobody here lives near Kilburn, though Charlie might be going, or could go that way if he's going out to his place in Northants.'

They both looked at Charlie, red-faced with his thinning, blond hair damp and stuck to his head showing the pink scalp beneath. He was shouting limericks across the table vainly seeking a rhyme for 'Stoke Poges', but succeeding with 'A young man in a punt'.

'Oooh, lovely. I hope he is going there.'

'On second thoughts the bus might be safer. At half past one or five and twenty to two.'

'Is he a bad driver then, when he's had a skinful?'

'My cousin is a bad driver at all times, he's a bad man altogether.'

'Doesn't seem like it.'

Around the table everybody seemed so jolly. Not like her dad who just got sad after a night out, sad and grumpy, or her Uncle Syd who liked to 'sort out a few of the lads' when in drink and, with no lads around, her Auntie Rita would do. Maybe it was beer that made the difference. 'What do you think, Nicholas? Do you think it would be a better world if everybody drank champagne instead of beer?'

He laughed and put his hand out to stop her drinking. 'That's probably enough champagne, however delicious – we will probably be having some fairly decent wine with dinner.'

'I shouldn't drink any more anyway. It's very expensive isn't it, and I don't know who's paying.' She sat back comfortably in her chair. 'This is heaven, isn't it? This room, all clean and pink and silver; someone else doing the cooking and the washing up. No worry about rations and coupons. All laughing and nice with each other and, lucky me, at the end of the table against the wall – no one to have to talk to on my right.'

'Iris, look at me.'

'Yes, Nick.'

'You look rather like Audrey Hepburn, you know.'

'Of course I do, you chump. I'm thin, no bust or not much, lots of dark eyebrows. You've got to look like somebody, haven't you, and I can't be Virginia Mayo or Diana Dors, I think she's going to be a big film star . . . Ooh, look. Lovely, shrimps and salad cream.'

'You are a dear.'

She picked up a rather thin fork after checking to see what Betty was using and started her prawn cocktail.

'I wonder who you were provided for,' he thought.

Upstairs in the club some of the party had drifted away to join other people, and two or three groups of diners from downstairs had amalgamated. Tables were pushed together; small intimacies had been formed; new love affairs seemed on the horizon. But at the same tables, the newly-made couples were flanked by boisterous men and shrill young women. Alcohol had subdued a few into glassy-eyed self-sufficiency. Mostly though, the same alcohol had produced a noisy need for company.

Iris sat on a red and white striped banquette, her back against the wall. She was nearly a part of the long table on her right and not quite part of the group at the table on her left. Without the anchor of Nick and Bébé, she was a bit at sea. Covering the awkward sense of not really belonging but not being totally unwelcome, she put on her perky 'I'm fine, don't worry about me' face. There was a small band playing such lovely tunes; all the latest and the nicest of the old ones too, the kind that made you want to cry without knowing why. Even Mum would have liked the music, they were the sort of songs she sang when doing the washing, keeping time with the scrubbing brush on the wash-board.

Turning to the right, she tried to look interested and casual. Should she join in the chat, or would that be rude without being introduced? She had turned down the offer of a drink, not knowing who would be coughing up for it. So far there was no way of joining in anyhow, talk was of the Festival of Britain and what a scream it was. Nobody had liked it but she couldn't figure out why. Holidays had come up; all of them had been abroad – France, Switzerland, even America. Food was better there than here, she learned, and they all had advice about getting round the rule of only so much money allowed to be taken. More than what Butlin's had cost Mum and Dad for a whole week. Not that that little bit of information would have interested them!

She turned back to watch the dancing. The floor was crowded so people had to dance very close, some more than others. Not much room to do anything fancy. The band was playing some songs from *South Pacific.* Maybe they'd play her favourite, one of her top favourites of all time, 'Some Enchanted Evening'. That's how she knew she would fall in love with a stranger across the room. It would needs be a small room on account of her dodgy eyes, and the stranger wouldn't fall for her if she was wearing glasses.

A very beautiful blonde girl, her chair tilted, was leaning against the wall singing softly with 'Bali Hai'. She was very pale and made up very old-fashioned; shiny dark lipstick and no eye make-up, or no doe-eyes anyway, just glossy lids. In front of her on the table was a silver compact. Once she'd had a look at herself in its little mirror and tidied her eyebrows, which was pointless as far as Iris could see. She didn't have any. Only a narrow, pale brown arch, which was drawn on. Now she picked up the compact again, opened it ever so carefully and took out a tiny silver something, maybe a spoon, like a mustard spoon. She scooped up a bit of the face-powder which was white – no wonder the girl was pale – and shoved it up her nose! How absolutely thrilling. It was like the pictures; that was definitely not face-powder. It was opium. Or something like that. The band ended 'Bali Hai' and went smoothly into 'Some Enchanted Evening'.

'Oh, lovely, that's one of my favourites,' she exclaimed.

'In that case I must take you round the floor.' The man sitting next to the blonde pushed the table out and stood up. He was huge; tall and with a big stomach. His jacket, navy blue velvet, was unbuttoned and his trousers, on red braces, were suspended above his stomach. 'Right, one of your favourites, little girl. Come on.' He pulled her up and led her to the dance-floor, putting his hand around her upper arm. 'They meet.' He stopped, looking at his hand on her arm. 'They meet, my fingers meet.' She examined her upper arm. Same old arm but he sounded quite surprised and very pleased. 'So what?' she said.

The way he took her round the floor was a bit of a surprise. Considering as how he must have weighed a ton and a half he was very light on his feet. It was a foxtrot and he did it properly. There was something a bit tangoish about the way he did his reverses but he was such a tidy dancer, there was even room for twirls. Judging it ever so neatly, as the band slowed down for the change of tune, he steered her into a corner. 'Now then, what's your name and how old are you under all that make-up?' There was no time to answer either question. The drummer started a slow drum roll, and the band-leader started counting down the seconds of the last minute of nineteen fifty-one, being shouted down by everybody, 'Fifty-eight, fifty-seven, fifty-six, fifty-five . . .' The lights were dimming; people were standing and beginning to link crossed arms all round the room. 'Thirty-three, thirty-two, thirty-one, thirty . . .' How wonderful! This was it. She was at a party. A proper New Year's Eve do. Lucky Iris!

'Better than Trafalgar Square, isn't it?' she shouted up to the man's big moon face.

'What, little girl?'

Excited, she crossed her arms and held up her hand to him, the lights were almost out now. 'Sixteen, fifteen, fourteen . . .' He took her hand and pressed it against the fly of his trousers, and bending down whispered, 'Rub my cock, little girl, and call me uncle.'

She snatched her hand away, shrinking from him.

'Three, two, one.' A huge cheer rose from the crowd, the lights were out, balloons descended from the ceiling and, after a second's pause, the crooner started to sing. 'Should auld acquaintance be forgot and never brought to mind . . .' It was next year – and she wasn't linked, would that bring her bad luck?

'Happy New Year, Iris.' Someone had taken her hand on the left; the lights were fully up again.

'Oh, thanks ever so, Nick. Happy New Year, to you and all . . . We'll take a cup of kindness yet, for the sake of auld lang syne.' Holding his hand, she beamed at everybody she could see, joining in the singing. Somebody gave her a glass of pink champagne.

'Don't look so concerned, Iris. It's on the house.'

'Oooh, how smashing.' She took a swig. 'Lovely. Here, you'll never ever guess what that disgusting fat old shit did – or what he said. I can't believe it. Cheeky bloody sod, beg pardon.'

'I saw what he did, poor you, but what did he say?'

'Well, not very nice, don't like repeating it really. Well, all right then. He said . . . he said . . .' She was laughing. 'He said . . .'

'What? Come on. If you're laughing the old shit can't be that disgusting.'

'He said . . . Oh, I am silly. I can't stop laughing. I can't get it out.'

'Is that what he said, "I can't get it out"?'

The girl had laughed till her mascara ran, and pushing her hand against her mouth had smudged the lipstick too. She was a mercurial creature, Nick thought. Downstairs at dinner she had been uncomfortable and boisterous in turn, throwing in quite bravely her comic opinions and flinching at any sense of social gaffes. Dancing she had been quite joyous, then trapped in the corner, tragic. It was as well the poor child could laugh. Beastie Baldwin, her disgusting old sod, had a taste for young meat that was usually met by the little chicks at Madame Fonselle's, runaways sometimes, but more often the children of her 'girls'.

'All right. I'm all right now. Are you ready?'

Nick nodded.

'He said, wait for it, he said, "Rub my cock and call me uncle." There, what do you think of that?'

'Oh God, Iris. What a way to start the new year.'

Those who'd paired off had gone. The Bébé woman had gone, Mr Fat had gone, thank Christ, and now she would have to go. It was gone one and she'd be hard pushed to get down to the bus unless she went right now. It would be nice to thank the man, Patrick, who'd invited her, but he'd gone too. Hardly saw him all night. But he had smiled and waved a couple of times. Never alone, she'd seen him skipping from group to group. It would be nice to stay here in the warm, but needs must . . . At the door she turned, hoping to catch Nick's eye. She could ask him about her coat; would sixpence be right for the tip? He was still standing by the piano, talking to the crooner.

'Bye bye,' she mouthed, waving.

He caught her up on the stairs. 'Of course, it's the witching hour coming up, isn't it? Five and twenty minutes to two.' Hurriedly feeling in his pocket he pulled out some money. 'Look, take a taxi.' He pushed a note at her.

'Nickelarse, Nickelarse, are you dumping me for a bitch?' the singer called from the top of the stairs. '*And* paying her?'

Embarrassed, she pushed his hand away. 'He isn't paying me and I don't suppose he'd dump a handsome bloke like you.'

'Oops, thanking you.' He skipped down the stairs. 'Why don't we, Nickelarse; me, you, and Miss Tinribs here, all go to the Corner House for breakfast and then – where do you live, darling?'

'Kilburn.'

'Perfect, darling. You can drop me off in Maida Vale and take the old man's darling on to Kilburn.'

'I would love that, if it isn't too inconvenient. Yes, please.' But Nick was disappointed, she could tell. 'Actually, no, no, I ought to go home and anyhow, I don't want to be a goosegog.'

'A goosegog?'

'A gooseberry, three's company, two's none. You two go off to Lyons' and drop me outside. I'll just about catch my bus. I'll be all right, honest.'

Nick shrugged ruefully, resigned to the fact that his on-again off-again affair with Bobby was off, for tonight. 'Iris. You are not going home on New Year's Eve on the bus. We will have breakfast, the three of us, and I will take you both home. And that is that.'

Her eyes were wide with anxiety as he collected her coat. 'Should I give her a sixpence?' she whispered. 'Or is that not enough?'

'I'll deal with it, don't worry. What's the matter? Put the coat on, for Christ's sake. It's freezing.'

'I don't feel the cold,' she said automatically.

Outside in Park Lane they waited for the door-man to bring the car.

'Funny, you camp little thing, that you don't feel the cold but you're shivering.' Bobby pulled the coat off her arms and draped it over her shoulders, lifting her hair over the collar. 'You know, you've got bona riah. And – may I ask – where did you get the coat, pray? It's a schoolboy's, isn't it? Get you, Ada. You like young trade, don't you?'

'I ate a lot of dinner, but a coffee would be smashing.'

'Not here it wouldn't, chicory and gravy browning – Camp coffee.'

'Isn't that nice then? Isn't it . . . right? That's what we have at home. Though to tell the truth, we hardly ever have coffee of any kind, it's just for show.'

She was just a little bit drunk, Nick could see, and even more ingenuous. Patrick had found her somewhere. Patrick the pander, Patrick the pusher, Patrick the pimp. Clever of him, quite a change from the usual.

'What are you thinking, Nickelarse, and what are you having? I am having – baked beans on toast and an orangeade.' Bobby ordered his simple food with a flourish, implying the choice of champagne and caviare.

'Just a coffee for me, please.'

The waitress tapped her pad impatiently. 'And sir?'

Nick didn't reply. She let the pencil drop to hang from the string at her waist and started to go.

'Two poached eggs on toast and tea.'

She turned, wrote it down without looking at him and trudged slowly away.

'Can't think why they call them Nippies.'

'Really, you two. Lyons' is known for its tea. Lyons' Tea. You don't hear people talking about Lyons' Coffee – or – Lyons' Orangeade.'

'I need the orangeade to put in my gin, darling, see?' Bobby revealed a half bottle of gin in his inside jacket pocket.

'Don't take on, Nick, please,' Iris begged. 'Tea is all I ever get at home so it's a change, even if it does taste like Bisto or gnat's piss.'

Nick smiled. 'Do you know what a putto is, Iris?'

'Is that north-country for putty?'

'It's what you look like when you're cross, a bad-tempered cherub.'

'I dunno about that.' And she didn't. Was it a compliment or not?

'What do you think, Bobby? She's a diamond in the rough, isn't she? An unpolished jewel.'

She brightened up. 'Oh, it's a compliment, is it?' She sipped her coffee. 'You're right, it does taste like gravy only bitter – that must be the gnat's piss.'

*

'How did it happen? An accident. Not a real one, chance. You see, Nick, I'd been standing at a bus-stop one evening, December, just after Christmas Eve. I go on the bus up to the West End – Regent Street preferably, somewhere up west. I love it. It's very grown up. I sit on top sometimes and smoke a cigarette nicked from my dad. Best of all is about half past six. There are more people about. Going home, going to work, going for a night out. Lots of people in pubs, men mostly, young men who can spend their money on a beer instead of the wife and kids. And quite a lot of blokes who have whisky money.'

She settled down in the comfort of the warm car. She liked telling her stories but hardly ever got the chance.

'Mostly I go on my own and just walk and look or I'll walk all sort of busy as if I was going to work or as if I was going home after work. And I imagine people looking at me, men, wanting to say, "Like a coffee, miss?" Yanks was what I used to be most interested in. "Got any gum, chum?" "Hi, honey, you wanna soda?" Nobody did. Not any of that. I don't look the sort. It was all bollocks anyway. Films. Lies from older cousins. Bollocks.

'Sometimes, three or four times to tell the truth, I went somewhere and actually ate dinner – something to eat in the evening – with my friend Beryl. I never had the money for that, so she had to pay, and she hardly ever had the money either. She worked at the Kardomah coffee place in the Kings Road. She paid for me, though, because she couldn't go out on her own, not likely. On top of that, she paid for me because when we were in the cafés, men would give me the eye, on account of my clothes I suspect, and she then would get a glance too. She didn't mind. Not at all, very practical. The places we went were nicer than pubs, yes, nicer class of people. Christ, I sound like my mum. It was Lyons' Corner House and the Quality Inn. It all worked out for her, she got what she wanted. We let a man and his mother share our table at Lyons'. He got talking to me, quite nice I suppose. He'd got a good position in the linen department at Marshall and Snelgroves. A bit weak though. A bit fat and soft, a bit . . . oh, you know. Beryl got talking to his mother meanwhile. She insisted on buying us our coffee. Beryl looked more of a safe bet than me, all in grey, medium length, touch of white – that sort of thing. Me, I'd got my circular felt skirt on, peacock blue, very tight waist, and very tight polo-neck black woolly jumper. And that was that. They got married three months later.'

'I think I'd like your felt skirt, Iris. Peacock blue! Go on.'

'Where was I? Standing at the bus-stop, right. Well, it was raining, pouring. There was a big lorry parked so I couldn't see what was coming and it was a request stop so I had to keep stepping out in the road to have a look. There were a couple of people looking for taxis. Not many about. All taken because of the rain. I popped into the road to have another look for my bus and a taxi stopped – for me! I laughed and was going to wave him on when a man came up to me, well-dressed gent. He'd been trying to get a taxi for ages, pissed off he was. So I said, "Go on, it's yours." Then the driver said, "No it ain't, it's yours, miss." He felt sorry for me I reckon because I was wet and at least the gent had an umbrella. Well, the upshot was, he pushed me in the cab and said if I dropped him off he'd pay for wherever I was going. Blimey! I was over the moon, Iris's lucky day. The driver said OK by him as long as the man saw me right. He was well-spoken, lovely clothes, a bit like George Sanders, very sophisticated. Not much time for a chat, just "Where are you going" and "awful weather", but he was looking at me, not cheeky, serious-looking. Then he asked my name, which I told him, *and*, if you please, my telephone number, which I didn't. Couldn't. Hadn't got one. I told him, in an emergency next door would take a message then we'd go to the corner telephone box and ring.

'He got out in a little street off Portman Square. Really nice, small houses, not properly paved – the street, very dinky houses, I don't know, like big dolls' houses. In any case, he kept his word. When I got home the taxi-driver told me he'd paid for the whole way and there was change. For me! He had already seen the driver all right so my divvy was three pounds. He gave it me all in half-crowns. I can tell you that was one of the best things that had happened to me, ever.

'Then, I didn't think about anything coming from it, anything else. Nothing could. He wouldn't remember my name, why should he? That's all. I hadn't said my surname even. So I went to work a couple of times when asked, a sort of snack-bar trying to be a coffee bar. I only stand in when regular staff can't. They don't consider me up to the mark, not enough "Here's your coffee – swing away haughty on your high-heels, like it or lump it" sort of thing.

'So tonight came with the family in, all listening to the wireless. There was a chance that Beryl and her young man and I would all go to the Quality Inn in Regent Street to eat our supper, with perhaps a friend of Beryl's friend, who was an assistant buyer in drapery at Marshall and Snelgrove. And then we would all walk down to Trafalgar Square. Nothing said definite but, just in case, I curled my fringe and put on a full make-up. We all sat there and bickered. Dad trying to get the reception better and making it worse, Mum moaning in advance about Dad getting a few too many pints down, Sam asking them to shut up so he could listen. I was keeping an ear open in case Beryl did come by and knock on the door. Then, lo and behold, round about eight o'clock, next door walked in, straight in to the lounge. She'd fished the key out from the letter-box.

' "Couldn't you hear me? I've been knocking for ages," she said.

'Liar. I'd been listening like a hawk. Anyway.

' "Emergency they said, a gentleman, very nicely spoken. 'Sorry to bother. Could I speak to Iris?' "

'Well, of course, it was him. "Last minute party," he said. "Dinner and dancing!"

'The car came so quick he must have known I'd say yes. Clothes were no problem because I have no clothes. I invented and hoped it would do. This is my school gym-slip, dark blue, pleated. No blouse underneath. Blue belt from Mum's mac round my hips and twinkly earrings, huge, pinned to each shoulder, see? And lots more make-up, specially doe-eyes, see?'

'Yes, indeed.'

'I didn't look like Barbara Goalen, but I'd do. There wasn't a coat in the family that would do so I took Sam's new school raincoat bought much too big and which he'd have to wear till much too small. It didn't fit but I'd carry it over my arm, all casual. If anyone mentioned it, like "Put your coat on it's cold", I'd say I never felt the cold. I'm always saying that, for the reason I never waste much money on coats. After all, you don't wear them all evening. But I do feel the cold and one day I'm going to have more than just one coat that has to do for everything, you know?

'When he saw me come out the driver started to open the door next to him but I stood my ground and waited by the rear door, the rear nearside door. I know about that from the pictures. I'd brought a Senior Service with me. Dad had been given a couple of packets for Christmas, a change from his usual roll-ups, so I lit it when we'd got up West, near where we were going. I thought I'd be smoking and sophisticated when I handed my coat to the hat-check girl – or is that only in America? Anyway, it drew quite quick, and we were held up in the crowds walking all linked and singing, at Hyde Park Corner. By the time we got to the restaurant, this'll make you laugh, more than half of it had gone and when I got out of the car, the ash had fallen all down my front, showing up of course on the navy. So, I looked like a right fag-ash-Lil. And the rest you know, Nick, you were there. Didn't we have the most lovely time?'

'Did we? What about your parents, didn't they mind, a girl of your age going out with total strangers, a man they had never met?'

'No, they didn't ask, most likely thought it was Beryl as arranged.'

'And getting back at four in the morning – that won't disturb them?'

'I won't disturb them and if I do they won't give a monkey's. I'll let myself in and, in case they hear the door, I'll pull the toilet chain so they'll think it was that.'

He waited till the heavy front doors were closing and called, 'Iris.' She turned.

'Would you like to see a show?'

She nodded and with a shy little smile, said, 'Don't mind if I do.'

Don't mind if I do. That was when he had first noticed her. Funny girl.

Chapter Two

'I GOT YOU A bloater for your tea.'

'Me? What did you get the others?'

'Bloaters. You got a funny half hour on?'

'I hate bloaters, I hate the smell. Anyway, I had my lunch at the coffee bar and because I'm new I got my break last; didn't eat till three, so I'm not hungry.'

'You ought to stand up straight, Iris, and stop pulling those faces. One day they'll be permanent. What did you have to eat?'

'Stuffed cabbage.'

'Stuffed cabbage? What did they stuff it with?'

'Christ, Mum, I don't know.'

'You don't know, and you ate it?'

'Well it wasn't stuffed with bloaters.'

'You get more like your father every day.'

'I'll take that as a compliment.'

'I've never in my life stuffed a cabbage, I don't see the point.'

'Yes, well, that's because you're not Austrian.'

'What's that got to do with it?'

'The café – is – called – the – Café – Vienna, Mum. Vienna – is – the – capital – of – Austria. See?'

'I still don't see any point in stuffing a cabbage.'

'Bloody hell!'

'Language, Iris, please.'

She wandered into her bedroom, colder in there. Buttoning up her cardigan, she went back into the kitchen. 'Is that kettle on for tea, Mum?'

'If you want to make it. I've got the ironing to do, unless you want to do it, miss?'

'Yes, I'll do it. Don't look so surprised, it will warm me up.'

The washing was suspended from the ceiling on the wooden clothes horse. Loosening the cord, she lowered it. 'On second thoughts, I'll do it tomorrow.' She folded the sheets, shirts, pillow cases, underwear and kitchen cloths neatly. 'I'll put it in my room till tomorrow.'

'And why, pray? Here's your tea.'

'So as it doesn't smell of bloaters, of course.'

Her mother banged the cup down, spilling the tea in the saucer. 'Iris, I'm warning you, no more of your lip. If you so much as mention the bleeding word bloater I'll . . .'

'Language . . .' Iris dodged the slap but couldn't rescue her tea.

'Honestly, Mum! You've knocked my tea over all the washing. All your hard work up the spout. All that washing and scrubbing, rinsing and wringing out, all that mangling, all that folding, all that . . .' Her mother's normally pallid face had two red blotches on the cheeks. 'Sorry. Honestly, Mum. I'm sorry. I'll rinse it through and iron it tomorrow.'

*

Her room was icy cold to sit in and cold to look at. Black curtains; there from the war. Green and grey wallpaper; there from forever – there from when they moved in. Bits of dark green carpet on the cracked, brown lino. One small, hard armchair covered in worn, green rexine, and yet a different green piece of material strung up on a line to conceal the hooks on the wall that served as her wardrobe. The only quite nice thing in the room was her kidney-shaped dressing table, given to her when her gran died, and in that, the drawers were missing. Used for firewood her dad said. Things must have been truly awful in those days. Not that much better today. After her lovely, most wonderful night out – nothing. Two weeks gone by. Was that it, then? Was that all she was ever going to have? New Year's Eve. NEW YEAR'S EVE FULL STOP. HERE LIES THE BODY OF IRIS WINSTON. 1934 – NEW YEAR'S EVE. R.I.P.

'Iris, Iris!'

She unlocked the door. 'What?'

'I have been knocking and calling . . . Were you asleep? Anyway, there's a note for you.' It was more of a letter size than a note. Cream paper, thick, in a stiff envelope. 'It was brought by a man – in a hat – more of a driver than a man.' Her mother hovered, too excited to hide it under her usual indifference.

'He's waiting, he's got to wait he said, either for you or a reply. Well? Well, Iris?'

'Tell him I'll be about half an hour – please.'

*

'Except for being so washed out you don't look half bad.' That's what her mother had said, but she was holding her own here, chiefly because none of the other women were under thirty. Nearer to forty – or even fifty – to look at them. They were all wives in the main, just herself and another girl weren't, although she could have been a wife like the others from the way she looked, proper and respectable, tidy. They had started off not being friendly; not rude, but not very sociable. It wasn't easy to get the hang of what was going on. She was here to make up for someone leaving; bit of an upset, it was a birthday party and nobody wanted thirteen at table. It had been a relief to sit down. The gin and Dubonnet was a mistake, or was the whisky and ginger ale a mistake? Whatever. She wasn't quite drunk, but definitely tipsy. The trouble was, standing at the bar, trying to fit in, she kept saying, 'I'll have the same,' but as everybody was drinking different things, she'd had a right funny old mixture.

They had all eased up a bit, having a laugh at her, when she'd asked the man at the head of the table, 'What sort of captain did your friend say you were? Army or navy? Or airforce?' After the laugh he'd explained, ho-ho-ho, he was a 'captain of industry'. Then she'd gone back to eating what she would call brawn but they called pâté. It kept her occupied, and she listened, waiting for someone to say something so she could join in. Some hope!

The wives across the table were talking about television. Three hundred thousand people had them, amazing, it was really catching on.

'Excuse me.' She put her elbows on the table. 'Can I ask you a question? I've never seen one, nobody I know has got one, how big is the box, please? Is it ever so big? Our radiogram at home fills up the corner of the lounge, so, if you've got to squash in all the stuff for the picture as well, it must be really big.'

'Well . . . er . . .' The woman she'd spoken to seemed a bit flummoxed. 'Ours is roughly three foot square, I'd say.'

'Right. Not bad. So, does it have the wireless, the voice part, all in with it, or does that come separate?'

The woman was laughing now but quite nice with it. 'Ours comes separate, the wireless, I mean.'

'Right, so, you switch on the picture, and the voices and music come separately out of the wireless then. If it's that complicated, in my opinion it's never going to catch on.'

'No, no, dear girl.' The captain of industry spoke slowly and clearly. 'The television set comes with picture and sound all in the same container. The sound synchronized with the picture – is that clear?'

Trying to imagine it, she stared at him intently. 'Are you telling me that people speak as you're looking at them, and they are in the television place, and all that comes out into the air and goes into three hundred thousand boxes all at the same time?'

'That's exactly what happens. You just ask your boyfriend, he'll explain.' He looked around the table to identify somebody who might be her boyfriend. 'Or your father.'

She looked too. Her father? How could he be here?

And she hadn't got a boyfriend. 'Just a minute.' Confused, she waved her hands to get his attention. 'Where are the others, please?' She hadn't noticed before but there were only ten people.

'Others?'

'Yes, Patrick said I was a last-minute thing. Someone had dropped out, or pushed off really after an argy-bargy, and it made it only thirteen, and *I* was the lucky fourteen.' They were all giving her a real once-over now – not talking, not drinking, not eating. 'See?' she said, not with much hope that they would.

'Aah, I think I see.' The woman opposite smiled gently at her. 'You are with the wrong party . . . Iris . . . was it? I did wonder, so did you, didn't you, Deirdre?'

Iris sat frozen. 'I'm ever so sorry. How awful of me. Patrick said everybody was at the bar and that I . . .'

'Don't worry, dear. Robert, have a word with Mr Stavras. Find out where this child should be.'

'But, I feel, well, so terrible. I've eaten all that pâté and toast – *and* the drinks at the bar. Let's see. I had three shorts, yes. I must give you something towards it. Would half a crown cover it, do you think? Oh, I do beg your pardon.' Near to tears she stood up. 'Beg pardon everybody, please. I'd best just go home. I've spoiled absolutely everybody's night out.'

'Not ours. I have enjoyed talking to you.' The captain beckoned the head waiter.

'You're only saying that, being polite.'

'No, no.'

'I've been the odd man out here and brought bad luck to someone else.'

'You should be upstairs, miss, with the Welford party.' The waiter led her away. Through the laughter that exploded behind her she heard someone say, 'Poor child, a lamb being led to the slaughter.'

First thing she wanted was a drink. 'Thanks,' she said, accepting the wine being offered by a rather floppy-looking young man. 'Where were you sitting before? I don't remember you, sweetie-pie.' He put his clammy hand on her shoulder, sliding his fingers under the cap sleeve and fingering the strap of her brassiere. 'I usuary, usarilly, notice all the crumpet.'

Wriggling away from him, she topped his glass of wine up. 'Here. Cheers! What's your name?'

'Yes, what's in a name?'

'Well, my name's Iris.'

'Oh, aaah, *you* are for *me*. You – friend of Patrick's?'

'Yes, why?'

'He, he said.' The boy drank the wine, a little dribble of red staining his chin. 'Can't remember what he said. What's your name?'

'It's Iris.'

He put his face close to hers, frowning. 'Cyrus? What? Bloody funny name for a piece of crumpet. Muffin. Muff-diver, that's me. Never understood crumpet. Crump-diver? No.' She shifted slightly along the banquette. 'Lizzie was here at first, and then she wasn't. She pissed off – cross. Not pissed though. Oh no. I was, I think so, and 'cause *I* was pissed, *she* pissed off. And . . . I was all alone. Bad luck.' Gloomily, he lifted the bottle of wine. 'It keeps going, this wine.'

'Cheer up.' Taking the bottle from him, she gently

eased him back, but he grabbed his glass and drained it.

'So I decided to get drunk. And tell you what, I have very nearly succeeded.'

He picked up a napkin and covered his mouth.

'Quick, take him to the gents', he's being sick.' She prodded the young man sitting opposite with one arm hanging heavily on a girl's shoulder.

'Oh, Christ. One good reason never to dine with children who don't know how to drink.'

Watching him stagger across the room holding his friend, drinking wasn't an art *he'd* accomplished either.

What a bloody evening. Standing outside the restaurant in the freezing cold waiting for a taxi, holding up this horrible boy smelling of the vomit that flecked his dark jacket. There was a bit on his tie like a slice of carrot. At a distance it could look like a tie-pin. Yes, a truly bloody evening. Too much to drink, only half a dinner and that eaten with people who must think she had escaped from Coney Hatch.

The doorman came running back, a taxi following him. 'Here you are, miss.'

The driver yelled out of the window, 'He ain't going to be sick in the back of my cab, I hope.'

'He's already been sick. He brought up everything from soup to sweet, probably chucked up his breakfast too.'

'That's all right then, miss. Hop in, and open the windows, love.'

'Oh, hell. I don't even know where he lives!'

'Not your boyfriend, then?' The doorman was concerned.

'No, he isn't, thanks very much.' She gave the boy a little shove.

'Careful now. You're new to this, aren't you?' The doorman opened the taxi door and helped her push the swaying figure inside and joined them in the back. 'Right you are, Sonny Jim. Let's see who you are.' He took a wallet from his inside pocket, carefully avoiding the stained exterior. 'Meet Francis Andrew Horton-Rigby, 43 Cranleigh Mansions, Little Seymour Place. That's off Baker Street, isn't it, driver?'

'Do me a favour, matey, I know where Little Seymour Place is. I know where Seymour Place is. I know where every bloody Place is.'

'That's all right, then, but watch your language, please, in front of the lady.'

Tempted as he was to say, 'Which bloody lady,' he felt sorry for the poor girl, only a kid, lumbered with this upper-class drunken twit. 'All right, all right, can we get going now?'

The doorman was riffling through the wallet, counting the notes. 'I'm just sorting out your bunce, mate. What's your name, miss?'

'Iris. Listen, thanks so much for doing all this.'

'I can't call you Iris, can I? Not when you arrive with your smart friends like Mr Horton-Rigby here.'

'You won't ever see me arrive with him, not in a month of Sundays. My name is Iris Winston.'

'And where do you live, Miss Winston?'

'Kilburn, and what's your name?'

'I'm known as Jim here, but my real name is Donald. One of us doormen is always called Jim and the other is called Jack, whatever your real name is, then all the customers know where they are, see?' He took a couple of notes from the pile of money.

'Here, Jim, you can't do that . . . you know, he might . . .'

'Don't worry. I'm not taking enough to notice, more than my job's worth. Just enough to cover the taxi and my tip for my time. What do you reckon, driver? Baker Street and then Kilburn. You can nip over to the Edgware Road, straight up to Kilburn High Street . . .'

'I know where Kilburn is, mister doorman. If I promise not to tell you how to open your doors, will you leave out telling me where everything is and how to get there? Let me tell you, I been cabbing since the war ended and I know every street in London from Petticoat Lane to Berkeley Square.'

'. . . Right, so, a fiver cover it?'

'Yes. Handsomely.'

The porter at the mansions showed no surprise at the condition of the tenant of number forty-three. He silently helped the taxi-driver haul him into the lift. With a voice posher than anyone she'd ever heard, including film stars like David Niven, even the king, he said, 'And where does Madame live?'

Before she could say 'Kilburn', the driver chipped in, 'Madame lives in Hendon.'

The porter had his back to them in his little room but they could see him unlocking a cash-box. He counted out three green one-pound notes.

'Ah, well, sir, that will see the young lady to Hendon but it won't see me back, will it? Stands to reason.'

Unsmiling, the porter removed another pound. 'Good-night.' The heavy, highly-polished, mahogany doors closed.

'Not bad, eh, Iris Winston? Cheer you up after a lousy night out? Half each, what do you say?'

'Lovely. What a lark.'

While she was waiting for the kettle to boil, she opened the small top window in the larder. If the door was left open all night, it would help clear the smell of bloaters. She could nip up early and shut it before Mum found out. No wonder it stank! There was a cold bloater, uncovered, sitting on a plate. Her 'nice' bloater. Which would be worse, hot or cold bloater? It was going to go anyway, hot or cold. The sash on the lower window was broken, it had to be propped open with the rolling pin. Out in the back alley, it was dark and silent. Not for long though. When the bloater hit the dustbin on the far side of the alley, cats slunk out of the night. Skinny, bony, half-wild, tabbies and gingers, black and white and even once-posh long-haired Persians. Very few had domestic lives or homes to go to. They had either been abandoned during the war or survived the bombs that had killed their owners and destroyed their houses. Poor things. One bloater wouldn't go far. There was the usual silvery, slimy trail left on the larder floor by the vile little insect correctly called silverfish. All fish were a bloody nuisance, except in restaurants, but better by far than ants, an army of which kept attacking the Golden Syrup tin.

She filled the old stone ginger-beer bottle with hot water. Although it was cold out, it was a nicer cold than in the flat. She got into bed wearing socks, with her nightdress over her knickers and vest. After the ginger-beer bottle had warmed her feet, she cuddled it, feeling the heat through the layers of cotton and winceyette. Would she be asked out again? Would it be held against her, turning up late? Would that silly drunken boy find out his wallet had been raided? Would the man she'd met on New Year's Eve – Nick – remember her and take her to a show? Would she ever go to Les A again, the lovely, beautiful, warm, nice-smelling restaurant? And would that doorman one day help her out of a taxi and 'Miss Winston' her? She fell asleep before the hot bottle cooled, convinced she'd had a really lovely evening.

Chapter Three

NEAR TO TEARS, her mother's face was prettier, gentle, the tight little mouth eased out of its perpetual bad temper. Her watery, blue eyes were casting about, frightened and anxious.

'I dunno what I done wrong, I just asked him for my house-keeping, that's all. As per usual. If I don't get it off him straight away, half of it would be gone on beer and the bookies, you know your father.'

'He doesn't drink that much, Mum.'

'It isn't only as how much he drinks, it's treating, that's what he's like – the big "I am". It's pints all round when he's got a few quid.'

'It's how you ask for it, Mum.'

'Oh yes? My fault now, is it? You always took your father's side.'

Iris ignored this.

It was Thursday, the day her father was paid. Everything as usual except for the way he pushed off. Her mother always stood at the front door when she heard his key in the lock. No 'Hallo', no kiss, only her hand outstretched and, 'Give me my house-keeping,' snapped at a man tired from a long day's labouring on building sites. Usually he handed over his pay packet there and then in the hall and, while she counted it, made some wry remarks like, 'Oh, hello my darling, you must be tired. I've made your favourite steak and kidney pudding. Come in my love, sit down, let me get you a cup of tea.' Then she would grudgingly hand him back thirty shillings – his spending money. Spending money, most of which went straight to the money-lender in Chancery Lane to service his pathetic debt.

'Mum, I've got to get ready.'

'Oh, never mind me. You get ready, Iris. You get yourself ready for whatever it is you get up to. Don't mind me, you've got your life ahead of you, mine is over and done with. Now your father's pushed off . . .'

'Mum! He's only been gone twenty minutes, probably gone for some fags and the *Evening News* for the racing.'

'You don't care about me. Your brother hardly notices I'm here except when he's hungry. I'm going to get myself a live-in job where my life and my money are my own.'

It wasn't about money, all this, not all of it anyhow. She was punishing him for Winnie Taylor. And she, poor cow, was the one who suffered just as much from the punishment. She wasn't a cold woman naturally, her mum. There was a time when she laughed and was singing when she came home from work. She would hold her hand and skip with her to the shops.

'I could get a good job easy enough, it wouldn't take me long, pack my bags and be off. I'd be gone days I expect before you'd even notice.'

'Mum! Please, shut up!'

'Don't speak to your mother like that, that's not the way you were brought up, I'm glad my mother isn't alive to hear you. It doesn't run on my side of the family, we always sat down together to our dinners all eight of us and none of us spoke until we were spoken to but young people today . . .'

In her pause for breath Iris filled in, 'Young people today have no respect for their elders . . . wait till you're my age . . . etcetera etcetera.'

'You'll laugh on the other side of your face one day, my girl . . .'

'Mum!' she shouted. 'I've got to get ready. All right? I'm asking you to come in while I get ready. All right?' She opened the door of her bedroom. 'Come in and sit down, for Christ's sake.'

'Language,' her mother muttered automatically. 'Well, I will, seeing as how you asked.' She tried to suppress a smile but failed, the little crooked teeth with one missing at the side of her mouth embarrassed her and, as usual, she covered her mouth with the back of her hand, a gesture that made her look like a geisha; feminine and insecure. 'Where are you going – if I might ask? To the pictures? And then the Corner House for a little something and a drink?'

Her mother's imagination produced what she would have liked herself and, thinking about it, she perched on the edge of a stool, crossing her long, slim legs. Even the thick beige lisle stockings couldn't disguise their elegance. Tilting her chin, she looked past Iris putting on her make-up at the mirror to the window, and beyond. 'Nice. A nice evening out. Jeanette MacDonald and

Nelson Eddy in *Smilin' Through* at the Gaumont, Leicester Square. Meet him outside Swan and Edgars maybe. Cross Piccadilly Circus, stroll down the Haymarket, a drink at Finch's – just the one – and then the pictures. I'd have to take my hat off of course . . .'

Iris powdered the thick, pale foundation and started to create her 'doe eyes'. She breathed on the black crayon to warm it up. Her mother was still living in her imaginary evening. 'After the pictures, he'd say, "Oh, don't put your hat back on, Miss Bellington, your hair is so lovely, it shouldn't be covered."' Patting her thick, dark brown, wavy hair, she adjusted the tilt of her non-existent hat. 'We'd have poached eggs on toast and a pot of tea, he might have a light ale. The talk would be all lovely and friendly, and a few laughs with our cigarettes.' She blew an imaginary smoke ring.

Iris could see her in the mirror. Well away she was, and here *she* was, crying. Thank God she hadn't started on her mascara.

'Aren't I silly?'

'Well, you're a day-dreamer, Mum, always have been. It isn't good for you, you know. If you do it too much real life is bound to be a let down.'

The hopeful little look in her mother's face had dimmed, the corners of her mouth resumed their usual discontented droop. 'What have you got if you don't dream, eh? A lifetime of disappointments and betrayals, of . . . of . . .' She looked out of the window again but the wistful dream of 'a nice night out' had gone. All she could see now was the drab alley, cluttered with dustbins and old cars, the high brick wall blocking the grey light.

'. . . Of Kilburn all dreary and dirty outside and no love inside.' She rubbed her forehead feeling the two deep lines between her eyebrows. 'I'm old, Iris.'

'Oh, Mum, for Christ's sake, you're forty, that's nothing these days.'

'Easy for you to say. Don't you dream sometimes?'

'No. Well, hardly ever, if I do I stop myself. I don't like it when the dream stops.'

'No. I reckon you don't, why should you? Your life is a dream – compared to mine.'

'Don't, Mum, please don't. Don't go down memory lane. I've heard it all before. I know it by heart. "I brought my family up single-handed after my mother died . . . I was an unpaid skivvy . . . Wasn't allowed to take up my scholarship – and what thanks did I get? A backhander from my father when he'd had enough on a Friday night – only one pair of shoes to my name . . ."'

'Sorry to bore you I'm sure.' She said this with less than her normal frozen sarcasm and, though she stood as if to go, hesitated at the door.

Iris put her make-up and comb in her handbag – black patent, went with everything. 'How do I look, Mum?' She took her mother's hand. 'Sorry,' she muttered. 'What do you think?' Her belt was too tight and the stiletto-heeled shoes too small but, once there, she knew she would forget all the small discomforts.

'Well?'

'You look like death warmed up – but nice.'

'It's all the rage. You've got to be ever so pale, no mouth and lots of doe-eyes.'

'In that case you've got it down to a T.'

'You smiled! Tell you what, Sunday, after dinner, I'll do your face and we'll go up to the West End together. We'll go to the pictures, take Sam and Dad too, OK?'

'If your father comes back. Off you go then, don't worry about me. I'll be all right. Haven't read my *Woman's Own* yet. Pot of tea and a tin of pilchards on toast, listen to the wireless. Expect I'll go to bed early. Mrs Crowthorn got me to do her ironing today when I'd finished cleaning through and my back's giving me gyp. Car coming? Or are they sending you a taxi?'

'No, I'm getting the fifty-three.'

'Bus? Ooh, you have come down in the world.' Her mother was pleased, she could see. It reflected glory on the family, the taxis and cars, especially the cars because of the chauffeurs, but she was envious. Her daughter was being treated like a toff, a lady. She needed 'taking down a peg', make her see 'life isn't all roses'.

'It isn't the usual crowd, see, it's my friend, Bobby, the singer.'

'The nancy-boy? What you going out with him for?'

'It's a party, in Soho, in a club.'

'Is that why you're wearing slacks, haven't got your glad-rags on?'

'Right. This is glad enough for tonight. Ta-ra then, Mum. Don't worry about Dad, he'll come back.'

'That's what I'm worried about, my girl!'

It was a really peculiar do. Not bad, quite enjoyable in fact, but definitely out of the ordinary. Bobby said the party was being given by the brothers because one of them had just come out of hospital. For the life of her she couldn't understand why he'd asked her. There were a few men she knew by sight from Le Routier, the Dive, the usual places. And, lovely surprise, two young film stars, gorgeous, usually played servicemen who were killed in the war, that sort of type, and a couple of older ones too who took the parts of generals and top airmen who sent the others to the war. She'd recognized a very famous politician; as she knew next to nothing about politics, he must be just as well-known as the film stars. Nick was over there, drinking and laughing with one of the brothers. Were they all poofs? She hadn't realized there were so many in the world. Apart from herself there weren't many girls there. Some older, ordinary-looking women, the pale, skinny girl who kept cocaine in her silver compact, a couple of dancer friends of Bobby's. But why on earth would the brothers have all these sort of men here – they couldn't be queer themselves, after all. Now she knew who they were and what they did, it stood to reason, you couldn't have a fairy demanding 'money with menaces' or getting sent down for GBH.

'Hello, love, shove up.' The brother who'd been ill sat next to her on the padded bench. 'So you're Iris, Bobby's mate. He talks about you a lot.'

Pleased as she was that anyone would talk about her, how come that Bobby did to Steve Brown? 'Nice, I hope,' she simpered, feeling a bit out of her depth, a right idiot.

'Very nice indeed.' He lifted the fringe off her brow. 'You've got lovely minces when you let anyone see them.' His smile was friendly and nice. She didn't mind him touching her hair and if anybody had lovely minces it was him. They were very pale blue, like the paper the Co-op used to wrap sugar, and his eyelashes were long and jet black.

'When did you get out of hospital?'

'Friday.'

'You don't look at all bad considering. What did you have?'

'I got three years on each charge to run concurrently.'

She laughed. 'What? I thought you'd been in hospital.'

'Nah, I've been in the Scrubs.' The blue eyes were really taking her in, he could have been checking her over like a car or a horse, but still smiling affectionately. 'You are just as Bobby described you, and you look terrific. Not many girls do in slacks. Here, I've got an idea; have you eaten anything yet?'

The room was lined with tables covered in white cloths with loads of stuff to eat on them, anything you fancied just about. All the usual: potato salad, ham, bread and cheese, Russian salad, beetroot slices in vinegar, pickles, cakes, jellies – it looked like a cross between a wedding do at a church hall and a children's party given by some sort of 'Help the Poor Kids from the Slums of London' organization, but with no worry about ration books.

'Well, actually, I am a bit peckish.'

'Tell you what, I'll get you a nice big plate of smoked salmon to start off with, how about that?'

'Oooh, yes please, thanks, but don't you bother, I'll get it.'

'Oh no you don't, only I don't want to leave you here on your tod, all alone. You come and sit with me and my mum over there and meet the family.'

He took her hand as she rose and led her across the floor. 'You'll like my mum, and she'll take to you, I know.' He paused before they reached the table. 'You're a good girl, aren't you, Iris?' He was very close to her and though he spoke softly, his voice was strong, she wasn't sure if it was a statement or a question.

'Yes,' she said quietly, with a little laugh.

'Of course you are.' He brushed aside her thick fringe again and gently kissed her forehead.

Mrs Brown, his mother, was very nice to her, made Steve sit on one side and her on the other. Kept telling her to eat up, all the usual stuff, 'Young girls today – no figures – starving themselves – look more like boys.' Steve shrugged and gave her a wink. The food was brought over by a young boy. Iris thought they must have had a row, Steve was really quite rude to him – 'Get this, get that,' and hardly looking at him. She caught the boy's eye and tried a sympathetic little smile but he only gave her a quick glance, nasty and cold.

'How long have you two known each other?' Mrs Brown patted her hand approvingly.

'A lifetime,' Steve exclaimed. 'Right, Iris?'

'Well . . . er . . .' and taking her cue from him she said, 'it certainly seems like it.'

Oh, no. He didn't appear too pleased with that, though it got a bit of a laugh, and she wanted to please him, she liked him. He was an easy safe-feeling sort of man in his way. 'But, Mrs Brown,' she said gravely, 'I hope we *will* know each other a lifetime.' That went down a treat with him. And come to that, it went down well with everyone; Mrs Brown, his auntie, one of the older brothers across the table, everybody gave her a nice approving smile.

Steve took her hand and held it. 'That's such a beautiful thing to say, Iris. Thank you.'

The other brother gave a sudden quick look at the door and gestured to Steve, mouthing 'Go.'

'Excuse us, Iris, but we've got a little business to sort out, won't keep him long. All right? I'll send over some sweets for all you ladies, an assortment. You take care, Mum.'

The men left, trailed by the hard-faced boy.

She looked tired, his mum, and a bit pale. Her clothes, though obviously good, well cut navy costume with a pink and navy blouse, didn't fit her. They were too big and they didn't suit her either. She was the sort who'd be happier in a flowery dress and an apron.

'Business,' Mrs Brown sighed. 'They're so keen to get on, my sons, got no time for anything else.'

'Steve thinks the world of you, no question about that.'

'Maybe, maybe. You're a nice girl, Iris. It's a change to see him with someone.'

'Well . . . er . . . Mrs Brown, not much chance, where he's been.'

'Not one of them, ever, ever brings a girl home. None of them started a family yet . . .' She was talking to herself, playing with her meringue, pushing it round the plate.

Iris poured some cream on the woman's plate. 'There you go, you tuck into that. Everything will probably change now, he'll more than like go straight now. Wouldn't that be smashing? No more worry about him and prison and all that.'

The aunt muttered to the woman on her right, 'There's straight and straight.'

Mrs Brown pretended not to hear it but looked pained. Her meringue broke under the attack from her fork and became a pile of white ash and tiny chunks, like masonry after a bomb. 'Now then, Iris, you don't want to believe all you read in the papers. People are jealous. My boys are successful at all sorts of business. They're businessmen. You take this here,' she waved her arm round the room. 'This is theirs. A chain of nice butchers they've got. A lovely farm in Essex. A very respectable bookmaker's.'

'Bookmakers?'

'Yes, a bookie's, you know – horses.'

'Oh, yes, right. Isn't that wonderful. You must be so proud of them.'

'I am. And they help their own, you know. Anybody

give anyone any grief in Stoke Newington and they sort it out.'

'Are you seriously trying to tell me that Vernon Brown is queer? Do me a favour, Bobby, he's a criminal, one of London's most notorious "shakers-down". He's the Al Capone of Stoke Newington, no matter what his mum thinks. If it wasn't true, how come the *Daily Herald* prints it all over the front page, eh? And he set his little brother a fine example, I don't think, got him into trouble and more than likely let Steve take the rap for what *he* had done. A hard case, nasty piece of work.'

'Those pictures you see, Iris, that's where you get that from.'

'You tell me how a bloke who's bent gets the respect of all his . . . his gang? You've been gulled, Bobby Brighton.'

He shook his head, amused at both her language and her naïveté. 'You're a camp one, Iris. Why do you think the room is full of poofs? Do you think we're going to do a number from *Soldiers in Skirts*, as a cabaret turn?'

She laughed. 'Your trouble is you think everyone is queer, your imagination runs riot. Look at the other night at Les A, there you were with your "had him, had him, had him" all evening – and half of them were married!'

'So?'

'So you're kidding yourself, you'll be saying that nice Steve is next!'

He ignored that. 'Take it from me, Vernon Brown is as bent as a corkscrew. He's a vicious queen.'

'What about the middle one, Artie?'

Bobby shuddered, 'The black sheep. Or ram.'

She looked across the room, the table was empty where she'd been sitting. The mother and the auntie were gone and a few others had pushed off too. But more people had arrived, more men. Poor old Mrs Brown, maybe it was true and that was why she looked all thin and worried. No wonder she'd been happy to see her youngest son with a girl, and she'd said so sadly none of them had started families.

'What are you thinking, Iris?'

'Don't know, nothing really. Funny old world.'

'Cheer up. Steve took a real liking to you, I could tell. You could do worse going out with him.'

'Yes, I liked him too,' she said absently.

'He'd take you to a show, nice trips, that sort of thing. His mother took to you too.'

'Mmm, she was very friendly.'

'And he's quite the gentlemanly sort.'

'What do you mean, he wouldn't always be grabbing at my tits?'

'Not much point in that, dear, they are about as big as two poached eggs – ooh 'scuse me, that delicious sailor is twinkling at me.'

He was off, making his way across the room, taking tiny steps and swinging his bum like some old-fashioned tart, she thought. Sure enough, he'd clicked with the sailor, hands on hips, giggling like a girl. When they were alone he wasn't like that, or not very. Last week they'd had dinner at the Quality Inn, both of them broke, they'd gone dutch, eating the cheapest things. Soup of course. Soup was always the cheapest whatever it was made of, that time it was French onion with a slice of cheese on toast floating in it. A meal in itself, odd but tasty. And after that, sausage pie. A nice change from the roes on toast the night before with a posh Indian. Posh and rich. He had treated everybody to the roes which were black and cost more than everything else on the menu put together. Caviare it was. She'd read about it being very rare, but black roes would take a bit of getting used to. Bobby told her that the Indian being a maharajah made him a big shot, like a duke, useful to know that. They'd had a good laugh, he knew lots of funny stories, real ones, not jokes. She was lucky to know him and he was always good for advice about manners and words and stuff. Not as good as Nick though. It was a pity about Nick. There he was chatting up one of the actors. She could almost fancy him, not as much as James Mason, but anyway what was the point? Perhaps she should go over and join Nick and the actor, it would be something to tell Mum. She'd loved him in his last picture. Something about a dangerous flying mission, flying at night and not enough parachutes to go round and he had sacrificed his life because all the others were married and had children and were intelligent and had useful jobs on civvy street and all his life he'd been a 'Jack the lad'; played truant at school, never kept a job and broke girls' hearts. Not a good enough reason, as far as she was concerned, not to give him a parachute. She'd tell him.

'Iris, there you are.' Steve touched her arm.

'Hello, business all done?'

'Oh – yes. Listen, my mum wondered if you'd like to come over to us for your Sunday dinner. Just the usual, big roast with all the trimmings. Most of the family; me and my brothers, my auntie you met and a couple of friends might drop in. And you I hope.' He smiled, crinkling his eyes.

'Well, it sounds lovely, a real family dinner, thanks very much. If you give me the address, I'll figure out how to get there.'

'No need, a car will pick you up and take you home, you'll be properly looked after. Were you off?'

'Well . . . not really . . .'

He beckoned over the boy he'd been ordering around before.

' 'Ere, you – take Iris home.'

'Oh no, now?'

'Now.'

'Where does she live?' he whined. 'Far out, I bet.'

'Doesn't fucking matter where she lives, arsehole. Take her home and then come back here, pronto. See? Excuse me, Iris, but some of these cunts can't understand the Queen's English!'

★

She sat in the back of the car, a brown envelope on her lap. 'That's for you,' the boy had snapped as he almost flung it at her over his shoulder. It felt either like a very long letter – or what? A small magazine? Maybe it was a map and an address, instructions how to get to his mum's on Sunday, but why, if he was sending a car? Christ, she hoped it wouldn't be this boy. He was ducking and diving in and out of traffic, accelerating, jamming the brakes on till she was feeling a bit sick. Probably what he had in mind. And she never got to meet the film star, Steve had steered her out of the club, chatting and giving her no chance to say she wouldn't mind staying on for a bit. He was trying to protect her, most like. Didn't realize she had nothing against all those queers. Of course, if he was under his brother's thumb, it might have been orders to get her out. She squeezed the envelope again. She wasn't going to give the boy the satisfaction of seeing her open it, no fear. It was best to be all casual. It was quite thick and soft like a duster.

'If you turn left here, please, it's the second on the left and the flats are at the bottom on the left.'

He didn't get out and open the door, just sat there with the engine running. Before she shut the car door she said, 'Thank you very much. You are a terrific driver – I'll tell Steve on Sunday.'

Surprised, he flashed her a quick glance, pleased but a bit suspicious. Yes, think about that, my son. I'm not some casual bit of crumpet; here today and gone tomorrow. She pushed open the first set of heavy doors, deliberately making a noise, in case anyone was using the dark space between the two doors. Last week Mr Williams from number ten had been doing it with the lady who served in the baker's shop. Up against the wall, grunting and puffing, wedged between her legs. Horrible. Poor things though, nowhere to go.

Right, now she'd have a look. There was sticky tape sealing the flap, he hadn't trusted the boy. It was the softest leather, dark cream. A wallet! Very peculiar. But – there was a great wadge of money in it and a note. No 'Dear Iris' or 'Love Steve'. *There was a dog running tonight at Hackney called Iris so I put something on it and it won so here's your share. Thanks for bringing me luck. See you Sunday.*

Five, ten, fifteen, twenty, twenty-five, thirty ... Blimey! A hundred. From a dog. She wiggled her hand inside the letter-box, no key, the string was there but no key. Her mother must have cut it off. It was a long walk to get round the back of the flats, up to the main road, left, and left opposite the bus terminal.

There was a low light on in the front room and that was all, everything else in darkness, which didn't mean that everyone was asleep. Levering the heavy window up, she wedged it with her shoulder; on one side the rope of the sash was frayed and on the other side broken. Pushing aside the dusty blackout material that now served as curtains, she completed the manoeuvre by leaping quickly off the sill into her bedroom. In the hall there was a faint smell of cigarette smoke. It must be her dad.

He was slumped in the uncomfortable armchair that belonged to the three-piece suite, pulled up close to the electric fire with only one element switched on. The room smelled of the dozen or so Senior Service stubbed out in the green glass ashtray. The light of the radiogram was on and records in their brown cardboard jackets were lying on the sideboard, but no music was playing. He hadn't looked up when she came in but, even though she had closed the door quietly, she knew he'd heard her.

'No music, Dad?'

'What?' He was startled. 'Oh, it's you, girl. I thought it was your mother come for another round of fisticuffs. No, no music. It needs a new needle, this one will scratch the records.'

She bent over to kiss him; he needed a shave. His beard was like his hair, strong and fast-growing, but the beard was dark and his hair prematurely grey, almost white.

'Why did you push off, Dad? Mum was worried about you.'

'Worried about her money, that's all, as well she might be, I don't blame her.' He gazed at the single glowing element as if he were seeing pictures in a flame. 'But where has love gone?' He said it so softly she could only just hear.

What a heart-breaker he was. Not just the man who pissed out of the window on a Friday night after a skinful. 'Love is in a safe, Dad, with all the money you want to borrow, in Chancery Lane.'

'Leave me alone, girl, I don't need you to rub it in. Be a good girl, go to bed and leave me alone.'

'I thought I'd sit a while, keep you company.'

'Suit yourself. Do you want a snout?' He pulled a half-empty packet of cigarettes out of his trousers.

'No thanks. I don't really smoke, not for pleasure. Only when it's handy – on social occasions.'

'I didn't know that. Very sensible. Waste of money.' He lit a fresh cigarette, drawing the smoke deep down and expelling it in a series of rings. What else didn't he know about her? A great deal. There wasn't much room for her and Sam in his life, complicated as it was by overwork, self-perpetuating debt and a marital war that see-sawed between passion and apathy.

'Have you always owed money, Dad, been in debt?'

'Always. As far back as I can remember.'

She wouldn't normally have spoken to him so plainly, but he was worse than usual, really sad.

'I'd just left school, fourteen. Your gran introduced me to her money-lender, he lived in the Buildings, her credit had run out, see. So I got enough to give her two weeks' back rent, and the deposit on a bike. That was that. It all seemed so easy. And then you can't stop.' The sardonic little smile didn't quite conceal the fear and shame. His mother had involved him at fourteen. He had involved Iris at nine.

They had taken a bus to Holborn and walked to Chancery Lane. She was wearing her old grey coat that she'd nearly grown out of. When it got too short Mum had let the hem down, but it was uneven and there had been no turnings on the cuffs so they stopped well above her wrists. Aunt Betty had sent round her Frieda's old coat which was lovely – powder-blue and only a bit too big. Her cousin was a year older and quite a bit heavier so her cast-offs always came in handy, and they were softer somehow, not so 'utility' as the few things her mum bought her. When Dad had said they were going up West together she'd put on the powder-blue coat and her summer sandals, even though it was February. Her heavy, leather, winter shoes were cracked and scuffed, not smart enough for being with her dad going up to the West End. But he had made her change, both coat and sandals. Rotten. Not fair. She forgot to sulk once she was sitting next to him on top of the bus. He wasn't very chatty, smoking in quick puffs, but when the bus lurched he put his arm round her to steady her and left it there. She leaned against his warm body, safe within the circle of his arm.

At the corner of Chancery Lane and Slate Alley he gave her a ten-shilling note, tucking it into her glove, where it felt like a crumped piece of paper. 'Ask for Mister Forsyth, all right? Mister Forsyth.'

'Yes, Dad. Mister Forsyth.'

'And all you have to say is, that's all my dad can manage this week, he's off sick. Don't smile, just think of me being very ill, right?'

'Yes, Dad.'

'What are you going to say?'

'Ask for Mister Forsyth and tell him that's all you can manage this week.'

'And?' he snapped at her, nervous and cross.

'And . . . you're off sick.'

He was pale and awful-looking. Last night he and

Mum had had one of their Friday rows, shouting. Mum had shouted, 'We'll all be on the streets, beggars.' It was easy not to smile remembering that. Mister Forsyth had been quite nice, said he had a little girl of her age, and ended up giving her sixpence. 'Don't tell your daddy, it's for you. Just tell him Mister Forsyth says – this won't do.'

She hadn't told Dad about the sixpence – or given him the message. They had stopped at the Lamb and Flag for Dad to have a beer, 'just the half', and he'd brought her out a ginger beer and a big biscuit, 'for my clever daughter'. He was jolly now. The day had ended gloomily though, nothing hot for tea, and Mum had waved her left hand a lot so everybody could see her wedding ring was missing. It had been pawned.

'How much short were you this week for Mum?'

'It adds up, girl, you see, and there's nothing I can ever do about it, short of winning the pools. Give us this day our daily bread, that's all I can manage.'

'Would this help?' It was one of the five-pound notes but she would give Mum one too, and that might buy some peace. No point giving him any more, it was water down a drain. Next week she would give him a quid or two. And the week after.

'Course it would help. Are you sure?' For the first time that evening he looked at her straight, fearful. 'Where did you get it, girl? I know you give your mother a couple of quid from time to time, but you haven't got a steady job and . . .' Helplessly he said,

'You're not . . . well, you know, no, not my daughter . . .' Wanting to keep the money, he willed her to deny his insinuation.

'No. I'm not on the game.' She was angry. 'Here.' She showed him the letter. Thank God it didn't say how much or he'd have touched her for more.

'Greyhounds, good for him, boyfriend of yours? I've never reckoned "the dogs" as giving good odds, the whole business a bit bent, but maybe I should have a go.'

'No,' she shouted.

'Only pulling your leg, girl.'

'I get good tips at the coffee bar, Dad.'

'That's nice. You get off to bed, I'll tidy up in here, and thanks, Iris. Bring your boyfriend home some time, your mother would like that.'

Chapter Four

The dressing-room was small, all the artists were squashed in there together, men and women. They were separated but only by an old torn blanket nailed to a curtain pole, and that had been pulled to one side. It was hot from all the little lights that edged the mirrors, and smelled of make-up, what Bobby called 5 and 9. When she had seen theatre dressing-rooms in films, they'd been like rooms in hotels, very luxurious and glamorous, but as she only knew what hotel rooms looked like from films, maybe that wasn't true either. This was very – interesting was the word – but you couldn't call this crowded, grubby little room either luxurious or glamorous. She was sure that backstage at the Hippodrome in Golders Green where they'd seen the panto was more what one expected.

She hung back shyly behind Nick. There were two other visitors there, filling the room to capacity. One, a tall, thin man with long, limp, floppy hair, was speaking rapidly with a bit of a stutter, gesturing with a black cigarette. He'd liked the show, said it was 'subversive'. She'd have to look that up. The woman with him was examining the cards and telegrams stuck round the mirrors and on the walls and laughing. Iris bent forward to read the telegrams. 'Do you mind?' she said to the dark-haired actress who, already plastered with what Iris presumed was the 5 and 9, was adding even more to it and widening her red lipstick mouth with a brush. Funny that. From the audience, even though it was a tiny theatre, she appeared beautiful and the pale blonde sitting next to her, taking make-up off, a bit dull. Now, here in the strong lights, you could see the pitted skin, broad nose and lines round the eyes. Her face was big and rather coarse. But the blonde was really lovely close to and the colour of her straight, silky hair was natural.

'Help yourself, darling. You can see I've come down in the world. There are telegrams here from Binkie, Gladys, Sybs – Sybil, you know, Larry and Vivien . . . I've worked with them all in my time.'

'Crumbs!' Iris widened her eyes, pretending to be impressed, and maybe she would be if she could find out who they were. What she did discover from the telegrams was that Deedee was loved, adored, admired. She didn't need 'good luck', she 'had it in her', and would get 'a warm hand on her opening'. 'You were so good as all the characters, ever so funny, especially the Russian lorry driver . . .'

'Oh, darling, sweet of you but I look so dowdy in that babushka,' Deedee pouted.

'Not at all, that . . . babushka couldn't hide your beauty.'

'What a little diplomat. So, what are you, darling? Actress? Model?'

'Well, no, I'm afraid not.'

'Here, help with the drinks, darling, will you?' She

gave Iris a bottle of gin and a tea-stained mug. 'Help yourself then help the others. Dancer, are you? Ballet or cabaret?'

'Actually, I'm not in the business at all.'

'Oh, a civilian!' Losing interest, Deedee turned to the other woman. The blonde gave Iris a little smile of commiseration in the mirror.

'Isn't Bobby camp? Did you see that telegram from "Mickey" Redgrave? He sent it to himself. I *do* know Redgrave and nobody ever calls him "Mickey",' Deedee trilled, loud enough for all to hear.

Iris felt uncomfortable for poor Bobby, but he was totally unaffected. 'And who pray is Gladys then, Deedee? Your aunt, is it, or mother's cousin second time removed? Come up here, and give us all a drink.'

They all accepted the gin, warm as it was, neat, in a variety of glasses, cups and mugs, the old comedian even holding out a small vase. She shrank back in the corner listening to the chatting, trying to catch on. Nick had told her off for not knowing things, not reading the papers. She'd got to keep up with everything and join in. The show had been terrific, very funny and clever, but it was the actors had made her laugh, not so much the sketches which she hadn't altogether understood. *Satire Tonight*, it was called. She wasn't sure what satire was. From this show she guessed it was a kind of rude teasing, 'specially about the government, the royal family and Noel Coward. Very near the knuckle about the Coronation and the Queen and 'Phil the Greek'. But they were all very good, not so much the blonde. She had a lovely voice but that was about all. Although, she made a change; she was a bit of a rest after the others who were all so . . . big.

'We must go.' The thin man gave her a lovely smile and stuttered a good-bye. 'We flew in from Washington overnight, fascinating, lunch at the embassy then we dined with a friend of Guy Burgess and his lover. What a rich mixture; dinner with a spy last night and *Satire Tonight* tonight. A laugh, a song and a manifesto!'

This was her chance to join in. 'Me too. Tea yesterday with a gangster and his mother and my first time backstage today!' It went down a treat and the Deedee woman said, 'What timing, darling. You should be an actress.'

'I didn't like to say in front of the others, Bobby, but you were definitely the best. They were all good but you were terrific. What I thought was . . .' The taxi was slowing down, negotiating the traffic in Wardour Street. 'It would have been cheaper to walk, it's only a few streets.'

'Oh, are you paying?' Bobby laughed and gave her a little push. 'Go on, darling, you were getting very interesting.'

'Oh no,' she wailed as the taxi turned right into Meard Street. 'You said we were going to have something to eat, a club, somewhere fun.'

'So?' Nick pushed her out.

'Isn't this Steve and Vernon's place? It isn't another do for "the family" is it? Because quite honestly, I've had it.'

'Stop whining, Iris.' Nick paid the three shillings fare with a five-pound note, gave the driver a shilling and thrust the rest at Iris. 'Here, go home if you want to, go back to Kilburn. Is it likely that Mrs Brown would be here at midnight? Where else are we going to get decent food?'

'Les A,' she said with a hopeful smile.

'That's not easy for Bobby, they don't really like, er, employees sitting out front, you know,' Nick said softly.

Bobby put his arm round her. 'What were you saying in the taxi? Go on, you're a good critic, you know.'

Once again she was aware of tarts hanging around other clubs, other doorways, but not this one. Inside, the whole place looked different from before. The lighting was dim, just small lamps on each table, brass with amber-coloured shades. The room was so smoky, shafts of light above the lamps were dark yellow like the shades. They sat at one of the small tables against the wall, holding the menus under the lamp. A few couples were dancing very cheek-to-cheek on the small dance floor, their dance having little to do with the music, which was being played by a pianist, a negro, in a white shirt and a cravat. There were three drinks lined up on the piano, and as he drank with one hand, he kept the tune going with the other, drifting from song to song without varying the rhythm, giving 'Night and Day' the same value as 'Alexander's Rag Time Band'.

A cigarette girl appeared at the table. 'Cigarettes for the lady, cigars, gentlemen?' She was absolutely gorgeous, like a chorus girl only better; black and white satin shorts and top, fish-nets and loads and loads of lovely make-up.

'Come back after we've eaten,' Nick said. 'We might have a cigar. Do you need cigarettes, Iris?'

'Not really, thanks. I only smoke a bit. Sometimes I take a couple off my dad, that's all.'

'What does your father smoke?'

'Rolls his own or Woodbines, mostly.'

'We don't do Woodbines, madame,' the girl said, attempting to be haughty.

Iris laughed. It didn't wash, being all superior when your bum was hanging out at the bottom and your tits were sticking out at the top.

'Give Miss Winston forty Players.'

Ha! Nick was on to her airs and graces. 'Thanks, my dad will be thrilled. I've taken home quite a few things lately, useful things.'

When they had finished their supper, the pianist waved to Bobby.

'Do you know him, Bobby?'

'Know him? I've had him!'

'Do me a favour, you're having me on, as usual. He's coloured.'

'What odd ideas you have, Iris. Do you think homosexuality is exclusive to the white English male?' Nick seemed a bit cross.

'Of course not, don't be daft. I know Americans are as well.'

'He,' Nick indicated the pianist, 'he, my good woman, is American.'

'Actually, to be fair to Iris, he isn't a poof, he's AC-

DC. So, darling, if you fancy him you could probably have him.'

'No thanks.'

'On second thoughts, better not. It wouldn't please Steve.' Bobby sniggered but looked around him anxiously. 'Two or three of the "cousins" here, I see – make the place look busy, keep an eye on the girls.'

There were two tables, Iris could see, with girls sitting together.

Bobby stood. 'I'm going to point at the porcelain, and I might give you a song on the way back.'

'Nick, are those girls hostesses?'

'Yes, most of the girls here are. I'm amazed one hasn't offered to join us.'

'If you're a regular, they'd know nothing's doing, right?'

'They never give up, all females think queers can be converted.'

She screwed up her eyes to get a better look. 'Not bad-looking. In fact they're all really attractive. Funny.'

A girl loomed out of the smoky haze with a camera hanging round her neck. She was dressed like the cigarette girl. 'Souvenir of a happy evening?' she chirped.

Surprisingly, Nick said, 'Yes, why not.' Putting his cheek against hers he took her hand. The flash-light illuminated the room for a second and the misty glamour vanished, revealing a tawdry prettiness, fat men and tired, over-made-up women.

When the photographer had gone he kept her hand folded in both of his. It was a small step away from the precarious life she was leading; a night-club hostess. The route there was failure: a dancer not quite good enough; a model not sufficiently photogenic; an actress between jobs; a hairdresser who couldn't manage on the wages. No, they never 'went home' with the customers. It was against the law, they were told, and the boss wouldn't like it. And they didn't when they started, but to supplement the tips, just once – not a bad-looking bloke – ten pounds. And then somehow the boss found out, and after that he expected her to do a favour for special customers. It was never ten pounds again, and he took his cut. How far down the line was it to joining 'the girls' outside?

'Aren't they terrific together?' Bobby and the pianist were singing in harmony, 'The Last Time I Saw Paris'.

'Iris, what did you mean, you've taken home some useful things? What things?' He was frowning. 'Forty Players cigarettes I can accept as useful.'

'Don't worry, Nick. I've got my head screwed on. It was at Steve's mum's. First I went for my dinner on Sunday, lunch you know, and when I went home she gave me a bottle of port for my mum.'

'Oh, very useful.'

'Sh, sh. Bobby's looking at us, he'll be hurt.' 'I've Got You Under My Skin', they were singing to each other, very camp as Bobby would say.

That first time had been all right, lots of people, very jolly. Lovely dinner, bit of a knees up. Like Christmas – when it worked. His mum was busy seeing to everyone. She'd had a good chat with Steve about old times; the war, the blackout, all the laughs in spite of the bombs. Then his mother, looking really tired, had gone up to bed. Steve said the car was ready and that was that, off she went. It hadn't been that sharp young driver, thank God. The next time was not jolly, not at all. He'd sent her some flowers to say thanks for coming and he'd pick her up Thursday, ten o'clock, for a spin in the country. All very well, nothing like 'take it for granted'. What did he know about her social engagements? Still, it was something to look forward to. But when he picked her up, his mum was in the car sitting next to the driver, he'd been there on Sunday too. She'd sat in the back with Steve, nobody talking.

'Lovely day,' she put in for starters, it was cold but the sun was shining.

'Yes,' Steve said, looking out of the window.

That was all! Try again, Iris. 'Hope you're warm enough, Mrs Brown. That's a nice jacket but you ought to be wearing a coat.'

Nothing. Bit of a smile from Mrs B. 'Ne'er cast a clout till May is out. I've always wondered if it meant May month or May blossom.' Nothing. They were driving down the Old Kent Road, through Lewisham, past Beckenham where her old gran had lived.

Finally, at last, somebody spoke. Mrs Brown sighed, 'It's very good of you, Iris, to take an interest. I'm not surprised though, dear, from all I hear you're a good girl. It's in Orpington that he's buried, eight years ago today.'

Iris gave her shoulder a pat. 'I know,' she said, looking daggers at Steve but he just gave her a smile, with nothing behind it. Orpington! Not what she'd expected, not like the pubs on the river. And a graveyard, lovely, I don't think. Still, if it was doing her a favour, fair dos, no skin off my nose. But he might have said.

There had been flowers in the boot, a huge bunch of white lilies. Mrs Brown placed them on the grave.

ARTHUR VICTOR BROWN
R.I.P.

It was nicely looked after, covered in a layer of pale grey stone chippings to keep it tidy. The men, Steve and Dick the driver, stood back. This was women's business. The churchyard was quite a shock. Some of it what you'd expect, old stone and marble headstones and mounds of grass, the older the stone the weedier the grass. Quite a lot of new ones with clear epitaphs, young people and kids. GONE TOO SOON – TAKEN BEFORE HIS TIME – BELOVED CHILD OF – all killed in the war. But worse was the crater. Slap bang between the church and the pond, engulfing half the graveyard. Looking down into the immense hole she could see a broken monument, cracked slabs of stone and marble, an angel with no head.

'Terrible, isn't it, dear. Thank the Lord my Arthur survived that.'

'Well . . . yes, Mrs Brown.'

'Couple of yards to the left and he'd be gone.' That he was 'gone' already didn't seem to matter. 'It might have shifted him though, still, this must be roughly where he is.'

'Are you all right, Mrs Brown? You shivered, are you cold or was it . . .?' It was difficult speaking when you wanted to laugh.

'He didn't like lilies, but Steve wasn't to know that, he was only fourteen when his dad passed away.'

'Was it the war? Was he in the forces?'

'It was the war in a way, but not in the forces, no. He wore glasses, you see. No, he had a heart attack in Finsbury Park underground. The air-raid warning had gone off as he was walking down Seven Sisters Road and everybody rushed to the tube for shelter, him with them. Crowds started pouring down the stairs and it seems he had a panic and tried to get out, go against the tide. It was all over very quick they said.'

The men were standing at the edge of the crater talking, their heads close together. He was really handsome in his own way, Steve, those blue eyes, hard cheekbones and nice soft-looking mouth, the dark suit and tie set him off very well.

'What did he do, your husband?'

'He was a greengrocer, high-class fruit and veg. I wish he'd lived to have met you, Iris, he'd have been so pleased. I'm pleased, you seeing my Steve regular. I hope I live to see him settled.'

Then, no lunch, back to London, starving. After dropping Mrs Brown off in Stoke Newington they'd taken her back to Kilburn.

'Thanks for coming, Iris. It's been very hard on Mum, she never had a daughter, see.' More than he'd said to her all day. 'Give this to your mum, all right?' He pushed an envelope at her.

'I don't need paying to see your mum. I like her.' But he forced the envelope on her as he gave her a quick hug, jumped back in the car and was gone, sharpish.

It wasn't money, it was coupons. Mum said she couldn't afford all that meat so she kept some to get scrag for a stew and sold the rest to next door.

'Aren't you exhausted, Bobby? A whole show and now cabaret?'

'Darling, I'm always fizzing after a show. Is it too late for more drinks, Nick?'

'I'll try.' He made some complicated gestures to the waiter across the room, who nodded and went through the swing doors into the kitchen.

'Are you going to ask your friend to join us?'

'Iris, if it's difficult for Bobby to join us at Les A when he's singing, it is obviously out of the question to do it here, especially a negro.'

'Not true! I've heard about things like that, Bébé said the other night it was absolutely no problem these days since some duchess had been having it off with a coloured man. These are modern times. And look at Roger.'

'Roger?'

'The maharajah. I call him that because it sounds like Rajah. Anyway, he's Indian but he goes anywhere, he even knows the Queen.'

'Shut up, shut up, shut up. You witter on with an insane confidence when all your information and opinions are based on the utter tosh printed in the yellow press or gossip bandied about at midnight by drunken trollops.'

'You shut up, Nick. The poor cow's only seventeen, for Christ's sake!'

'You have no sense, Iris, of the subtleties of class, birth, behaviour, caste . . . anything.'

She nodded carefully. 'I dare say, but you're going to put me right now, aren't you, Nick?'

'As for the duchess, an H.R.H. can do whatever they like. It's considered a bit eccentric, a few eyebrows would be raised, but no restaurant or club is going to discourage them from visiting their establishments. And as for 'Roger', he has an old title as important as any duke's, his sister is married to the premier maharajah in India, the whole family are close friends with all the royal family and . . . and he was educated at Eton and Oxford. A little more acceptable, you will agree, than your white, ill-educated English father.'

He had gone too far, her little face was pinched with pain.

'Here,' she scrabbled in her bag. 'Here. My white English father doesn't need your fags.' She placed the two packets of Players carefully on the table and turned her head to the dance floor, feigning interest in the desultory movements of a woman dancing with a glassy-eyed younger man. Nick wondered if the long neck and firm jaw gave her a false dignity, or was it real.

The waiter appeared, putting a coffee-pot and cups on the table. Winking, he poured brandy from the pot. 'Not too strong, I hope, sir.'

'I'm inclined to agree with your cousin Charlie,' Iris said, giving him a brief disdainful glance. 'He said you are ageing unattractively into a pathetic old queen.'

'I like the girl but she irritates. They all do inevitably, people who intrigue you for a while from that class, even when educated, and God knows, she isn't.'

'Don't play with her then, Nick. You didn't have to come tonight, she asked me if she could come to the show, you added yourself uninvited.'

Nick ignored this, pouring brandy into the coffee cups. 'It's the pleasure they have in their superficial opinions, never formed by themselves. The self-importance at having an opinion. A half-remembered headline from a rag is trotted out as a valuable piece of analysis of thought or behaviour or . . .'

Bobby yawned. 'With all due respect, Nick . . .'

'Meaning you have no respect, rather lazy little phrase that, don't you think?'

'I think I'll ask the ciggy girl to check on her, she's been in there a long time. Perhaps you'd like *The Times Literary Supplement* to jerk off over while you are waiting. 'Scuse me, sweetie.'

Nick watched Bobby as he crossed the floor. It took one minute, but it was time enough to blow a kiss to the pianist, circle a couple dancing with a few neat steps and pause at a table where a hostess was trying to encourage a man to drink. He, too old and too wise, was doing the same to the hostess. The drink in question was champagne cider, with the emphasis heavily on the cider.

After a few words with the cigarette girl, Bobby turned, waved, and was gone. Had Iris gone too? No taxi money, no cigarettes – she must have taken it seriously, his little diatribe.

One of the girls sitting at the round table in the centre of the room was giving him the eye, a rather cold malevolent eye. She was large-boned and heavily made up even for a night-club hostess, glamorous though, a touch of the Linda Darnells or Margaret Lockwoods about her. Silly cow, she must be new, couldn't recognize a pansy when she saw one. And now she was approaching the table, walking slowly, swinging her hips, the whole attitude confident and cool. 'Is that brandy in the coffee-pot? I'll have a cup, if you don't mind.' She sat, poured herself some brandy and sipped it with a daintiness at variance with her coarse appearance. 'So, what do you think? Suck you off for a fiver?'

He winced at the grotesque thought.

'Don't look like that, you might be pleasantly surprised.' She grabbed his hand and forced it under the table, pressing it between her legs. 'Yes, dear, it's a cock. So put your money on the table and I'll get under the table or would you rather go to the gents' toilet?'

He looked at her/him sadly, the prominent cheekbones and coarse skin. What had Iris called him? A pathetic old queen. Indeed. 'I think the toilet would be more discreet.'

Chapter Five

'"A rude man atones for his lapses," that's what it says.' Sam put his nose in the big bunch of flowers. 'They smell nice, how much would they have cost?'

'How should I know?'

'Who is he? And how rude was he?' Sam squared his shoulders, doing a bit of 'I'm your brother' stuff.

Iris smiled and shook her head. 'Nothing like that.'

'I think Mum's right, it's about time you got yourself a proper job.'

'Mind your own business, Samuel.' She sorted out the flowers, untying the ribbon and delicate wire that held the white roses and scented freesias. 'Get me a couple of milk bottles, there's too much for this.' She held up the pale green ceramic vase decorated with a zig-zag of orange. 'It's so ugly it makes these beautiful roses ugly.'

'He must be in love with you.'

'Ha!' she snorted. 'Not likely. Anyway, Mum has no need to go on, I give her about two quid a week, and she's had a bottle of port, meat coupons, and a big piece of proper made birthday cake, all in the last month.'

'More useful than flowers.'

'Yes, maybe, but . . .' she held the freesia against her face, '. . . not as romantic.'

The birthday cake was from Mrs Brown, it had been cut carefully so that some of the icing message was on it, . . . PY BIR . . . and a little iced rose. After the tea party, Mrs Brown had stood at the door waving 'Ta-ta' to her. She was pale and quite shaky but smiling. Steve had been walking her to the car but stopped, drew her to him and gave her a lovely kiss. Full on the mouth, not rough, but firm and lingering; not unlike Paul Henried and what's her name in that beautiful, sad film. Turning she saw Mrs B give a last little wave

She opened her eyes. Sam was staring at her, puzzled. 'You're squashing the flowers. Why don't you go to the pictures, Iris, like other girls, like that stupid sister of Lenny Chester? She goes out once a week with a boyfriend. And she's got a job with prospects, Mum said.'

'Will you stop it; stop it, stop it. Job, job, job. I don't know anyone to go to the pictures with. I don't know anyone. What with us moving after the war and Dad changing his job and moving again and new schools – I haven't got any friends, not real ones. And it's too late now.' It was too late. She couldn't sit in the back row of the State cinema and kiss some local boy, things had changed. Would going to a dance at the Irish Club on the Kilburn High Road, having a jitterbug with cheeky

Terry from the ironmonger's, something she had once longed for, work out to be the fun she'd anticipated? Half a shandy, the bus home, sitting on top smoking. Kissing in the corner up against the Anderson shelter. Him trying to get his tongue in her mouth and his knee between her legs and undo her brassiere at the same time. It was no longer what she wanted, any of it. Posh men were no easier to deal with but it was everything else that made it her other lovely world. She tried to imagine if she saw Terry at Les A and he bought her champagne, would that work? But she couldn't do it. It wouldn't fit. Like putting the wrong bit of a jig-saw in the picture, you couldn't force it.

'These blokes,' Sam gave the flowers a push, 'flowers and cars and telephones, would they marry someone like you? Mum said to Dad you should think of settling down, it's about time.'

'Lovely, isn't it? What they want is my room for a lodger again. I'm still quite young, you know.' She put one of the milk bottles full of yellow freesias on the window-sill above the kitchen sink. 'This might do something for the smell of boiled cabbage. Put the wireless on, it's nearly time for Dick Barton. The roses are going in my room, and the rest of the freesias too.'

'What smell are they going to get rid of there?'

'Damp. And dry rot. And dustbins from the back alley. She's got a cheek, Mum, I'm only seventeen, still got some life ahead of me. She wouldn't get as much from a lodger as she does from me.'

No regular job 'with prospects' would give her as much as the bits and pieces of taxi money.

His sister hadn't 'filled out' as some of his friends' sisters had, she was smaller all over. Good job he'd taken up boxing at the youth club. 'Iris,' he shouted outside her room. 'If that bloke lapses again I'll sort him out for you, never mind the flowers.'

It was easier being nice to someone else's mum. At the start going to see Mrs Brown had been part of a sort of deal with Steve, nothing said mind, it was a way of seeing him sometimes and getting a bit of credit. But when the poor old love was really ill, not just poorly, dropping in to the Royal Free Hospital for a bit of a chat, or just sitting there holding her hand had been really nice. Funny, the Lady Almoner had told her she could apply for bus fares as a daughter-in-law, so long as she passed the means test! Not being married to Steve was one thing, and if she was she definitely wouldn't pass any means test.

All the horses, what a sight, black with tall black plumes on their heads, big, shaggy hooves making a heavy clop, clop on the partly cobblestoned street. The carriage they were drawing was black too, of course, and huge; the roof covered in a cushion of flowers – bunches, sheaves, wreaths and crosses. Loads of lilies, she'd smelt them as the procession approached. Now it was here, the smell mingled with that of the horses. Pride of place was on the front, an arrangement of red, white and blue carnations, M-U-M. Among the men flanking the carriage in their tight black suits was the nasty little sod who'd driven her. Iris dodged between a couple of onlookers, no point in letting him know she hadn't been asked. She stood close to a woman dressed like all the others, flowery print cotton frock and big, not quite clean, apron. Some of them still had their hair in curlers, the rags and iron rollers showing under turbans or snoods. The woman smiled at her and wiped away tears with her apron. 'Lovely, isn't it, dear? She was a wonderful mother to her boys, and they appreciated it, always took care of her they did, nothing too much for their mum.' The carriage carrying the coffin passed and was followed by another horse-drawn vehicle. Inside you could see the brothers. Steve sitting by the window, looking at the crowd, pleased, not smiling – no – more of an acknowledgement of their presence. Paying their respects, as was expected.

Then came the cars. Big serious grand ones, navy blue or black. Then the more ordinary cars, at least a dozen. Big turn-out. Loads of people going to the funeral, the church service at St Saviour's and then to Bethnal Green cemetery. After that, the whole lot, and many more besides, would be at the wake. A slap-up do at the enormous church hall in Clerkenwell. But not her. Not Iris Winston. And she wanted to know, how comes this? *She* was one of the last to see the poor thing in hospital. And one of the last things she said was, and painful too because the disease had spread to her throat, 'Take care of my Steve, won't you, Iris? He loves you, you know. He told me.' So hoarse, it hurt to listen. She'd nodded and whispered, 'Of course, Mrs B.' It was all very upsetting. And surprising. That was it, she died that day. Then, just a short note from Bobby – bet he was there – why not, every bloody person was there – 'Don't go to the house, don't go to the funeral, Steve will be in touch.'

Sunday afternoon was always rotten. Not like other bad times and days, rotten in its own special way. Stuffed with the big meal which you had to eat, and all of it, because Mum had been 'slaving over a hot stove and what thanks do I get'. An atmosphere, heavy with spoken and implied recriminations all through the roast, if they were lucky, and plums and custard because Dad was late back from the pub and the Yorkshire puddings were burned, or the onion sauce or the crackling, depending on the joint. Why she didn't plan it for a bit later so that Dad was on time and nothing was burned was a mystery. Though it reinforced her role as the Martyr of the Mansions. Then there was the awful gap between the big roast or stew and cheese and pickles with the radio, at seven o'clock. She always washed up and she and Sam always had a row about wiping up. Then Dad told Sam off, and Mum told her off. Then Mum and Dad had a row and Mum would go to their bedroom and slam the door. What happened next varied. With a bit of luck Dad would say, 'Why don't you take Sam for a walk, I think I'll have a lie down.' Which meant he and Mum were going to do it. But the walk was the worst bit. Why would anybody want to take their little brother for a walk? Anywhere. And certainly not in Kilburn, Willesden, Brondesbury or Cricklewood. The rows and rows of semi-detached houses with tiny front gardens all with the same bushes and shrubs. Dark green, dusty foliage, prickly leaves, gloomy trees, dustbins and bikes. And from every bloody house came the same smell of roasting meat and boiled cabbage. Anyone would think it was against the law to have boiled meat and no cabbage.

The whole walk was pointless. It didn't make any difference if you went forwards, back or sideways, if you crossed the street or went round the corner. It was miles of sameness and she always felt the same kind of sadness and a tight feeling in her chest as if she was going to cry, only she never did. And so bored she was frightened it might last for ever. The only bit of change was the bombed-out bits where no proud owner had got rid of the daisies and dandelions and feathery grasses.

This Sunday had started a bit different, though it was likely to end up the same. Dad was back from the pub, on time, with a jug of Guinness for Mum. It was pork and Mum had done little bits of crackling separate, for them to pick at while it was cooking. No cabbage smells because they were having peas, which she had podded. A couple of small worms and some insect gunge but not enough to put you off. And the weather was still nice, so if Steve turned up they could drive to Hampstead Heath and have a walk round. The message as delivered from next door had been from Bobby: 'Steve will come by after dinner on Sunday afternoon.' Bit of a cheek. What was she supposed to do, keep herself free for a month of Sundays?

Dinner was all right, good in fact. Easier to eat when things were peaceful and there was some nice chat. Sam helped Mum clear away with no argy-bargy, Dad put the kettle on for a cup of tea and Mum said she'd have her tea in bed as she could do with a lie down. Then Dad said, 'You ought to get out, the pair of you, make the most of the weather.'

Iris checked the large copper kettle on the back burner for the washing-up.

'I can't take Sam.'

'I'd rather go out on my own anyway, thanks, stupid.'

'So as you can go to the shelter, I suppose, and smoke and talk dirty.'

'Why, Dad, is that what you used to do?' Sam dodged a blow that didn't come.

'Why can't you take him?' Her mother was suspicious. 'You two get on all right, considering.'

'My friend, Steve, might be waiting in the street to take me for a drive.'

Her parents smiled. 'That's nice, dear.'

'It's only a might, Mum.'

'Ask him back for tea, why don't you?'

'Yes, we'd like to meet him, your steady.' Her dad was probably remembering the money from the winner at the greyhound track. Steady boyfriend, steady money.

'No, I can't do that.'

They stood together, hurt, a defensive partnership.

'Of course you can. We've got serviettes,' her mother said proudly. 'I'll make some rock cakes.'

'Don't count on it, Mum. He's not easy to pin down, he's . . .'

'He's busy,' Sam said. 'He works all the time, that's how he gets the money to send flowers. He's a busy businessman.'

'Thanks, Sam,' she closed the front door quietly.

'For wiping up?'

'You know why.'

They stood outside the large grimy mansion block, indecisive.

'If you want to go off alone it's all right by me, Iris.' He didn't look as jaunty as he sounded.

'Tell you what. We'll walk down to the corner, to the old shelter; if your mates are there, OK, ta-ta. If not, we'll cross the road, walk up to the High Street, and if my friend isn't around, get the bus at the Green up to the Heath.'

The shelter was deserted, the interior stinking of urine, both animal and human, and cigarette smoke. Messages to Hitler chalked on the wall were fading. It wasn't quite clear now what the residents of Angleton Street had intended to do to him when caught, though it certainly involved his only testicle. Deprived of that pleasure by his suicide, local wits had changed Heil Hitler to: Hell Hitler, Vile Hitler, Heil Shitler. The cold, damp, hastily thrown-up cheap brick shelter had been built during the war before the blanket bombing of London and the invention of the flying bomb rendered it obsolete. She remembered the new bomb, the fear of the whining sound and the greater fear when the noise stopped indicating an imminent explosion. It was called a V1. That was bad enough, but would there be a V2 and a V3, even worse? When people started calling them Doodlebugs, although just as many people were killed, the funny name reduced the threat. After an initial enthusiasm, the shelter had been abandoned by locals aware that they were more vulnerable there than in the basements of flats or houses. The friendliness had been the big attraction – nobody wanted to die alone – so they shared flasks of cocoa and tea, and had sing-songs. But in the unhealthy atmosphere of walls beaded with moisture and damp floors they also shared flu, pneumonia and diphtheria and the social life lost its appeal.

'They call it the Youth Club now.'

She caught her heel on a used condom and slipped, steadying herself with a hand on the slimy wall. Youth club, Christ! Why weren't there any lovely places like the Yanks had, in films anyway; soda fountains, Coca-Cola machines, straws in frothy ice-creams, twirling on a chrome stool at the counter. A lovely friendly man making you a banana split. Nice music. Teenagers dropping in after school: hi! hi! they said hi!

They were half-way up the street when Sam noticed the car following them slowly. 'Don't look now,' he whispered, 'but there's a two-tone beige and brown Sunbeam Talbot behind, I think it's trailing us . . . I said *don't* look.'

Was it Steve? Hard to tell, he was wearing a hat. The

car drew ahead and stopped; as Steve got out she could see he wasn't only wearing a hat, he was wearing gloves too.

'You got my message then?'

'Bobby's message, yes.' She wasn't going to help him out, make it easy for him with a nice chat, a bit of this and that. No. Sod him. Sam was looking at him really close, almost rude, forgetting to be nonchalant, curious about one of his sister's new friends.

'You Sam? Iris has told me about you.'

'Yes. Are you the one who sent her the flowers?'

Steve gave her a cocky raised-eyebrow look.

'No, not him. It was Nick,' she explained to Steve, though where he got off eyeing her like that after all he hadn't said and done. 'It was after that time at your club, remember, when I bumped into you as I was leaving.'

Steve waited, expecting more. So did Sam.

'Well, we'd had a bit of a falling out, you know what Nick's like, he can turn as fast as "milk in May", so he sent me some flowers to make up.'

'Some? Huge! Big as the bunch in Farrow and Colleys.'

'What's Farrow and Colleys, Sam?' Steve was quite taken with him, smiling, sizing him up.

'It's the funeral parlour in the High Street.' Iris felt awful, but not Sam's fault, it was said, no bringing it back, she shrugged.

'Sorry.'

'Look, sonny. I want to talk to your sister . . .'

'. . . All right, all right, I'm off.'

'No, I got a better idea. Get in the car, we'll go up to

Hampstead Heath. Iris and me, we'll have a walk and you go to the pond and watch them sailing the boats, then we'll come back and get you and I'll drop you both back home.' He opened the rear door for Sam, no checking with her, lovely, so this is it. Right. The big brush off. She had half a mind to tell him to get stuffed. But what else was she going to do with the afternoon, and Sam too, he'd like going in a car, going for a drive. Maybe he'd have a 'goodbye' present for her. If he was true to form it should be something not usual – no chocolates or flowers – more, what? Utility, that's what. Half a ration book? Bottle of brandy and some cigarettes for Dad? Cash from a bet on a horse called Iris? A piece of cake from the wake? Wake cake! Even getting the brush off, the old heave-ho, was better than wandering around the dusty streets of NW5 and NW6.

Driving up the steep streets to Holly Mount he talked to Sam mostly. Sport. Football, boxing. Boring. There were a few young couples wandering over the Heath; behind Jack Straw's Castle, down towards the slopes leading to Highgate and across the stretch to Frognal. Hand in hand they were looking for somewhere private to do a bit of necking, or more if they were engaged. All the men carried raincoats – *not* that it was going to rain. Older couples were settled on benches, some facing the wide green spaces interspersed with clumps of trees and footpaths, and others across the road from the pond. Sam was there with half an eye on the little boats and the other half on a bright red kite hovering over the pond on a long, long string held by its fat, elderly owner who was wailing, 'No, no.' A puff of wind lofted it, the owner shortened the string and the little boats sailed on, round and round, free of the danger from the skies.

Here she was with Steve, like the others, part of a couple. Iris and Steve. Not that he looked comfortable in that role; no holding hands, no arm draped across her shoulders. Would the old dears sitting on the bench by the bus stop, facing the road, backs to the Heath, him reading the paper, her smiling placidly at everyone, especially kiddies, would they think she and Steve were a couple? They could be a couple who'd had a row.

'Steve, there's no need to waste your time. You just walk me over to that seat under the big tree and get it over with, it shouldn't take long. And I think I know what you're going to say.'

He gave her the once over and sighed, but it was relief not sadness.

'It was for your mum, wasn't it? A put-up job?' Christ, she hated men when they went all shifty; like her dad when he came home with drink on his breath and no money for the rent. He was sort of shuffling from foot to foot and clearing his throat.

'Your mum wouldn't have liked you to settle down with that girl – your girlfriend. Right? RIGHT?'

He pulled at his hat awkwardly and winced. 'It's . . . well, not as bad as it looks, Iris, and . . .'

'What's the matter with your head?'

'Nothing. What do you mean, my girlfriend?'

'And why are you wearing gloves in this weather?' She didn't want to go on and on, it would be more dignified to be aloof. 'That girl I saw you with at your club, very close you were, talking. Not the type to please your mum, what with all that make-up and being a hostess, and, well, not what you'd call a good girl. I was leaving fast so as Nick and Bobby couldn't come after me but I saw you all right.'

'Oh, I see.' He looked a bit surprised.

'But why did you kiss me so nicely, and why wasn't I allowed to the funeral?'

He took off his gloves ever so gently and carefully, and then his hat.

'I know that I'm not everybody's cup of tea and that hostess of yours is more Ava Gardner, more, oh, I don't know, sexy . . .' His eyes were closed.

'Steve – what have you done? What have you done to your hands?'

They were bandaged, swollen with lines of blood seeping through the gauze. And his head; it was shaved in patches and bits of hair were crusted with dried blood. Good job they were out of sight under the spreading branches of the tree. No nosy parkers.

'Part of my job,' he said, just as a matter of fact. 'Someone had a go at me with a knife.'

No surprise, really; as he said, that was his job. Someone had a go at him? He and his brothers had a go at someone else; not much fun when you got down to brass tacks. She would rather have Mickey Rooney's life than James Cagney's any day of the week. 'I came to see you, Iris, because you got to know first hand, you haven't got to come to our place again, ever.' He held out his hands in mute explanation. 'Not the club neither. And that's why I put the bar up to you coming to the funeral, see?'

'All right, OK, when I'm useful, no danger then?' She didn't feel bitter, it was just all too sudden, something familiar in her life gone.

'Our competitors, people in the same business, well, they have respect, as we do, for immediate family.' He was shifting again, all uneasy. 'Ladies, that is.'

'But not scrubbers?'

'Not what I mean. No, all due respect for mum and auntie, yes, but not for girlfriends.' A little bead of blood dripped from his scalp and dried on his brow like a droplet of red sweat. 'Not that they'd go the whole way but it could be quite nasty: little fire, broken arm, sort out your face, you know.'

It didn't feel like Sunday afternoon on Hampstead Heath, more as if the air-raid warning had gone off. He wasn't talking, nobody was, or you couldn't hear it. You couldn't hear anything. Just silence. She didn't look at him again.

'Put your hat and gloves back on, Steve, I've got the picture. You'd better go, before we get gunned down in the street.'

She sat on the bench and touched her face, the face which might get 'sorted out'.

There was a family sitting on a bench outside the pub, Jack Straw's Castle. Two boys, one girl, one mum, one dad. They were having a picnic tea. She'd seen them get off the bus from Golders Green, the dad carrying a cardboard suitcase. The picnic had been in the case: untidy sandwiches, squashed cake and a flask of something. If they took their time, the pub would be open at seven and Mum and Dad could have a beer before getting the bus back to Golders Green. Nice.

It hadn't been nice finding out from Sam. He had guessed immediately and she hadn't twigged in months.

'What do you mean, it runs in the family? If it ran in the family there wouldn't be any family.'

'One of the teachers at school is, you can tell.'

'Has he interfered with you?' She clasped him protectively.

'Get off, Iris, they don't have a go at everyone. Did any of your teachers have a go at you?'

'No, one of them put his hand up Rita Gordon's knickers, but nobody did it to me.'

'There you are then, it's the same with queers, see.'

So Bobby must have known. All those 'had him, had him, had hims', had he 'had' Steve? Most likely. Was the nasty little driver one? One of Steve's? Of course! Bobby set her up, introduced them. Wonder what he got – a few free dinners at the club? Meat coupons? A slice of Mrs Brown's birthday cake? Couldn't blame him really.

'What do you do when you go out? Iris . . .' Sam waited, she kept looking at the family sitting outside the pub. 'Why do you go out if they don't even take you to the pictures? Why did that bloke who sent you the bunch of flowers be rude to you – go on – tell us.'

She opened and shut her handbag, fiddling with the strap. It was getting worn; still, it was cheap, and you get what you pay for.

'Why go out with someone who's queer, even if you didn't know it? You must have known it, though, because he won't have kissed you.'

She smiled. 'Oh, but he did, you see, Mister Clever Clogs.' She sort of knew why she went out. It wasn't being in love or wanting to kiss or even do it. No, not with any of them, the silly drunk young men, or the older ones able to hold their drink, all of them pulling and pushing and pinching bits of your body. What was it then? Getting out, getting away from the flat, the cold smell. Mum and Dad. No hope, only sad for ever more, they couldn't change it because *they* couldn't change. Only sometimes, a nice Sunday afternoon. And the inside of yourself shouting – not me, not me – awful, awful they were, hitting and hating. And sad. So anything must be better. True. It was. Everything was better if you were not at home, not in the flat and not with them. She wanted 'Some enchanted evening', and if they didn't have it, it wasn't her fault. 'Not my fault' was the end of most rows in the flat.

They walked down East Heath Road, turning right at Downshire Hill. 'Keats Grove, see, Sam, that's where he lived, the poet, Keats.'

'Right, so a street's named after him, is it? I don't see why.'

This seemed to needle her, she frowned and walked faster. Pity, because he'd thought this might be the right time to get *it* out of her, she was off her guard. He followed her, lagging behind on his short legs. On

Finchley Road, opposite the coffee bar she sometimes worked at, they sat on a wall by the bus stop.

'What do you say, bus, or walk and save the money?'

He decided to plunge in and just ask her; being sly and pretending didn't work with Iris. 'Tell us about Mum and Dad and that woman. Go on, Iris, please. It's not fair, I'm older now than you were when it happened, so even if you tell me now you will still, and always, know for longer than me.'

'True,' she laughed.

'Winnie Taylor, wasn't it?' he prompted.

'Yes, she lived next door, in one of those Buildings in Holborn.'

'I remember the Buildings, everywhere crowded and noisy. I remember the rent man coming and people shouting up from downstairs so everybody hid as could, it was terrific fun.'

'I'm surprised he ever got the rent money back to the office in one piece.'

'Go on then, about . . . her.'

It had taken her some time to sort it out, what she'd seen, what they'd said and Mum shaking her, saying, 'Don't look, don't look.'

'I was ten when it happened. Not that much really if nobody had seen: just a bit of drunk and disorderly. If only . . .'

'If only?'

'Mum had done some overtime at the factory, wasn't expected back for half an hour or more, but someone gave her a ride home on the back of a bike.'

Looking flushed and pretty, Mum had collected her

from the street where she was playing 'statues'. It was her turn after the counting out ('One, two, three, a larey, I saw sister Mary, sitting on the wall, a larey, kissing Charlie Chaplin').

'The trouble was, she wasn't wearing a brassiere, see?' She didn't wait for 'No, I don't see.' 'So, when Mum caught them at it he had his hand up her jumper, kissing her as well, of course, and that done it. Well, in any case if only she'd been wearing a bra it wouldn't have mattered so much – Oh, it was such a long time ago.'

'Why, Iris, why did her jumper matter?'

'Bra, not jumper.'

'Bra, then. Why did her bra not being on make it different?' He knew the answer but the excitement of hearing her say it . . . though pity it was about Mum and Dad . . .

'Because, Dumbo, he was touching her tits, OK?'

He didn't like it, it wasn't exciting. He wanted her to stop. 'Shall we go?' he said. 'Walk, save the bus fare?'

He took her hand as they set off.

'It was the war, a lot of that sort of thing went on. And Winnie Taylor's husband worked a late shift, you see.'

Iris had known about carrying-on since she was a kid. People were doing it all the time with the wrong people, all over the place. Up against a wall, panting and grunting, doing it quickly in case someone came along; in a big old bath on a bomb site where a house had been split in two, and at dusk one evening a couple had hidden behind a line of washing to do it but had been revealed by a puff of wind.

'Why are you laughing? It isn't funny.' He ran ahead, kicking a stone. 'Women,' he shouted. 'It's all your fault.'

When the door slammed for the third time it meant they were all gone: Sam to school, Dad to work, and Mum off to Hendon where she was working part-time temporary for a friend who was off sick. Iris had left a note.

DONT WAKE ME UP. WILL DO
WASHING UP AND BEDS. Eye.

And Mum hadn't, not exactly. But a non-stop row with Dad was as good as an alarm clock. It was carried on in their bedroom, the hall and the kitchen and shouted through the bathroom door while he was shaving.

'Hot breakfast? Give me enough money and I'll give you all the hot breakfasts . . . You're useless, Bill, do you know that? If you had never been born nobody would have noticed.'

'Leave me alone, woman.'

'Leave you alone? I'll leave you alone, I'll pack my bags and go to the Isle of Wight.'

Iris pulled the blankets over her head. Christ. It never stopped. Or changed.

Last night had been extremely unusual. It was as if she was a girl from somewhere all right and nice the way it turned out. First off she took a bus to Hyde Park Corner, done up quite good in her navy with a tight belt. Not the high heels because if she didn't click with someone it was rather a lot of walking. Then she'd strolled past Les A slowly, not exactly looking in, but pretending she was searching for something in her handbag. If a crowd had come along she might have had the luck to slip in with them and if nothing happened, well, it was a bit of a trip up West. But a group came out and one of them was Deedee from Bobby's show and she said, 'It's you, Bobby's friend, *not* in the business.'

Then the others all said, '*Not* in the business?'

And Deedee couldn't remember her name and said she couldn't remember *anybody's* name. And a big roly-poly man with a rumbly voice said, 'As long as you remember your lines,' and he laughed so loud people across the street looked.

Then Deedee said, pointing to the roly-poly man, 'Obviously you know who this is,' and she said, 'No,' they all laughed and roly-poly most of all and he said, 'You could be the new Beatrice Lillie.' But as she didn't know who the old one was she just gave him a bright smile. And then they took her to a place at the other end of the Kings Road for dinner, where there wasn't any choice except for steak and chips – fine by her. The whole evening roly-poly, and the funny thing was his name *was* Roly, told stories that were long and very funny even though she didn't always understand them. Whenever there was a bit of a pause a tiny woman wearing a beret on the side of her head who was his girlfriend would say, 'Tell them about what Binkie said at Edith's,' or, 'Tell them about Wilfred falling off the stage,' and he'd be off again. Quite a relief someone like that being at dinner. You can get on with the food. When it was all over she shared a taxi with a couple who lived in Hampstead. She asked the man who'd been rather quiet all evening if Roly was on the Halls and he laughed more than he'd done all night. But the saying goes, 'If a laugh doesn't reach your eyes it hasn't touched your heart,' well, his hadn't arrived at his mouth either. She insisted on paying her share, so no taxi money but a really nice time.

Today, she was going to do Debenham and Freebodys and pluck up courage to go into the smart costume department. Last week she had gone up to the West End and done Selfridges. In the sales she had bought a blue linen-type dress which should do nicely for the lunch outing that Patrick had arranged for her. It was like a much more expensive one in *Vogue* that she'd noticed while reading it fast in the newsagent's before the man told her to put it back. He always said the same thing – this ain't a lending library.

After washing up, making the beds and scrubbing the lino on the kitchen floor, she did herself up, not to look attractive but to be ladylike, and got the tube to Oxford Circus. It wasn't as difficult as she thought it would be to saunter in because it was so different, she was in the room before she knew she was there. No racks with skirts and blouses and dresses, just a few dummies all nicely dressed, posed in a superior way, some with a hat. A saleslady, better dressed than anyone she knew, said, 'May I help you?'

Iris hesitated. 'Well, yes, I suppose so.'

'Is madam looking for anything in particular?'

She brazened it out, and described the dress in *Vogue*.

'Yes, madam, I think we have that in cornflower blue.'

She tried it on in a little room, it was lovely. Now she could really tell what was different with hers. Linen when it was real was sleeker, softer, and money made a difference with the colour too. The woman was right, this was cornflower blue.

'What do you think, madam?'

'It's lovely, but I don't think it suits me.' Stupid thing to say. It was perfect, very embarrassing.

'Come and see yourself in the double mirror.' The woman was smiling.

All at once Iris knew she knew and was sorry for her as well as herself. In the double mirror outside it looked even better. She shook her head, 'No, it really isn't me.'

A woman came out of one of the rooms, a bit plump, very brown, in a sleeveless white dress, it made her bleached dry hair even worse. She examined herself in the double mirror and was cross. Cross with the saleslady and cross with Iris as well.

'Do you know,' Iris said, 'do please pardon me for interfering, but this dress would be perfect for this lady with her cornflower blue eyes.' The nice thing was that in a few sizes larger it was, and the woman bought it.

It had been very good practice. One day she might even try something on in Fortnum and Masons.

On the way out she strolled through the handbag and wallet department. There was a dinky, soft kid handbag: suitable for both day and evening wear. Black. Just what she needed. It was about half the size of her patent one. She wandered idly round the S-shaped display counter and managed to move it with her elbow between two bigger bags; it was nearly hidden in the curve of the S. With her handbag open she pretended interest in a heavy sensible brown bag and just about got the little black one lined up to shove inside when a voice said, cold as cold, 'Which one are you interested in?' And a heavy hand fell on her shoulder. It was the spottiest-faced man she'd ever seen, tall, and with a mouth like a pair of slugs. She kept her nerve even though she was terrified and trembling.

'This one,' she said, holding up the almost nicked one. 'But now I can see it's the spitting image of one I've got in crocodile.'

Chapter Six

It all, you would have thought, looked quite usual if, passing by, you had seen them there – two people, eating and drinking, smiling and talking. A restaurant in Mayfair. Through the window you would have seen, at a table for two, a man and a woman. Normal, not unusual. The man, average height, average weight. Normal, but not ordinary. There was nothing ordinary about the small restaurant. No ordinary person could eat there, it was a private club and exceedingly expensive. Patrick had told her where to go and what to wear. He had described the man, five foot eleven, light brown hair – not much help, so ordinary, so normal.

'May I help you, madam, are you expected?'

The man had stopped her just as she stepped through the door. 'Yes, well . . .' She hesitated. He wasn't letting her in, barring the way. 'I'm meeting . . .' Damn, she'd forgotten his name. '. . . Someone.'

'Yes, madam? Of whom is madam the guest?'

It was so embarrassing, she couldn't remember and this condescending prick clearly thought she was having him on.

'Ah, Miss Winston, hello.' The man put out a hand.

'How do you do.' And there he was. Five foot eleven, light brown hair, nice, nice-looking.

'Your usual table, Minister? Follow me.' The waiter – no, more than a waiter or even a head waiter – led them to the centre table in the window. Minister? What sort? If he was, Patrick must be wrong about the whole thing. She had done as asked, but was certainly not going to bring the subject up. He waved away the waiter with the menus.

'Give us a few minutes, will you, Carlo.'

They chatted a bit, interesting things, not weather and the latest picture, but all sorts of news. He was good on news. All the sporting stuff too. He had seen Denis Compton get his hundredth century – very keen on cricket; he had seen Little Mo, the American girl, only seventeen, win Wimbledon. He was keen on tennis too. And he knew all that was going on abroad. He would, of course, because it turned out he was a different kind of minister than she'd thought. Nothing whatsoever to do with church, he was a cabinet minister and that was to do with the government and politics. She hadn't taken it in when Patrick had told her he was an MP. But all this news was terrific. If she managed to remember it all and trotted it out for Nick when they went out for the day in the country – well, his face would be a picture. 'Getting rid of King Farouk, although understandable in Egypt's circumstances, is yet another nail in the coffin of the divine right of kings.' Ha, Nick, top that. She must remember about all the different things in Africa. Some very violent stuff in one bit, the Mau Mau, and the really sweet thing in another where black people were only sitting down as a protest, not hitting or killing. She was eating her smoked salmon, heaven! Smoked salmon was probably the most wonderful food ever invented, and it might well be a fish, and a bloater might well be a fish, but really they ought to call it something else. He polished off his potted shrimps and drank a bit of the lovely white wine.

'As a woman, Iris, I expect you were a little sad at the death of Evita?'

'Oh, yes. No, I mean I wasn't sad, as a woman, or anything. Why?'

'You know she got the vote for women? And used her power to good effect in many cases. The poor loved her, and they had some reason to. Some.'

She finished the smoked salmon, running her tongue over her upper lip to savour the slick of oily salt. 'In that case, for what good it will do, I am sad,' she said brightly.

'And yet, Iris, she was also involved in torture and murder. A beautiful young woman, idealistic and corrupt. Corruption. Do you know what that means, Iris?'

The waiter brought their steak Dianes and a trolley with a flame thing on it. Throwing Worcester sauce and brandy all over the steak, he set it on fire. She watched, fascinated. 'Doesn't it smell wonderful? Yes, I know. It means bunging someone to do something for you that isn't on the up and up. Right?'

He ate the steak slowly. 'Yes, it does mean or can mean dishonesty but it is also the loss of innocence. And putrefaction, decomposition. This steak, this piece of beef, it has to be hung to give it flavour and make it tender. As with grouse, pheasant, all game, it is the onset of putrescence that makes it so delicious.'

'Er . . . yes, I see.' It was delicious, but this chat would have been more enjoyable at another time really.

'So we are, as it were, eating corrupt flesh.' He drank a little water and smiled. His teeth were nice, white and even. 'Tell me, Iris, what are you wearing?'

Oh, Christ! This must be it. Not the usual question that anybody might have asked. Well, so what, nothing much, especially for a fiver. 'Do you like my dress? I got it at Selfridges in the sale.'

'I like the colour, that deep blue suits you. And?' He ate a bit of his salad, still looking at her, his eyebrows raised in query. 'And?'

All right. Here goes. As per instruction. 'Well, my brassiere is white, cotton, with little loops round the edge, the straps are satin, quite wide. I do it up on the tightest hook. It's 32A.'

'Is it boned? Where is the seam?' He was still eating, nearly finished, sipping his wine.

'No, it isn't boned, and the seam is in the centre of . . . the . . . the cup.' The steak sat on her plate getting cold, the fat congealing. She didn't fancy it any more. Putrid. She remembered a lump of beef at the butcher's in the High Street. The butcher had offered it to her mum cheap and no ration book. He'd said the same thing, being a bit high made it tender. The lump of beef had looked green and shiny. Mum said, very kind but no thanks. 'Too many maggots,' that's what she said on the way home – how many was too many? She put her knife and fork together on the plate, neatly. 'I think I'm full.' He was waiting, expectant. 'My stockings are nylon, beige I call them, although it says "ecru" on the packet, medium denier because that's supposed to be stronger than fine, but they still ran when I snagged them. I put a bit of clear nail-polish on the snag. That stops them running, you know.'

His hands were folded on the table, relaxed. 'I didn't know. Where did you snag them, Iris?'

'On the bus.'

'No,' he smiled, 'where on the stocking, and which one is it, the right or left?'

'It's the left one, at the knee.' He waited. 'Just above the knee.' It still wasn't enough. 'On the front, just above the knee, it ran up, about an inch.' His right hand made a little encouraging gesture. 'My suspender belt is white too, cotton. And the straps again are satin. There are pieces of satin ribbon that hang over the doing-up bits.' He was interested but didn't appear any different, not dribbling like some dirty old man. 'Round the bottom edge of the belt part there's a little lace frill. I don't know what it's made of but it scratches.'

'Where does it sit, round your waist, or on your hips?'

'Suspender belts are usually too big to stay on my waist so they sit above the bone on my hips but below my belly-button.'

It had been said unselfconsciously, she had been distracted for a moment from the awkwardness and unease by working out where her suspender belt did sit, but the slightest flicker of interest had occurred on the word belly-button, the first sign of interest. A twitch that nobody else would have seen. Why be scared? This was a public place even though it was private. Nothing could happen.

'And?'

A waiter stood at the table offering small menus, another cleared the dishes away. The steak was gone now, thank goodness, and with it the memory of maggots. Nearly over. Not that bad really.

'Would you like something chocolate, Iris, pot au chocolat perhaps? That's a mousse. Or cheese? The Stilton here is excellent.'

'No, no.' He looked surprised. 'I mean no thank you.' Stilton, that blue cheese. Nick had told her about that. It had to be old before it got proper, age made it blue and it developed . . . ugh.

'Perhaps just an ice-cream?'

'Yes, please. That would be lovely. A lemon water one, please.' Something cold and not too sweet. It was called a sorbet, it cleansed the palate.

'I don't have to be back in the House – House of Commons – till half past three, so we have plenty of time for coffee too. Bring us coffee after the sorbet and my cheese.'

They were alone again, his hands folded on the table. Occasionally he looked out of the window. 'And what else are you wearing?'

He must know, it was what he wanted. 'Nothing.'

'So tell me what you are not wearing.'

What would happen if she shouted, 'Well, actually, as requested, I'm not wearing any knickers.'

The ice was perfect, sharp and freezing, she let it sit on the back of her tongue, the flavour deepening with warmth. 'Let's see. Well, aside from my navy suede medium-heeled shoes, my ecru nylon stockings, the white brassiere and suspender belt, underneath this blue, imitation linen dress buttoned down the front with blue glass buttons and cinched at the waist with a belt made of the same material, it would be fair to say – I am not wearing anything. I don't have my knickers on.' She thought she'd draw it out so he couldn't ask anything else. Again he looked out of the window; people were passing, a man glanced in, slowed down eyeing them and then walked on. It was then the little flicker, a twitch under his eye, happened again.

She hadn't wanted to get in the car. As far as she was concerned she'd done her bit to earn the fiver and, though it hadn't been as difficult as expected, she felt as if she'd done something wrong and wanted to be off in the nice afternoon. In the park perhaps or walking round a big shop looking at stuff, as if she had all the money in the world. But here she was in the back of his big, dark, official car and he was opposite on a little fold-down seat like in a taxi. All the windows were closed. She could see the chauffeur in his smart uniform – a nicer suit than anything her dad owned – standing by a lamppost. His back was to the car and he was smoking in secretive, short puffs, nervously flicking the ash.

'What do you say, Iris?' He was too big for the small seat but he didn't look uncomfortable; quite relaxed and dignified in fact, in spite of what he'd just said. She was sitting very upright, her knees pressed primly together, he wasn't going to get a look up her blue linen skirt.

'Iris,' he said, a bit impatiently. Anyone would think he'd only asked her if she wanted to go to the pictures. The whole thing at lunch had been unusual, it *must* be unusual, but this new idea was more, not that it meant going the whole way. How did he know he'd like it? Had he done it before? If only she could talk to someone about it. Nick would be best. Being a poof he might know about all sorts of funny carrying on. Odd sex things. But Patrick had said no one, not anybody, was to be told, ever. She wasn't to say anything because it could get back, and he could make life very uncomfortable for her. And quite right too! You couldn't expect people to vote for a man who was willing to pay a girl like her fifty pounds to have lunch on her own at a table set in the front window of a house in Wigmore Street, for everyone passing by to see. Whilst . . . Christ, it took some taking in, whilst *under* the table, under the tablecloth, while *she* was eating a meal, properly; knives and forks, glass, bread plate, napkin, salt and pepper, everything, nicely dressed too, well the top would be nice, *he* would be under her skirt, leastways, her petticoat, a very full rubber petticoat. And he would be doing what she knew from school was sixty-nine, or half of it because she wasn't going to be doing the other half on account of eating her lunch. And that wasn't all. The rubber petticoat had to touch the floor which meant no air could get in and she had to judge when to let him out, at the last minute preferably, he said. All very well but how could she tell, and what if she left it to the real last minute? She couldn't see herself saying to the police, 'Oh yes, sergeant, I often have a spot of lunch on my own, with a member of parliament stuck up my rubber skirt!' And shouldn't doing something like half sixty-nine be a bit more romantic? It was probably invented to stop people getting pregnant and with that in mind it was definitely much nicer than doing it the sailor's way.

He was looking at her handbag placed square on her lap, maybe he was thinking of upping the ante, or then again he might be thinking about what was underneath. He took a buff envelope out of his briefcase. 'I mustn't forget your expenses. No, don't put it away, please count it.' Five green one-pound notes. He watched her fingering them, a little nerve jumping in his cheek. Still she didn't speak. 'I will take your silence for a no, would that be right? You don't care to join me for lunch again?'

'Yes,' she whispered. 'I mean, yes, it does mean no. No, I'd rather not, if it's all the same to you. But thanks very much for asking.'

The five pounds were spent that afternoon. She knew she'd feel better when it was gone – got rid of.

£1 Dad
£1 Mum

2s.6d.	gas meter
2s.6d.	electric meter
£1	Post Office Savings Bank (just started)
13s.6d.	Black velvet skirt, full (but not *that* full!)
1s.6d.	Black elastic belt with silver buckle
7s.6d.	Black Merry Widow corselet
1s.	for Sam
2s.3d.	for Sam scout trip
3s.6d.	box of three bars old rose soap & talc
1s.	dictionary (CORRUPTION is nasty whatever way you look at it)
1s.6d.	record for Dad (Harry Roy)
1s.3d.	Lavender water and California Poppy for Mum
5s.	Beer for Dad. Guinness for Mum
17s.	scarf from Selfridges for next door. She would like the bag it came in as much as the scarf.

Chapter Seven

Going out for the whole day, and evening, with Nick. Terrific. Smashing! Long lovely drive, up the Great West Road all the way to near Bath, not very near, where they were going wasn't really near anywhere. So, basically she didn't know where they were going except west. And absolutely everything would be all right. Her clothes, for instance; Nick had tipped her off about what to wear, just about anything would be suitable as long as it suited her. But to remember it was the country, grass and stuff like that, high heels wouldn't do and though black was OK, not evening kind of black. The same with make-up, as much as she liked, doe-eyes, the lot. Probably having her on.

They were artists whose house they were going to, painting artists and statue-makers. So naturally, of course, they were a different kind of people. She went to the National Gallery on Thursday then couldn't pluck up the nerve to go in, but the library in St John's Wood next to the 53 bus stop was absolutely terrific. The woman in charge had been so sweet to her, not just 'can I help' meaning 'piss off who do you think you are', but 'you look lost' and a nice smile. She had settled her down at a table and given her two books to look at with photographs of artists in them and paintings by the artists, people who would be alive today. She hoped Nick's friends would be in there. Some of the paintings were a bit fuzzy and not true to life, not at all like photographs. These paintings weren't realistic, she remembered that, what she hadn't remembered was what they *were*.

'Stop bouncing, you're like a rubber ball.'

'Oh, sorry, Nick, I'm just so excited. I've never been on a long car trip, I've never been as far as near Bath, I've never been asked out to artists, I've never been out at half past seven in the morning.'

'Very well, just don't bounce as much.' He didn't really mind, she could tell, if he did he would have made his prune face.

'It was ever so nice of you to come in, Mum was really knocked out, especially as I told her you were in the foreigners office.'

'Foreign Office.'

'Yes, sorry.' Was he cross? Bobby hadn't said not to say, and she wouldn't if he'd said, 'cross my heart', once said she always stuck to. Anyway, who would Mum tell? Breathing deeply, trying to control her excitement, trying not to bounce, she looked from side to side at the empty early morning streets of Knightsbridge. 'I'm having such a good time!' she shouted.

'Already? We've only been driving for ten minutes.'

They passed Harrods slowly, held up by a milk cart and a dog crossing the Brompton Road so leisurely he must know it was Saturday.

'Here, Nick. Beg pardon. Excuse me, Nick, but Harrods is posher than Selfridges, isn't it?'

'But not as posh as Fortnum and Mason.'

'I know, I've seen through the windows, all those men working there, all wearing gloves.'

'And Fortnums isn't as posh as Jacksons.'

She didn't believe this but no point in irritating him, as Bobby said she did. Sometimes. Couldn't be always or he wouldn't ask her out. 'If you say so,' she said diplomatically.

Breakfast out! And outside! They stopped at a place by the river, a grand roadhouse. Not like one of those she'd been to where it had been a bit tricky not going upstairs after lots of drinks at the bar and a slap-up lunch. They had all made her feel guilty. First the bloke who had taken a shine to her, quite nice really, and looking at it from his point of view, not fair, he'd treated her and got nothing in return. Then the twins made her feel worse, all her fault they said if they had to fuck all four of the men, considering as how Alicia had got the curse. Pretending to go to the toilet, she'd slipped out and got the Green Line bus back to London.

'Coffee or tea, miss?' The waiter put out the toast and butter.

'Both, please.' Nick raised his eyebrows. 'Like you said at Lyons' Corner House, I'll see which one is their métier.'

'I take it, jam *and* marmalade then?'

'Depends on the jam.'

'Plum jam, miss.'

'No jam then, thank you.' She sipped the coffee, tasting it carefully, and then the tea.

'What do you think, Iris, what is your considered opinion?'

She looked at the river, the little black ducks with white faces, the larger swans like royalty in ermine capes, the tiny birds pecking at the crumbs under their table. 'Well, to be quite honest, the grub's not as good as the setting, but that's true about most of these places.' He touched her bony shoulder, laughing. 'Or so they say,' she added.

'Have you been here before?'

'No, but same sort of place.'

'With?'

'With some of the usual gang, Peter somebody, that American friend of your cousin Charlie, the twins. You know.'

'Christ, you get away with murder, girl. Coming to a place like this in a gang like that means only one thing. You do know that?'

'I know, I know, well, I know now. I had to get the Green Line bus back.'

'You're still a virgin, aren't you?' She blushed, touching her red cheeks. 'I'm sorry if I embarrassed you.' What an odd little creature. 'You don't turn a hair at "fuck", but . . .'

'*Virgin* is so personal.'

'Of course. Sorry.'

'No, I've never slept with anybody. You see, I've never been in love.'

'And it's never occurred to you to go to bed with somebody – a body – just for the pleasure of it?'

'No, never felt like it.'

'Is it that you've simply never fancied anybody?'

'Just about, I have a bit, but it was out of the question.'

'Married?'

'No,' she laughed. 'That's never out of the question. No, more like . . . it's hard to say.'

'Ah, you're protecting my feelings; he, or they, were queer. Right?'

'Right.'

'Then I would say you had a "safe" crush.'

'Not as much as that, not what I'd call a crush. I know that because I've got a crush on James Mason.'

They went fast on the open roads, whizzing past grass, hills, trees, animals and fields full of unknown stuff, well, wheat, barley and corn, Nick said, but she didn't know which was which. It was slower but more interesting going through the small towns. Everybody on a Saturday queuing for the Sunday joint. Queues at all the butchers, greengrocers, bakers, men queuing at tobacconists, kids hanging round outside sweet shops, but mainly women queuing for food clasping the handbags that held their purses and ration books. Did the Sunday afternoon streets of Reading and Maidenhead smell the same as Kilburn and Cricklewood?

They were quiet after Marlborough. Not talking but all nice and friendly. Knowing him for about eight months, a long time, but not really truly until today. Discrimination, he said, is the core of our friendship. It was all very interesting and needed some sorting out. Neither of them could cross a barrier and nothing could change it because of the people who knew them now. If in the future they tried to pass themselves off in different company there was always the chance of a tip-off and that was dangerous, and better to live without fear even if it wasn't the life you wanted. Fancy thinking like that! All very well at his age, settling for something, and anyway what a lot he'd already got. And why think yet about the years ahead? Eighteen his god-daughter was, just a few months older than her, today's do was a birthday party. When *she* was eighteen her godfather wouldn't be going to her party, for the simple reason she hadn't got one. And that wasn't the only reason. What Nick didn't understand was it didn't piss her off, that was the way it was, for always. And all he said about going out and be careful, well, most of it was lovely in spite of the drawbacks, and she couldn't afford 'dignity', and in any case it wasn't much fun.

'Why are you laughing?'

'It was that sign, TO THE DOWNS, only the lane was going up.'

Zig-zagging through high-hedged lanes, occasionally a stone farmhouse was revealed lying back off the lane surrounded by flower-filled gardens and cow-studded fields.

'See, there's another funny one, UPPER DOWN-SIDE FARM. Here, Nick, your friends' house, is it as big as that?'

'Well, bigger actually. More of a manor house.'

'You told me they were nice ordinary people.'

'I did no such thing. The Chiltons are nice easy people, but certainly not ordinary. Don't worry, you will, well, fit in all right.' He patted her knee. 'Did I offend you just now, darling?'

'No, not really, I don't think so; I agree I *am* a very faulty type of person.' She was extremely pleased at the 'darling', it wasn't Bobby's camp 'darling', it was a real one. 'To tell the truth, Nick, I was a bit browned off at first. I offer to be your beard, your cover, and meet the family, *and*, may I say, a well experienced and successful beard, Steve Brown's mum never twigged that I wasn't his true love, well, his girlfriend, and you, all scornful, give a high-falutin' laugh and tell me your mum would rather you turn up with a posh poof than a bit of rough like me.'

'You're not a bit of rough, Iris.'

'A scrubber, then. Anyway, say no more, because I understand, I think, it's just that you don't put things very nicely.' Frowning, she tried to figure it out. 'Your mum could pretend to herself that a posh poof was just a chum and that he wasn't queer. But, me, she couldn't pretend about because of my voice and not knowing what people are talking about, especially when it's all "He's MFH of the Whaddon Chase," "Did you see Piers at Corbishley?" I was having dinner at Les A the night before last with some real nobs and they were talking about horses and hunting and racing and the going being soft and in the middle someone said Felicity was a real goer, yes, yes, you know what I'm going to say; not a horse, a stable girl they all knew. I ended up being a laughing-stock.'

There was no self-pity in the girl, his mother would like her, but not as a consort. He turned off the narrow bumpy lane on to a track. 'There, you can see it through the trees.'

It was the best she'd seen during the whole long lovely drive. The sun was turning the stone all pink and making the long windows look like crystal – like lots and lots of vases. And all round the house, instead of beds of flowers and lawns and borders, the flowers were all muddled up with veg, like a lot of fancy allotments.

'It is a bit big, bigger than you made out, Nick, but it's smashing. I've never seen anything like all the potatoes and lettuces being in with the bunches of flowers.'

'Yes, I forgot, I'm used to it. They did it during the war, and didn't stop.'

'You haven't said anything about how I look, and you look smashing, you do, honestly, casual and bohemian, it suits you. Yes, if you had a beard you'd look like a cross between Augustus John and . . . whatsisname Strachey. Not the old food minister, I don't mean.'

'I am surprised you know of either.'

'Don't be so bleeding condescending. Augustus John was in one of those books at the library.'

'I see, you know what he looks like but not his work.'

'And I am not disinterested in politics,' she added loftily.

'I am pleased to hear it – turn round. You look

wonderful, very Twenties.' The dress was grey muslin, unlined and floaty.

'Can you tell I'm not wearing a bra?'

He hesitated. 'No, I don't think so, and so what, if I wasn't a poof I'd fuck you into the middle of next week.'

'Would you honestly? Oh, thanks, Nick.'

It wasn't easy, not like he'd said, fitting in didn't happen just like that. After he'd introduced her to Cordelia – 'lot in common', 'same age', 'boys and dancing', bollocks like that – off he'd gone. She was lovely and nice but it was her party so in between being polite to people she didn't know, she was trying to have a good time with friends.

First there was 'This is Iris' to a group and 'How do you do' all round. 'Did you motor down or come on the train?' someone said, then gradually they all drifted back to their private chit-chat. Another couple joined the group on the edge, so she did, 'Hello, I'm Iris,' and shook hands, then the man did the 'motor or train' question, but they knew the others in the group so without being rude she was sort of shoved out. There was an older man looking at a sundial, all alone. She'd try him. Tall and thin, even older close to, grey hair, bit of a beard, slightly humpty-backed.

'How do you do, I'm Iris.'

'What did you say?' He cupped a hand behind an ear.

Well done, Iris, you've picked a deaf one. She smiled, holding out her hand. 'I'm Iris Winston.' He shook her hand unsmiling and turned back to the sundial.

'Did you motor down or come on the train?' she shouted.

He looked round, bewildered.

'Did you motor . . .'

'Yes, yes, don't shout. Why the hell would I do either? I live here.'

There was no one else to join, it was a large garden and the little clumps of people were dotted about with quite a bit of distance between them and all turned in to face each other. Right. She'd have to keep this going. 'Excuse me, beg pardon, but would you mind telling me about the sundial, please?'

The old man sighed, a little impatient puff of air.

'You see, I don't think I've ever seen one before, and seeing as how this one is yours and you must be used to it being here I wondered as to why you were giving it the eye – giving it the once over – giving it an awful lot of attention. See?' It was putting her all on edge, this ignoring her. 'I mean to say, you can give it a quick look-see any old time, right, so then, it stands to reason that if you can be bothered to keep on, it must be really special.' She waited. Rude bastard. Nearby from a big old tree came the squeals and shouts of kids; perhaps she could pretend to love children and join them in a game. Somewhere a clock struck twelve, like from a church, slow, and very serious.

'See.'

Christ! He'd spoken. 'What?'

'It's twelve o'clock.'

'I know, I heard it from the church.'

'Yes, but that was late, this – ' he pointed to the shadow falling on the sundial, 'this, as ever, was on time.'

She circled and inspected it from every angle. 'I don't mind telling you I am absolutely knocked out. It's so clever. I wonder who thought it up?'

He gave her a little sort of nod and bow and left, walking towards the house. The children she'd heard before came spilling out, running towards her, ignoring the old man.

'Have we missed it?' 'We forgot.' 'I heard the clock and I remembered.' 'Ha, easy remembering after.' There were six of them, between the ages of three and eight she thought.

'Does it only work at twelve o'clock?' she said.

'Best at twelve, Greatpappa likes the shadow best then,' the older boy said. 'You saw it?'

'Yes. Tell you what, why don't we make a clock ourselves?'

The younger ones stopped their leaping and screaming. 'How, how?'

'Lie in a circle. Sort of evenly, every ten minutes, say, I'll be twelve o'clock and the rest of you can take it in turns being the hand.'

It went down a treat; after resisting for a minute on the grounds of age and superiority the oldest boy joined in as the hand, and accompanied by shouts of 'tick-tock' he rolled from one to twelve. Then they had a fight about who should take over and should there be a pendulum and what sort of clock was it, and if it was a cuckoo clock who was going to be the cuckoo. Iris got a bit of a titter from an observer when she said, 'Too many cuckoos spoil the clock,' but the kids were bored, the game was too passive unless you were a hand or a cuckoo.

'Hide and seek,' they shouted. Iris decided to be 'it', she needed a rest and it was a bit more dignified hiding somewhere nice and quiet than running around with a pack of hollering kids. She settled down at the back of a long barn, not far away, easy to find. They were counting down in shrill excited voices: 'Nine – Eight – Six – Three – Five – Two.'

'Seven, you forgot seven.' That was the little girl in glasses.

'Didn't, DID NOT, Four.'

'What about seven?' And then it was quiet.

About five minutes should do it, they were bound to have cheated, opening their eyes as she ran off. Pity there wasn't a mirror round here, her handbag was by the sundial, she was hot and all this make-up had gone on at half past six. There were some glass panes leaning against the black planks of the barn, come from the nearby collapsed greenhouse, she guessed. Not bad, they made quite a good mirror, her eyes had run a bit, she looked like Claudette Colbert – or was that the dust? No sight or sound of the kids. She peeked round the side of the barn, the girls were jumping with a skipping-rope, and the boys were playing leapfrog. They had forgotten.

She could walk out there as if she meant to join someone and by the time she got anywhere there might be someone to join. No sign of Nick, he must be in the house. Those kids, those little shits, not a thought for her. And if she just strolled away from the barn on her own, now, would they think she'd gone to the toilet? So much bloody easier in a room.

Something was up, people were drifting towards the house. Good, she could nip over and then drift with them. Smashing, really good luck.

'Iris, I'd like you to meet Sarah Marshall,' Nick took her hand and pulled her to him. 'Where have you been? Having a good time?'

'Yes, thank you.'

'Sarah, this is Iris Winston, we motored down together.' Ah, how sweet of him, really sort of saying, 'Iris is my friend.' And the lady was truly lovely, browny-gold hair all wavy, crinkly laughing eyes and dimples when she smiled.

'How do you do, Iris. I saw you with the children. Wonderful idea, that clock, it must have kept them occupied for at least half an hour. Very noble of you.' That was nice, she had been noticed, made it worthwhile. 'I'm just going to find John, will you get us all a table, Nick?'

After getting their food from the buffet, bit of a laugh, 'Don't take all the mayonnaise,' jostling in the queue, 'Now then young lady, you need more than that,' all very good-humoured, they settled at a table. Not too big, people would have to talk to her. And anyway she'd got together a few bits and pieces to chat about, not just 'Did you motor down or come by train?' The cold salmon came from Caroline's father's place in Scotland where someone at the table had a rod, Caroline being Cordelia's mum, and a rod meant the man was allowed to fish. The old man at the sundial was the owner of the place, the painter's father, who was Caroline's husband and obviously Cordelia's grandfather – or something like that. And he was known as being very eccentric so that was all right. The lovely friendly lady was married to one of Nick's bosses and the wife of the man with the rod was having a baby and she was a relation of the Chiltons so they were staying the night and she was an artist and dyed silk.

The food was right up her street, very good and easy to understand but a surprise here and there. The mayonnaise for instance was green, and the potatoes didn't have mint but something just as good. Nick was pleased with her because the thin blond man sitting opposite him said she had a lively intelligence and agreed she looked like a putto and they were going to show her one on the local church.

The wine was good, she knew because everyone had said so; she tried to copy the way they drank, something in between dainty sips and big mouthfuls. Then her heart was beating fast and she felt funny. Behind her someone was talking, lovely voice, low and beautifully spoken in the way of the BBC. He laughed, 'Sorry I'm late,' then a figure bent over the Sarah woman and gave her a quick kiss. He was saying hello to everybody, sitting next to Sarah, opening his napkin and picking up his knife and fork. As Nick leaned forward pouring the wine he finally saw her, took her in. The smallest, smallest, speck of anxiety flickered across his face.

'Hello there, I'm John Marshall. I don't think we have met.'

'Of course not,' she said firmly.

If it had been before lunch it would have been simple, no problem; slope off, find a toilet, be sick, have a kip in the barn, and nobody any the wiser. Now, everybody was milling round the room all talking together, and try as she might as soon as she made a move, not easy considering how giddy she was, someone would come up and have a word or people would turn round and include her. A bit bloody late in the day. She was aiming to get upstairs out of the way. There was a cloakroom downstairs somewhere, but someone waiting to go might hear the awful sound, and know she was being sick.

Edging away from the little group she faced Claire, the rod man's wife, smiling a little worried smile.

'Are you all right?' she whispered.

'Not really, no, I'm a bit dizzy.' With a flash of inspiration she said, 'I've got the curse rather badly.'

'Poor dear, the one thing to be said about pregnancy is you don't get your period for nine months. Come up to our room and I'll give you a couple of aspirins, have you got a thingy?'

'Yes, thanks ever so, I would like that please.'

What a relief. Claire had drawn the curtains and gone. In case someone came in she pushed the big weighing machine against the door, which didn't lock, she meant to be sick in the toilet but it happened so sudden she only just got to the sink in time. Still it was better than putting two fingers down your throat, which made you feel sick – though of course that was the point; except being sick wasn't quite the same as feeling sick.

It had been the drinks with the coffee that had done her in, finished her off. After the minister had arrived, tell the truth, she had drunk a lot of wine, it was to keep herself occupied, along with eating more too. Then Nick, ho ho ho, said you don't have to choose port or brandy you can do what you did at breakfast, have both. Well, they all laughed at the story and to be a good sport she'd drunk the brandy, port, and a green thing.

It wasn't going down, bits were lodged in the plughole. Poking it with a finger didn't work, the handles of the toothbrushes were too wide, but there was a steel comb with a nice thin tail, just the job. Christ, her breath was disgusting. After washing her hands she rubbed a bit of soap on her tongue. Not a good idea. This time she managed to get to the toilet.

Sitting on the bed propped up by big comfy pillows (lying down had given her the whirlies) in the darkened room, the picture of him at lunch: eating and enjoying the salmon, laughing about a political thing with Nick, talking nicely with his wife, all ran together with having lunch with him before. Sitting opposite her he was then too, enjoying the food, chatting all political and amusing, polite and gentlemanly, and her with no knickers on.

That pretty wife, Sarah, did she have a long rubber skirt? As they were married, would they do all of sixty-nine instead of half? No, not on your nellie, he didn't do those sort of things with her, no, they probably did it all comfortable and pleasant, in bed.

Must be nice to have your own church. This one belonged to the Chiltons and was very handy if you felt like a bit of religion. Thank heavens for the two aspirins and the cup of tea, else tipping her head back like this to see the little statues on the church would really have done her in.

'You are rather a pale putto this afternoon, why?'

'Do I look awful? I had to take my make-up off, it had all run.' Not true, most of it had come off being sick.

'Not awful.' He wasn't going to tell her how lovely she was with or without make-up, he was too angry.

'I don't think she looks like these scary baby monsters, her face is too fine.'

'Yeah, thanks.' He was OK this man, obviously an old chum of Nick's. Or an old boyfriend? A posh poof!

'You should see her when she's angry, she puffs out her cheeks like a guinea-pig.'

It all sounded fine and dandy but it wasn't, he was pissed off, no doubt about it. Good then that they were giving the bloke a lift back to London. His name was Hadrian, at first she thought it was a joke – Adrian said by a cockney – but no, it really was Hadrian, you'd have to be rich and posh to get away with a name like that.

*

The drive back was faster at night, the villages and towns they'd crawled through in the morning were now empty and Nick sped through them. She sat behind Hadrian, warm and sleepy, hardly joining in their conversation, grateful for what she knew was a lull before the storm.

He exploded the minute Hadrian got out of the car in Chiswick. He lived in a beautiful big house right on the river, very nice, but a peculiar place to live if you could afford somewhere in Mayfair or Chelsea, but then so was the country. Nice to go to but not for all the time. And she said so. It was like as if he was a tin of petrol and she'd thrown a match at him, not that it was anything to do with Chiswick or Mayfair. He had guessed.

'Sarah Marshall is one of my best friends, she is a charming, intelligent, attractive, kind woman. A marvellous woman; a good mother, wife, excellent hostess, she would help anyone, she . . .' He fumbled for more adjectives.

'Yes, isn't she? I loved her, she was ever so nice to me.'

'Be quiet. Don't give me your faux naïf performance you nasty little slut.'

She let him go on, there was no point in denying anything until he let on what he knew.

There was a tube near here in Hammersmith by the Palais but would there still be trains after midnight? And wouldn't it be better in the long run to sit here and put up with it, all the insults? He didn't need her at all, it made no difference to his life, he could take it or leave it. The 'it' being her. Whereas, with Steve gone she couldn't afford to cut off someone like Nick who gave her a good time now and then with no bother about going to bed and was part of her lovely other world.

There was a sad little noise from the river like a bird calling, or a duck. Could ducks be sad? Anyway there was no way she could let on anything about Mister John Fucking Marshall (not that he had fucked her or even wanted to). Patrick had been extremely serious about keeping her mouth shut.

He'd stopped talking. Was he waiting for an answer? What had he said? Mr Marshall was one of his oldest friends, perfect marriage, etc., etc.

'Nick, I told you this morning, and you knew it was the truth, I'm a . . . well, I've never done it. Now . . .' She spoke carefully, choosing her words, she'd got to protect herself from Patrick's threat and keep Nick as her friend. 'Are you saying that I went off somewhere today with him and we slept together? Are you saying that I was a virgin this morning and . . . not this evening?'

'Iris, we all know you are a prick teaser. I believe you have hung on to your maidenhead but there is a reason why you were shaking at lunch the minute you heard his voice. You have met him before, I know that, probably sucked him off or gave him a hand job.'

'Not me, Nick, isn't that what you do? You don't think much of your happily married oldest friend to think he'd stick his prick in the mouth of a nasty little slut like me.' She felt for the handle of the door. 'As for shaking when I heard his voice, I'd come over a bit funny as Claire – another one of your friends – noticed and kindly took me up to her room for a lie down.'

She was trembling again; her face, dimly lit by the street lamp, was pale and frightened. Who had frightened her? He had heard John Marshall referred to obliquely as a 'chancer', indirect gossip, vague enough to make it possible for him to ignore or forget. She was still scrabbling for the door. Poor cow, she could find it quick enough if she wanted to. He reached over the back and opened it. 'Thank you.'

That was that then, there'd be no flowers tomorrow, she was the one who had lapsed. Chin up, Iris. Bobby owes you for setting you up with the Browns, he might be able to straighten things out with Nick.

At least she was wearing flat shoes and it wasn't raining. How long would it take her to walk home? Up Chiswick Mall and Hammersmith Mall by the river, then left at the roundabout down Shepherds Bush Road, right at Holland Park Avenue, left at Ladbroke Grove; safest to stick to the big roads which might be lit, no short cuts, right in Kensal Rise, to Brondesbury Road and then she'd be in Kilburn High Road; lucky if she'd got any shoes left.

'Where do you think you are going?'

There was just a little smile on his face as he opened the car door at the front. 'Get in!'

Chapter Eight

A PRIVATE COCKTAIL party to do with a newspaper or magazine, she couldn't remember. Or both. If you had all the machines and all the paper and the writers you might just as well do both and keep it all going. She was to be there at the beginning and stay till the end and circulate. Patrick said they wanted it to be crowded and successful. With a bit of luck there would be dinner after somewhere. A crowded do would make it easier to become part of a group.

Half past six prompt she got there, a nice private room upstairs at Da Fredo. Nobody was there. Not one single person. Not a guest or a host. There was a very long table covered in a white tablecloth to the ground that was covered in bottles and bottles of all sorts of stuff, mainly whisky and gin, and glasses. No food at all, not even crisps and nuts. And no waiters around either. It made her feel more awkward being alone in a room than walking into a crowd of people and not knowing anyone. If she stayed there and people came in they might think she was a waitress – or even worse, a hostess. Waiting in the ladies' room was the answer. Thank heavens, no attendant, she could save her threepenny-bit, and put on some more make-up. When she went back upstairs, like a miracle it was jam-packed. Lovely. Loads of noise. talking, laughing, shouting. Even those whispering were doing it loud. Absolutely everybody was smoking, lots of different kinds, the smoke changed from person to person and group to group. American Camels, Players, the French strong ones that came in blue packets, big cigars, thin cigarillos. As people smoked they puffed the smoke away, some in the air tipping their heads back, some straight ahead. The cigarettes and cigars they held to one side, so basically you might be smoking a Camel and the person talking to you a Cuban cigar and someone next to you a French Gitane, but the smoke you all inhaled was a mixture.

It was a crowd of proper drinkers. Not a sign of a cocktail. It was all gins, whiskies, and brandies, in small tumblers. She did what she was told and circulated, standing on the edge of knots of people nodding and smiling. Once or twice she managed to get in one of her useful sentences: 'I quite agree' came in very handy. And depending on who she was talking to, a very nice sentence was 'The government needs a left-wing element,' or 'It didn't.' As it was a Labour government anyone would have thought it already had a left-wing element. Questions were the best. 'What do you think about . . .?' Then add Bentley who'd been found guilty of killing a policeman though he didn't actually do it. The Mau Mau, that was in Africa. The train crash, so horrible what could you think about it. Anything in the papers would do. Over in the corner she could see the twins chatting with Alice, not fair really if they were invited so as to circulate. She was standing very nearly part of a group of men. All with posh voices and talking fast about everything, all sorts of stuff. The only sentence she could try was, 'How interesting, I didn't know that.' Somebody pushed through, elbowed her aside, and turned to apologize. It was a man she'd met at a couple of big dinners and danced with.

'Hello, Robert.' He was the sort of person who always used his whole name, insisted on it, never allowing Bobby or Bert, but who couldn't remember anyone else's name.

'Oh, hello, Lucky,' he said and turned his back. It was Lucky or Cheeky or Sweetheart.

The man facing her turned from chatting and said, quite serious, 'Lucky?'

'Yes, that's right,' she said with a bit of a smile.

'What are you doing? Would you like to come to the Pearthies?

All ever so commanding he took her shoulder and led her away. Not led, more *pulled.*

In his car, which had been waiting for him slap bang in front outside, there were piles and piles of newspapers. He didn't say hello or anything to the driver when he opened the door, just 'The Pearthies.' Then he leafed through the newspapers fast, throwing them aside and muttering and biting his nails, they were down to the quick on both hands.

'Have you been to the Pearthies?' he said, lighting a thin dark cigarette.

'Not actually, though I have heard of them, of

course.' It sounded like a place, the Chilterns, the Cotswolds, the Pearthies.

'Why do they call you Lucky?' he said, still going through the papers and throwing them to one side.

She would keep quiet about the fact that nobody called her Lucky except the bloke who couldn't remember her name. Well,' she said brightly, 'I *am* lucky, you see.'

'How?' He looked at her now, dumping the rest of the papers. 'Do you bet?'

'Yes,' she said firmly. 'I bet, and I win; on horses, the dogs, you know.' It wasn't a total lie. She had won a lot of money, for those days, on the Derby in 1948. My Love, the horse was called. 'And I bring luck to other people too.' She had really got his attention now.

'What is your name?' He touched her hand, not affectionately, more like you do when you say 'Touch wood.'

'My name's Iris. Iris Winston. But they call me . . . Lucky Winston.' She didn't half want to laugh, it was all very Rita Hayworth or Rosalind Russell, though she did quite like it. 'What's your name, please?'

'Me? I'm David Selsdy.' He said it as if she ought to know.

At the door of the big house in a square near to Belgrave Square he rang a bell. The door was opened only a little bit by an unseen person.

'It's D.S.,' he said. 'With Lucky W.'

If it was going to go on like this she would either

laugh or wet herself. Inside there was a lovely big room, two rooms really, divided by an arch. All comfortable looking, big long squashy sofa, nice shiny polished furniture, paintings and mirrors in curly gold frames and a marble fireplace. That was one half of the room. In the other half – it was a gambling den! Two tables with roulette wheels spinning round and French words being spoken and pearly discs instead of money, and two other tables with cards, not poker or gin-rummy but something else. The place was quite full. Everybody dressed like ladies and gentlemen. David Selsdy went straight to one of the card tables and sat down, saying 'hello' to people and introducing her as Lucky. She got the hang of the game pretty quick, it had a French name but it was only twenty-one. Two other girls were standing behind men playing at these tables, but at roulette there were more. Two pretty young women were sitting on the sofa drinking champagne and eating sandwiches. She would consider herself 'Lucky' if she could join them.

After about half an hour D.S. was doing quite nicely, a good pile of the pearl chips in front of him. Then one of the players left and a man with ginger hair took his place. The next game was going really well, D.S. should win it, she could see an ace in his hand and an ace showing on the table. He bet a lot, then two men dropped out and 'Ginger' was left and the man dealing the cards, 'The House'. But then the next card was a big one and took him over twenty-one, so 'Ginger' won. Then he lost again – very big.

'Mr Selsdy,' she whispered, 'that ginger bloke has

brought you bad luck, you should knock it off for a while.'

It came in handy because it meant she could have a drink and a sandwich. It was all free, the food and drinks. But if you counted it against the lost betting money it was very dear.

'Room for a small one?'

The two women smiled and moved up.

'Very exciting, isn't it?' Iris said. 'Specially if it's not your money.'

The one with straight rather oily hair pushed behind her ears held out her hand. 'I'm Flora.'

'How do you do, I'm Iris.'

'You are quite wrong, Iris,' she said, 'it's only exciting if it *is* your money. Rather a lot of David Selsdy's money is sitting in Oliver's bank account. That's Oliver.' She pointed to the man who'd opened the door. 'And it would appear he is going to lose more tonight. And that excites him very much.'

Why does he bite his nails then? And where is he? Gone to the lav, right? Got the runs.'

Flora laughed. 'Of course not, silly. He's on the telephone calling his paper.'

'What paper does he work for, please?'

'*The Hour.* And he owns it.'

'Oh, no.' Iris was abashed. 'I've been so rude, I should have known. I bet he's laughing at me. Who are you with? Which man?'

'I'm not with anybody. Oliver has quite a lot of my money too.'

'Poor thing. I'm so sorry,' Iris said sincerely. 'But fancy having enough to have spare money to lose.'

Oliver came over with a glass, a bottle of champagne and a plate of tea-time-looking sandwiches. 'There you are, Lucky, and how are you, Flora?' He filled all their glasses. 'I was surprised to see David tonight, with all that's happening at *The Hour.*'

'Oh, I know why he came.' Iris felt important with knowledge, and had a bite of sandwich. Crab paste, she thought. In a place like this though it could be real crab.

'Why?' Flora was interested.

'Well, you see. There was a party and I was in a group with him, by chance, and someone came up, a man I know, and he said hello to me, only he said "Hello Lucky", that's my nickname.' She was beginning to believe it. 'And he, Mr Selsdy, got all excited and insisted we came here. All on account of me being called Lucky. I didn't know we were coming somewhere so nice. Just as well he didn't say we were going gambling, I'd have thought he meant poker.' She took a big swig of champagne.

'Well, Lucky, we do play poker too.' He topped up her glass.

'Yes, but there's poker and there's poker. Now. The poker I'm used to – well, seen it twice – is played in an old basement which you get to from the kitchen and it's all very serious. No style like this here.' She smiled contentedly around the lovely room. 'Not nice sofas to sit on. You've done this up all very attractive. And they wouldn't let me stay and watch, perhaps because I wasn't eighteen yet – I'm still not, but very nearly.'

Oliver had put the bottle and plate on the side table. 'Where did you go to . . . not play poker? The Brown brothers?'

'Yes. Do you know them? You see, I used to know their mum quite well.' No point telling them about Steve. Except this Oliver was doing something against the law just the same as the Browns. Gambling was illegal in this beautiful house as well as in a basement.

Neither of them were smiling at her now and before she'd finished her champagne and sandwich they had walked her to the door saying goodnight. Flora took her out to the street and waved down a taxi.

'Excuse me, Flora, but why do I have to go? Because I'm only seventeen?'

'Partly. A word of advice, Iris. Enjoy the protection of the brothers but don't talk about it.'

'Don't know what you mean,' she said sulkily.

'You were a friend of the mother? I think you do. Here . . .' Flora gave her two pounds for the taxi.

Sitting on the bus with the taxi change, £1 16s. 6d. – she had stopped the taxi once they were clear of Belgravia – she thought of D.S. with regret. He could have been truly useful. Other men who were winning gave their girlfriends small pearl chips, and he was interesting too, he must know items of information that would be good for a chat. As it was she'd been shoved off home with no pearl chip and £1 16s. 6d. Next time Lucky would keep her mouth shut.

'Happy new year, Iris.'

'Ouch! That hurt.' Somebody tugged hard at her plait, the man's voice was sharp, it didn't sound as if he really wanted her new year to be happy. She ducked away, protecting her breasts. She knew who it was from experience, he always did something like that, distracted her from his real intention by pinching her cheek or pulling her ear. Once he even kicked her behind the knee and as she bent to rub it, put his hands on her bust and pinched the nipples till she almost fainted. Nick had told her about him the first time they ever met. 'My cousin is a bad man in more ways than one.' She didn't want to know about that but he was definitely very nasty.

'And a happy new year to you, Charles,' she smiled sweetly. 'If you do that just once more I'm gonna give you a bunch of fives.' She held up her fist. 'You fucking little sadist.'

He loved her swearing; well, they all did come to that. He surveyed her from head to foot, taking in the clever, discreet appeal, nothing revealed but everything showing; an emergent schoolgirl. It must be calculated. 'Have you done yourself up like that for Beastie? Is he finally going to get your cherry?'

'What do you mean? What's wrong with how I look?' It was beautiful what she was wearing – in a dull sort of way. The lightest of taffetas, tissue taffeta the shop woman had called it. Full skirt well below her knees, the tightest of waists – she'd had to wear a Merry Widow for it – and a fitted bodice of fine jersey going right up into a polo neck. Bloody difficult to do up. She blushed remembering trying it on – and the other dress – and the look on the shop woman's face. Awkward, it had been. All of it.

Charlie was interested. 'Are you blushing, little girl? Ah ha. I thought I was only teasing but . . . well, make sure he pays a commensurate amount for the loss of your hymen. He's been after it long enough.'

'What would be the point?' She had recovered her poise. 'I wouldn't live to spend it, he would suffocate me.'

He snatched her wrist as she walked away, pulling her arm up behind her back. 'There is more than one way to skin a cat, silly girl.'

Bobby had found a good table and rescued her.

'They aren't all like that, Bobby. I have lovely times, you know, and what's more I have been out at least once a week on average since last New Year's Eve and . . .'

'Yes, darling, I know. I've seen you, don't forget.' He took his hands off the shoulder he'd been rubbing. 'Is that better?'

She nodded.

'All I'm saying is, it will catch up with you one day. You can't get away with it for ever. Even I have been known to put my face in the pillow for a hot dinner and a taxi home.'

Her eager little face showed that his advice was being ignored.

'Wasn't it wonderful, Tuesday. They played *my* song when we walked in. I thought it must be for someone else but when Ricky bowed to me, I knew it was for me – me!'

'Yes, dear.' No point in telling her that any girl who arrived with England's richest and classiest businessman got the treatment, and when his actual girlfriend arrived from a stop-off in the ladies' room, Iris's song was quickly changed to 'You're My Everything'. 'I'm going to get some of that Coronation chicken before it goes. Shall I get some for you?'

'Please. And I'll get our wines topped up, OK?'

'Right. Sit with your back against the wall, Stan, and if anyone tries anything on, keep your hand on your halfpenny and tell him tits first. Won't be a min.'

Stan. She hadn't liked it at first. Now though it fitted in with what Nick called her persona; she was a bit of a character. All her life from ever remembering anything, but most of all in school, she had wanted a nickname, but there was nothing you could do with Iris. Then she met Bobby and he called her Stan. He wouldn't explain for ages, said she had to guess. Even when he did tell her, it took forever to get it. Iris = Flag = Standard = Stan. 'Stan without the dard on,' he'd said, then Nick had been really rude to poor Bobby. 'Like you, Bobby, without the hard on.'

*

There was Bébé, leaving before midnight. Maybe she didn't feel well, or she might be going to the Milroy, like last year. No, the man she'd been talking to was following her, carrying a bottle of champagne. They most likely wanted to be alone. He was very nice, the man. Canadian, not American as she had thought at first. Ever so polite; stood up when you left the room. After a really nice chat, he'd been easy to talk to, all about Mum and Dad and how rotten it was living in Kilburn. He insisted on sending her home with two fivers for the taxi. 'So long, Cinderella.'

She hadn't seen Bébé since the business about the model job, but they had said hello as normal tonight so that must have been a mistake all that stuff and it was daft to be suspicious about someone doing you a good turn.

A couple of weeks ago, someone had bumped into a waiter serving Iris a gin and Dubonnet. Poor Iris, fresh out of luck, it went all over her best cream imitation silk blouse. Might have known. Wear black or navy, nothing ever goes wrong, nobody spills nothing, anything. 'Oh my God, look at me,' she shrieked. The waiter looked anxiously at the head waiter, more worried about him than her blouse. A couple of people at the table laughed and went on talking and there she was soaking wet. 'Don't worry,' she mouthed to the waiter. No point in him losing his job over her blouse. It would probably dye. There might even be a colour called 'Dubonnet', after all, there was a 'burgundy'. She didn't want anyone to see she was a bit tearful, so she nipped downstairs to the lovely little ladies' room they had at La Panache, all done out like a velvet tent. The woman could dry it on the radiator but she'd have to go home. Nice night out! All that bleeding money down the drain. No taxi money, pay for the bus, and a tip for the woman, and the blouse, if truth be told, had had it. She hated the colour burgundy. It was just a fancy word for maroon.

'What a fuss, Iris, crying over an old blouse.' Bébé had followed her down to the toilet. She'd been nice, though. Suggested she might try out for a job as a house model at Lamasse. The models there were about her size, though she might be a bit too short. So she'd gone home on the bus, very uncomfortable, fed up, the woman wouldn't dry the blouse.

'My ladies don't want washing all over the place.'

It had dried on her, all sticky. Still, she'd learnt her lesson. Never ever would she drink Dubonnet again.

The next day she met Bébé at Le Routier after lunch, had a glass of champagne and walked round the corner to Lamasse. They were taken through a room where a couple were waiting, man and woman, sitting on sweet little gilt chairs. There were more chairs, a nice big sofa and a big gold and blue mirror. The couple didn't say anything, just nodded and smiled. She was beautifully dressed, no doubt she got her clothes here, or some of them. Iris thought they were part of the crowd that went to all the places, she might have seen them somewhere. The shop woman, Madame something or other, led her and Bébé through to another room with lots of clothes hanging on a rack, an armchair, more of the dainty little gilt chairs and another lovely big mirror. Bébé suggested a dress for her to try on, strapless, straight skirt, very narrow. After taking her jumper and skirt off, the woman said she had to go but she'd come back when Bébé rang through to the salon to say she was ready. Because it was strapless, her bra had to come off too so, for decency's sake, she turned her back to Bébé and faced the mirror.

'How modest,' Bébé laughed, and laughed even more watching her wriggling herself into the dress. 'It's so elegant, Iris, I think I'll try it on. I might even buy it for New Year's Eve.'

Her undies were gorgeous, pale grey silk, all to match, with tiny white rosebuds on her bra and suspender belt. Her knickers were almost see-through they were so sheer. 'Sorry, dear, but those bloomers will have to come off, they are as thick as school knickers.'

'Aren't they awful.' Comparing herself in the mirror with Bébé, she was quite ashamed. 'Turn your back then and I'll take them off. The skirt should go on easier then.'

Bébé turned away, laughing again. It was smashing having such a big mirror. She preened, admiring her nice tight bottom, pulling in her non-existent tummy. The dress slipped on easy without the thick knickers. 'Would you do me up, please?' That was when the odd thing happened. Nothing much, and maybe she was old-fashioned to mind, but as Bébé, pulling at the zip, got to her waist she put her hands inside the dress and put both her hands on her bust.

'You have to lift your breasts in a dress like this to show it off properly,' she said.

Not true! Her bust didn't need lifting by anybody or anything. She stuck out without the help of a brassiere what's more *and* they weren't big enough to drop.

'I know about this sort of thing,' Bébé said. 'I used to model sometimes, here in fact.'

'Shall you call Madame whatsit now?'

'Mm, no, not sure, it isn't absolutely you is it? Quick, let me try, OK?'

The dress was too tight for Bébé and try as she might she couldn't get the zip up, all very well her saying 'pull'. She bent over the back of one of the chairs – to help she said, but it didn't. So there she was in all her glory, except for her suspender belt and nylons, tugging away. You could see the funny side of it. Then the woman came back and after she'd slipped the strapless number back on had said, 'Thanks for coming in. We'll keep you in mind.' But after all that she had been a bit too short. It all ended well though because they suggested she try on the black one, which fitted perfectly lovely and as it was one of last year's it was given to her to make up for not getting the job. Very nice of her, very nice indeed.

'Here's your chicken.' Bobby squeezed in next to her. 'And where, pray, is our wine, darling? I've done *my* bit.'

'Sorry, I was day-dreaming, or thinking.'

'Thinking? That's an improvement on what you usually do – which is nothing. Don't look so hurt and humble, Stan. You're a scream. You don't know what day it is, don't know your arse from your elbow.'

'If you're going off after eating this to do "Auld Lang Syne" does that mean this party stops or I've got to go? I mean seeing as how I came with you?'

He was eating quickly, looking at his watch. Couldn't be late at the Browns' party, and wouldn't be able to take her with him. 'I'd take you with me but it's strictly a queers' do. You'll be all right here, the Maharajah's dos go on for ever, even after he's been put to bed pissed.'

The sooner she sorted herself out a boyfriend the better. Someone older, married, and with money. Set her up in a nice flat. She couldn't go on for ever being a fag's moll.

'So it's OK if I stay?'

'Of course. Happy New Year, I'm off.' He was seeing Steve, she could tell. 'A queers' do', 'Can't take you', all uncomfortable, no need for him to be uncomfortable, nothing to do with her. Very nice of Steve to send the cash for Christmas. A superior gesture, classier than paying her off when he said all through, thank you.

The bathroom she chose was big, all marbly and sweet-smelling with enough towels to stock Swan and Edgars. They were all big. Like the beds were big and the wardrobes that were all fitted in. Three whole suites in the hotel he had – and he didn't even live here full time. His main place was in India, naturally, but here in London he had a pretty little house, a whole one not a flat, as well as all this. Easier to look after him in a hotel, that secretary man said. The front door opened, you could hear the lift and voices and laughing. She hurried out but they had gone. There were fewer people now, and Roger was sunk in an armchair, his head lolling, half asleep.

A quarter past eleven. Not long now. It wasn't so good if you didn't click with someone, you were on the edge of it all. The problem was that all the men who were out at parties were on the look-out for a girl who would end up in bed with them. After dinner and dancing and drinking they got practical, you might be a lot of fun to be with, you could be the prettiest girl in the room, they liked to swank about that, but if you started pushing their hands away they dumped you. If she had the nerve she'd go to Les A and just go up to the bar and pick up a drink as if she'd left it there while going to the toilet. Most there would be a bit drunk and merry and not notice. But special occasions like New Year's Eve were difficult to manage. So many of the usuals were at their homes, older men with wives and families, younger ones doing their duty with Mum and Dad.

She couldn't stay here perched on the arm of a sofa pretending interest in a conversation she couldn't hear. It was better to perch than sit, she'd learned, easier to move off.

'I came I saw I conga'd, I came I saw I conga'd. It's plain to see you conquered me.' A line of people led by the twins appeared dancing from one of the bedrooms. 'I, I, conga, I, I, conga, I, I, conga – Aye Aye!' Good opportunity to join in and mix. She tagged on the end. 'Each time I shake a shoulder, I get a little bolder.' Another man slipped behind her and lightly touched her waist. 'I, I, conga, I, I, conga.' They snaked round the long sitting-room, picking up people as they went, and danced into the hall. This was more like it! She swayed her hips and sang, 'Oh, I came I saw I conga'd, and now it's time to go.' Still led by the twins, they made their way in and out of rooms, gathering coats, and left, dancing and singing down the stairs, across the grand reception hall of the hotel and out into the street. Some of them drifted drunkenly away, still singing and dancing, crossing Park Lane and disappearing in the dark.

'Eight of us, two taxis, where are we going?' The man behind her took charge.

'Les A?' Iris said wistfully.

'The Sheffords,' someone shouted. 'They always give a good party.'

The doorman whistled up two taxis and deftly pocketed the pound note offered, ignoring the prior claims of a couple whose money wasn't on show.

In the taxi nobody knew each other; the two men talked about business and the girl, who was very pretty, dyed ash blonde hair, shivered in the corner, her nose pink with a cold. When the men said something about Africa Iris tried to join in. 'My friend, Nicholas Wytham, who works for a foreign office, is in Africa at the moment, or in Kenya, I think.'

It went down like a lead balloon. They smiled, nodded and went on talking.

There was nobody from the other taxi outside the block of flats in Kensington, but the name Shefford was on a bell and they were let in, no trouble, by a porter. Up on the fifth floor, number twelve's door was open a bit, not much noise considering there was a party. Music, all slow and dreamy, but no laughing and shouting. Two or three glanced up as they came in, someone pointed to a long table covered in bottles and glasses and said, 'The barman has passed out, help yourselves,' then waved vaguely at other doors. 'Coats . . . etc.'

The bed wasn't only piled high with coats, there were couples lying on top of the coats doing it – on-top-of-the-coats. Disgusting. She had heard about those who liked doing it in front of each other or all together, all well and good, if that's what they wanted, none of her business, but on top of other people's coats! She clasped her own tightly to her, she was not going to take it off and leave it here. Not her first purpose-bought coat, paid for by some of Steve's Christmas money. They were humping and heaving, in the gloom she could see a big pink bottom rising up and down, then a voice panting said, 'Keep watching, sweetie, I'm about to come.'

It was silly and scaring and funny. Nobody hardly looked up as she slid back into the main room; the same man pointed to the bar. 'Help yourself,' and nobody said goodbye as she left.

As she walked past the porter's cubby-hole he smiled. 'Happy New Year, miss, only a quarter of an hour to go.' He was tidying up the little office and changing his jacket.

'Thanks, same to you.'

Was she going to be stuck alone in the street at midnight? Might as well have stayed at home. This wasn't like last year, sitting in the front room all grumpy and nothing to look forward to then quite late all of a sudden the phone call from Patrick.

'Excuse me, please, can I use your telephone? I'll pay, of course.' She took two pennies from her purse.

'Help yourself, miss. No, no, not necessary.' He pushed the money away. 'I'll get it for you, know the number?'

Of course she did, she knew three people with telephones and she knew all the numbers. And next door's best of all.

'Kilburn 4219.'

'Ringing.'

'Hello, Mrs G, it's Iris. Not too late, I hope. Oh, oh, yes, thanks, lovely. Yes, ta and the same to you. Oh, how smashing.' She twirled, hugging herself. 'I've been asked out.'

'A bit late.'

She ran to the door. 'Which way would I go for Hyde Park Corner?'

Following her out he banged the double doors shut. 'Where exactly are you going?'

Impatient, how would he know Les A? She eyed the street for a taxi. 'A place called Les Ambassadeurs.'

'Les A?'

'Oh yes, that's right.'

'And you want to be there by midnight?'

'Yeah, fat chance.'

'Every chance, miss,' he said calmly. 'Get on the back of my Vespa.'

She put her arms round his comfortable waist using his back to shield herself from the wind. He smelled a bit like her dad, smoky, something nice slicking his hair down. The motor-bike accelerated up Kensington High Street, weaving its way between cars full of shouting and singing people hanging out the windows and trailing balloons. Before Knightsbridge he overtook a dawdling taxi and nipped smartly into the park exiting at Hyde Park Corner. In Hamilton Place he stopped smoothly in front of the restaurant.

'Go on, don't waste time, enjoy yourself.' The porter waved away her thanks and disappeared into Shepherd Market.

'Good evening, Miss Winston, he's right you know.' The doorman ushered her in. 'Six minutes to 1953.'

All sorts were there from all the places, all the restaurants. The Club, Le Routier, the Panache, the Dive in Gerrard Street. Men who had danced with her, bought her drinks, those she'd fought with in cars and taxis, the white-haired drug girl, and when the drumroll announced midnight she was linked with Beastie on one side and little Francis Horton-Rigby, drunk as usual, on the other. Except for missing Nick and Bobby it was just as lovely as last year. Pink champagne, laughs, compliments, dancing, and then a proper breakfast: scrambled eggs, smoked salmon, everything – anything! And it didn't look like stopping, the band was still there with the singer, very slinky in black sequins.

'I'll be seeing you' they played. Who would the *you* be for her? Someone romantic and tragic. Married, forbidden. In all the old familiar places. Here? His wife would be in the country with the children in her long cotton dress, smiling in the garden, waiting for him. She was nice but she didn't understand him. He would be in London on business, delayed. They would come here for dinner and dancing, him and his business partner, one of the big nobs, to discuss work. The big nob would dance with his wife, he would sit alone. And she, Iris, would walk in. And that would be it. Then they would see each other deliberately, by chance, again and again. In an old café, across a crowded room. Lovely. Francis she could see was asleep, fallen sideways on the banquette, a small glass of brown stuff that he'd spilled spreading a stain on the white tablecloth. No surprise.

People had started to go, couples were leaving, perhaps she should go after this dance.

Then everything changed. Patrick cut in on her dance with Beastie, just as if it was an 'excuse me'. Good job too because it was a slow and holding tight dance and though he was definitely a very good ballroom dancer, when it came to the more smoochy things he was absolutely disgusting. Pressing herself against the younger thinner ones and shutting her eyes and thinking abut someone lovely like the new singer Johnny Ray was one thing, but having Beastie's enormous stomach rubbing all over you was another, and what with that and all the stupid revolting things he whispered wetly in her ear – I want you to play with my cock in your liberty bodice and school knickers – she'd willingly kick him in the balls, if she could find them under all that lard. So when Patrick slid her away gliding neatly across the floor to the far side of the room it was a relief.

'I've never seen you dance,' she said.

'No, I don't. I wonder why I am?' He wasn't asking her, he was more thinking it. As they passed the band the singer eyed her watch discreetly, she must be tired.

'So, then, why are you dancing, and do you want to stop? I hope not, because you are good at it.'

'Thank you.' He guided them past a table where a couple were standing up and nodded goodbye. The man was rather messy looking, untidy clothes and dark shaggy hair falling all over his face; he was leaving with Alice, the so-called model.

'Did you have a good time at His Highness' party? I suppose he fell asleep?'

'Yes, he did. Poor bloke. It was nice, lovely food, but

I felt awkward when Bobby had to go, you know, being at a party without the person who'd asked you.'

'Come and sit down,' he snapped.

'Oh, yes, right.'

'It was you, Iris, who was invited to the party. Not Bobby. I merely asked him to let you know because you don't have a phone. Pushy little fairy, not very wise; they don't use him here as much as they used to. No, he is unwise.'

She smiled awkwardly. 'No, I'd noticed. Oh, look, poor old Beastie, sulking in the corner.'

'And another good reason for you to get a telephone,' he laughed, 'is you are the only person in my address book who takes her calls "next door".'

They had really delicious smelly coffee, much better she knew now than the bottled stuff.

'That will keep you awake, won't you want to sleep all day tomorrow?'

'Today. Not me, Patrick. I'm working at my coffee bar, no one else will go in.'

This was the longest time he had ever talked to her, and it was quite OK, he didn't want anything, she could tell; if was as if he actually liked being with her.

'That man, the dark one, who left with Alice, who was he?'

'Nat Chievely, the racing driver. What do you think, Iris, do you find him attractive?'

'Yes,' she said doubtfully. 'No. I can see he's handsome

and like a hero in a book or film, all brooding and smouldering, but I don't find him attractive. The sort of man I like . . .' she enthused, 'is someone I don't meet, like in films or in the papers.'

'Nat is in the papers. Second at Le Mans last year.'

'Yes. And in the papers with that famous girl who knew everybody and always went out a lot and then all of a sudden committed suicide, and not even doing it easily like putting your head in the gas oven which is what I'd do, but stuck a bread knife in her bust. Very peculiar.'

He nodded and laughed a bit, but didn't say anything; was he going to ask her to do something with the driver? It wouldn't be easy saying no, it never was, but he was sitting there all nice and chatty and maybe it was only conversation, after all it was she who had brought him up.

'What I like in life, Patrick, is: nice dinner, a dance and a bit of a laugh. If I ever came into money I'd still like the same, only not to have to go back to Kilburn and worry about taxi money.'

'And when will you let your dreams step into your life? And I don't mean NW6.'

He was only chatting, kind of a relief. She wasn't going to say anything about the MP or the man who gave her stockings, all the arrangements were kind of hinted at, and he must know, the men would have told him, she didn't exactly come up trumps.

'Have you figured out why you wanted to dance?'

'Yes. My work was finished. You looked cool and

beautiful. I didn't like seeing you in the arms of hot fat Beastie.'

She kissed his cheek, surprised. 'That's a lovely thing to say.'

The driver watched her lean forward. He'd been eyeing her in the rear-view mirror, wondering what her game was. He always twisted the mirror a bit when a nice-looking bit got in. She'd been fiddling around with herself, twisting and doing something to her frock. She knocked on the window.

'Yes, miss?' Slowing down he turned his head. Ah, now he could see what she'd been up to. She'd been wearing one of those things his daughter had got. Got it for Christmas – a waspie or something – black, made your waist smaller.

'I want you to stop at the next corner. I've changed my mind, sorry.' The voice was a bit rougher, more common, than when she'd said 'ta-ta' to the bloke in evening dress.

'Not very nice for a young lady like you, miss. Dodgy manor, this.' He gave her his best I've-got-a-daughter-your-age kindly old dad smile.

'I'll be all right, thanks.' She gave him two pounds. 'Keep the change.'

The black wasp thing had dropped in the gutter as she got out.

'Never mind "keep the change" you cheeky cunt. Here I am, New Year's Eve, four in the morning, stranded on the Edgware Road, no chance of a fare . . . that fellow give you a fiver, I saw.'

'That's right, he did. Two for you. Three for me.' She waved. 'Bye-bye, happy new year.' She walked off briskly, her stiletto heels clicking, her taffeta petticoat rustling. I only need castanets and I'd be a dead ringer for one of those girls at El whatsits, she thought.

The taxi passed her slowly and stopped. ''Ere, you,' he called, 'you dropped your corset.' He threw it at her.

Damn! He must have seen her wriggling out of it. 'Thank you,' she said dismissively as she caught it.

'I seen up your skirt, dear. Nice legs you got, and down your bodice, nice tits too. Nah then, what about a bit of the other in the back of the cab and then I'll drive you home for nothing.' He waited, cheery, hopeful. 'Nice way to start the new year.'

'Nice way to start the new year,' she repeated slowly, examining the eager face, white and sweaty, the broken veins stretched across his face like cracked china. 'No, I don't think so. You are not really my cup of tea, you see.'

'What about a quick plate then?'

Ignoring this she said, 'More my cup of arsenic.'

'Cheeky cunt,' he yelled again as he did a fast 'U' turn and headed back to the West End.

It was cold but not freezing. Her feet had been killing her in the high narrow shoes so she'd taken them off, to save her nylons, the last pair, she'd taken them off too.

Perhaps the cold pavement would take down the swelling. Only five more streets to go. Left at Macfisheries, she could smell it now. Always reeking of whiting and kippers, even when it had been shut for a couple of days. Probably it reeked of cod and haddock too but as her mum only bought whiting and kippers, or a 'nice bloater', that was the only reek she knew. Down the bottom to the fork that went right to the school, which she'd left on the dot of her fourteenth birthday, and then second left for home.

Nearly there. Round the corner where the library used to be. One of the saddest days ever when that was bombed, worse than when Uncle Phil was killed. Right again at Angleton Road. It was still dark. Nobody up yet anywhere. No lights on. You'd think the war was still on and the blackout curtains up.

She was fed up. Nothing much was going on. Most were away either freezing or boiling. Some off in the mountains skiing, and others lying on the beach millions of miles away. She knew what she would choose. *Not* putting sticks on your feet and sliding down snowy hills catching a nasty cold. Nick had gone to Venice, to look at churches, he said. As if there weren't enough in England. Only one nice night out in three weeks: a huge party at the Dorchester. She went on her own. Patrick said she was to mingle as much as possible, which she did; as soon as she got bored she moved on. They were all talking about the same things. The Olympic games, of course, and far too much about Churchill and stuff going on in the world. The good thing was that when Nick got back she'd have a few topics up her sleeve. The evening went on all night, moving to supper in the hotel's restaurant, then some went on for dancing at the Dive. Then back to the hotel for breakfast. She hadn't clicked with anyone and began to get a bit worried about going home. Probably the first bus would have to do. Then a serious kind of woman, like a secretary, came up, gave her an envelope and said thanks. Inside there was twenty pounds! Only there was a slip of paper that said FORAYS ESCORT SERVICE. The woman shrugged when Iris pointed it out and told her to keep it.

After that, a few days later, there was supposed to be a really lovely big dinner party at Les A, but it was cancelled because the King died. But honest to God! People still had to eat. To top it all off, Sam had fallen off his new bike and hurt his leg, and of course, Mum and Dad had a real go at her, it was all her fault for giving it to him. Brand new. Over a year it had taken to save up for it. Sod the lot of them.

To cheer herself up she was going to do Dickins and Jones. Never having set foot in there, it would be nice to stroll around, keep her eye in on the fashions. As usual, nice simple clothes when she was going to do a big store. Grey pleated skirt, the new imitation silk blouse bought to replace the one ruined at La Panache, and the Coat.

It wasn't what she had in mind when she did it, it was just easy, like a piece of cake. But long term not a good idea, because Dickins and Jones was nice and now she could never go back. In case. The separates department was posh up one end and more her budget down the other. Having picked out two blouses to try on from the reasonable end, she'd moved along to have a good look at the rest, all open and above board. That's how she got away with it. In the expensive bit there was her blouse, only so much better, real silk, pretty buttons properly sewn on and the collar sitting just right. She'd taken that to try on too. And it was in the trying on that it happened. One of the cheap ones, black with a neck frill, was good and useful, she didn't try on the other so as not to be tempted. The real silk cream was even better on, worth the extra money, if you had it. Like the linen dress at Debenhams. Her cream blouse was hanging with the cheap ones when the salesgirl knocked, 'Everything all right?' and came in.

'Yes,' Iris said, 'I'm going to take the black.'

'Very useful, miss, I'll wrap it up.' And she took her cream away with the others. Leaving she buttoned her coat up tight to the chin. On the bus home she undid it. No point in sweating into a beautiful real silk blouse.

Chapter Nine

It was lovely going out to lunch on a Friday, even if it was only with Bébé. The weekend wouldn't be as dreary and flat as usual – nothing to do; nothing going on; nothing to look forward to. But Le Routier didn't look as pretty during the day and it didn't feel the same and, most important, who was going to pay? She was jolly hungry, almost nothing to eat last night what with the maharajah getting bored wherever they were, ordering smashing food and then either leaving the restaurant before it arrived or ignoring it when it did. At Les A she was just putting a forkful of potatoes and black truffle into her mouth when he'd grabbed her wrist and held it in mid-air. Bloody torture, smelling it and not allowed to eat it. He'd been talking to the blonde dancer with the funny name. She was supposed to be his person for the evening, not her. She was his type, long hair, tiny nose, but, oh no, like all men, really he wanted someone who paid him no attention.

'Why do you call me Roger?' he'd said.

'Because I can't remember or pronounce your name and Roger sounds like rajah.'

He'd liked that. Laughed. He always did. Every time they met he said the same thing. After lots of truly lovely wine. Then the secretary man had joined in laughing and, instead of just being there making up a group to be jolly, she was the centre of attention. And got no food. The good thing was he drank lots of wine and was no trouble. The bad thing – he sent her home in his car, so no taxi money. The secretary had put her in the back seat, very polite. 'You will always keep your figure if you dine with His Highness.'

Cheek. She could manage dinner and still keep her figure and who was he to look at her like that, as if his eyes were hands. Ugh. Anyway, Nick had told her he was queer, or half queer so what did he want with her? What's more, his boss was much better looking.

'What are you going to have, Iris?'

She glanced up shyly from the huge parchment menu the waiter had presented her. 'Don't know yet.' The cheapest was clear soup to start and then an omelette, but that was so boring.

Bébé waved the waiter away. 'We will be a few minutes yet. If it helps, I'm having asparagus and then scampi.'

Iris re-read the menu hoping to see something delicious for the same price as soup and eggs; something she'd missed before.

'What's the matter?'

'Nothing.'

'You're frowning horribly, something must be the matter.'

'Look, Bébé, it's awkward because you're a woman, see?'

'So are you.'

She laughed. 'I know that, but it's like this. When you telephoned me this morning and asked me out, I thought there would be two men as well, and, in that case, of course, they would have paid, all well and good . . . But now . . . as it's only us, well, I feel awful but I've only got two pounds and I can't really spend all that. I don't know how long it's got to last . . .'

'Do shut up, Iris. My God, you're still the little innocent, aren't you? Listen, foolish girl, you will never have to pay for lunch, Iris, or not till you're forty or so. Alex won't charge us. He won't give us a bill.'

Iris saw the owner, Alex, a tubby little man, unctuously bowing a favoured customer to a corner table. Catching her eye, he inclined his head and smiled rather sweetly at her. 'Gosh, wonderful. Why won't he though? And should we be careful?'

'No caviare, no Montrachet, but otherwise . . .'

Iris examined the menu again joyfully. 'So I don't have to have soup and omelette. Smashing! Seriously, Bébé, why?'

'Look around the room, it's full of dreary-looking people.'

'Not full actually.'

'Quite so. London's choicest restaurant, or one of them, is half empty and the people who are here are a few boring and bored married couples and some dull businessmen – not even Londoners, from the Midlands most likely.'

'Except for the big table under the mirror, they're all young and not bad-looking.'

'Yes, except for them. Johnny P. and his friends seeing him off the list.

'The list?'

'The bachelors' list. Johnny is getting married tomorrow. Alex would rather have two beautiful young women here eating for nothing than an empty table.'

'Beautiful? You maybe. I'm only attractive.'

Bébé ignored this. 'See the three men nearly opposite, next to the liqueur trolley?'

'Yes, they've been giving you the eye, haven't they?'

'Both of us. Now, when they want to go to a restaurant again they will suggest Le Routier, partly because Sir John Pilsherd is having a stag luncheon party that will probably be in a newspaper tomorrow, partly because Pepé the poor man's Picasso is eating over there with his extremely peculiar-looking model – she's more abstract than his painting. He won't be paying either.'

'And us?'

'Yes. Most of all us. They are paying their bill now, see, and they will be paying through the nose for their meal – but – they can ogle us for nothing.'

The waiter appeared bowing low. 'Madam is ready to order?' He hissed in Bébé's ear, 'I advise fish, miss, the gents over there have put a bottle of champagne for you on their bill.' He included Iris with a barely perceptible wink.

'Merci, Pierre, pour moi asperges et en suite le scampi.' Bébé said this loud enough for the three men to hear as they left the room. The last one paused and turning gave the two women a quick appraising glance, dwelling a little longer on Bébé with a questioning half smile. 'What about you, Iris?'

'Asperges for me too please. I suppose that *is* asparagus?' she said anxiously.

'Asperges, certainly, and to follow?' The waiter smiled at the girl, a sweetie pie she was. Pity she was mixed up with this lot. 'May I suggest the turbot, miss, hollandaise sauce, a few beans, new potatoes perhaps?'

'Mm, yes, lovely. Thank you.' When he'd left with their order Iris whispered, 'He keeps changing from mademoiselle to miss and asperges to asparagus.'

'He is Pierre in public and Peter in private. Like me, he finds a French name and a little of the language can be quite useful.'

'Ha! You're not a Betty, Bébé is much more you.'

Loud laughter and shouts of 'Hee-haw, hee-haw' from the young men's table distracted them.

'Hee-haw, you're an ass.'

'Who's he going to marry, Johnny P.? It's a bit sudden, isn't it? Last time I saw him he was with that red-haired girl who works at Lesperts, the model, and he wasn't going to marry her, I know, because I was squashed in a car with him coming back from the country. She was in another car and the car was so full I had to sit on his lap and I said why don't I sit on Nick's lap in case she saw. Nick had taken me down there just for the party, see, for the day. Most of the others stayed. Anyhow, Johnny P. said, "Not likely. You sitting on Nick's lap is a waste of cunt." Beg pardon, Bébé, but that's what he said.'

'Don't be so coarse, Iris. "Beg pardon", I mean, not "cunt". I've known Johnny Pilsherd for years and his use of a four-letter word is not going to shock me.'

'Yes, sorry then.'

'He would be likely to take to you. You're not

exactly a red-head but chestnut would still be in his range.' The champagne had arrived in an ice-bucket with a sealed note. Bébé read it, smiled and put it in her handbag.

'Was it to you then, Bébé?'

'Yes, but you are to share it, of course.'

'Thanks. So who is he marrying then? Somebody I know?'

'Hardly. He's been engaged to her for years – two or three years. Very rich, quite pretty, extremely well turned out. Bob Hagels's daughter – they live in Dorset. She's only allowed up to town to get her clothes and get her hair done.'

'He can't be that keen on her if he was off with Alice the model. And going home in that car when he made me sit on his lap, he tried to poke me through my knickers.'

'A divertissement, that's all. They get on quite well. She'll get an old title and an old house and he'll get new money and all his bills paid.'

'This is the life, all right.' Iris smiled contentedly around the room. 'Thanks, Bébé, I really appreciate it. That hollandaise sauce, is it Dutch? Whatever, it knocks spots off Heinz's salad cream.'

'Miss Bailey,' the waiter coughed. 'Sir John and his friends would like you both to join them for coffee and brandy – or champagne – or . . . er . . . whatever.'

The pre-wedding table had been getting noisier as the restaurant emptied. A game of flicking pellets of bread on knives had been replaced by batting chocolates and ice back and forth with dessertspoons. Some of the chocolate and ice and bread pellets had gone astray, reaching their table, always followed by elaborate protestations of innocence and apologies.

Bébé took the note that came with the champagne from her bag. 'I'm not sure if I can. I've got to phone somebody. You go, Iris, and I'll come and let you know.'

She slipped out of her seat, automatically straightening the skirt of her navy barathea suit and checking the seams of her stockings, and slipped through the half-curtained doorway to the telephone.

Iris thought she'd like to join them, if only not to stop the lovely day. This morning, quarter to twelve, when Bébé had telephoned, was her first proper call. The telephone had been put in and fixed up two days ago but anybody who wanted to talk to her that quickly had got the number of next door and didn't know about their telephone – their own telephone, and their own telephone number. No! Her telephone! She had paid and she was going to pay half the bills. If she could. How long would Bébé be? Not long. It would be better if she waited. 'Don't think I will either, Pierre, or not till she gets back. Can I have a glass of water please?' She refused his offer to top up her champagne glass.

Peter, the head waiter, was the only major staff member left on duty now, apart from the washers-up in the kitchen. Alex had gone up to his flat above the restaurant and would be asleep – DO NOT DISTURB hung on the front door. He was due to knock off in ten minutes but it might be as well to hang around. A good tip might be in the offing and there was no knowing what that table of buffoons might get up to. They would pay all right for any damage but best keep an eye on them.

'What's your name, little darling?' one of them yelled. 'Have I had you, my pet?'

Johnny P. had a vague recollection of some sort of intimacy with her. 'I know, I know! You gorgeous bit of crumpet. You're the bugger's beard, the poof's pet. You are Nick's bit, Miss Iron Drawers!'

They were standing some of them, shouting, laughing. She wasn't scared, it was all harmless high spirits – well, bottled spirits too – but she hoped Bébé would come back soon. Four of them lined up in front of her table.

'Come on, what's your name, darling?'

'Iris,' she said quietly, looking at them her eyes demure under her thick fringe. If they thought they were the big 'I am', they had another think coming. She wasn't afraid of them. Walking past the Feathers at closing time was more difficult to handle than this.

'Iris! You are the flag, the flagship. If I was your frigate I would never flag. If I was in your fleet my mast would always be up. Come and join us, little Venus.'

The tall thin one with a funny R in his voice muttered, 'Little Venus, suck my penis,' but she pretended not to hear. Suddenly, two of them picked her up in her chair and placed it at their table. The other two picked up her table and dropped it behind her, trapping her. Johnny P. was singing, 'I'll be seeing you in all the old familiar places' followed by the man sitting next to him, 'I'll be screwing you in all the old familiar places'.

She wasn't sure if he could have said that because he was smiling so nicely at her. They were off their rockers! She tried to stand up, escape.

'Oh, don't go, lovely lady.' One of those who'd carried her put his hand on her chin and pulled her face round. 'I remember you.'

She remembered him too, but couldn't remember his name.

'I appeal to you, Iris. Keep us lonely boys company. Pilsherd only has one day of freedom left. You wouldn't abandon a condemned man would you?'

She remembered his flat in St James's. After dancing with him quite a lot and much too close – her fault – it was tempting because it was nice to be told 'You're the sexiest dancer ever' but it made them expect more. They had gone to his flat, run out of money he'd said; wanted to see her all right; give her something to get home. No sooner in the lounge than he'd lunged at her, unbuttoning his trousers. She had asked for a drink. He had one too and that was that. Pissed, he'd passed out; fallen asleep. Until she was sure he was out for the count, she'd locked herself in the bathroom. So tempting, warm and clean, lots of towels, two huge ones, little flannels, everything all clean, not used. The bath was the best ever. So much hot water, her skin was all pinky red. She didn't want to pull the chain in case it woke him up, so she peed in what looked like a footbath but she knew now to be a bidet. He was sprawled on the sofa as she tried to creep out. 'Had a bath, sweetie?' he mumbled. Sitting up he felt in his trouser pockets, the flies still unbuttoned, and took out some money. 'Here you are, sweetie. Thanks, you're a sport.'

Taking the twenty pounds from him she noticed his breath – sickly; smelling of brandy, red wine, onions, cheese. Foul. Did he think she'd done it with him? What a cheek. What a fool.

And now he was remembering her. So was the stringy older man who had given her nylons a couple of times and usually gave her decent taxi money. He liked to be dropped off at his place in Mayfair – little mews house. It was a bit nasty that he wanted her to put the nylons on in the taxi, but that was it; he never touched her.

Johnny P. jumped on the table but stumbled as the tablecloth slipped under his feet. Kicking little coffee cups off in a fury he shouted, 'Goal, goal, goal!' as they hit the wall. That was going too far – but, well as long as they paid. The waiter was fed up, she could see, but it was probably all worth putting up with. The worse they behaved, the bigger the tip. Now Johnny was trying to pull her up on the table. Oh, no. She knew their game, she was no muggins, they'd look up her skirt. But they were being lovely in a way, putting all the little biscuity things and chocolates in the dainty basket made of sugar and putting that in a big white napkin. One of them wrapped up a big blue and white ashtray that said 'Le

Routier' on it and took a big spoon and a little spoon and put that in another napkin with the big wooden pepper-grinding thing.

'Wishing you many a good grind, Iris.'

Pity they didn't have a cruet. Would she be allowed to keep it all? She looked over at Pierre, still hovering by the entrance, keeping a distant eye on them.

He shrugged. 'Take it,' he mouthed.

A large cushion cover from the banquette had been unzipped and all the things were stuffed into it and presented to her. She supposed this too would all go on the bill.

The table behind her was pulled away and they were all standing up, still laughing, but now whispering things. Were they laughing at her? Nick had said not to worry about getting things wrong, that it intrigued people that she looked 'the thing, the real goods', but wasn't – that she couldn't quite pass.

'Stop it,' she yelled. Whoever it was had touched her breasts from behind.

'Oh, delicious. They stand up like stiffly set jellies.'

Pushing him off with her elbows, she caught a warning look directed at him from the skinny one. Well, at least one of them was a gent – a gentleman. But maybe that meant he was queer, like Nick. And then he looked kindly at her.

'We ought, I suppose, to take you home, but . . .'

She waited for him to finish. Obviously he didn't

want to drive to Kilburn, he wanted her to interrupt, to say, 'Don't bother, I'll be all right.' 'Don't bother, I'll be all right, honestly. I'll walk down to Swan and Edgar and catch the 28 or 53. There's loads of buses.'

'No, no, we'll drop you at the Dorchester and get you a taxi there.'

A taxi! Free lunch, all the presents from the table and a taxi. If she took the taxi up Park Lane she could get out at the bus stop at Marble Arch and get the 28 from there. They'd be bound to give her a fiver. Enough easily for the week and give Mum a couple of quid. 'Excuse me please, but why bother about dropping me at the Dorchester? Couldn't you find me a taxi here? I'll be able to get one passing by, won't I?'

'Because . . . it is cold. Because . . . Irises are bulbs that should be kept warm.'

They surrounded her and ushered her outside; she was clutching on to the big cushion-cover full of things. They were still laughing, laughing. Drink of course. Outside she saw Bébé in the back of a nice big car. A chauffeur all in grey and wearing a cap to match was closing the door. He grinned at the group of young men and put up his thumb, cheekily signalling approval.

'Where's the car, please?' Iris waved to Bébé as her car drove off but she didn't see, her head was turned the other way.

'Car? No car. We are going to give you a lift, a flying angel.'

She squealed. It was like being a little girl with Dad and Uncle Syd. They were holding her and running.

Running and laughing. Holding her high. Feeling safe, she relaxed into their hold, enjoying it. People passing waved up to her and they laughed.

'I'm not an angel,' she shouted. 'I'm an aeroplane, I'm a balloon, I'm a bubble!'

There was the Dorchester. Two taxis waiting. Oh, how sad. Now they would drop her, pop her in a taxi and, thinking about the wedding tomorrow, forget this and forget her. The fun, being the centre of attention, would end with her heading back to Kilburn on a 28 bus. Richard returned from talking to the doorman. She'd remembered his name. Yes, that was it, Richard. Dancing, pressed close to him. 'Richard is my name. Just keep whispering it in my ear, go on.' And she had. Richard, Richard. He'd liked that, very much.

'He says they are both taken. Says we'd be better off telephoning for one.'

From the shoulders of the two men, she called out. 'Honestly, don't bother. I really can get a bus.'

'No. We are gentlemen. We shall see you get home.' They carried her into a small block of flats in the side street by the hotel.

'What's this place?' She ducked her head as they entered, dodging the little chandelier. 'Careful.'

'This was borrowed for the last night.'

'The last rites, you mean.'

⋆

Only three could get into the small lift, the two carrying her and the one they called Andy who was holding a bottle.

'Handy you've got this, Andy.'

'Handy Andy.'

'Randy Andy.'

'Andrude.'

The other men were racing up the stairs, she could hear them, ahead of the lift. They were there when the lift stopped on the eighth floor. They had to turn her sideways to get her in the flat and finally put her down.

'I feel like a parcel.'

Robbie, the skinny one, took her bag of presents from her and gestured to a sofa. It was a lovely flat. Warm and warm colours. Not like the flats they called chambers which all looked and smelled the same. This one was bigger and looked like someone lived here, flowers and books, and the smell wasn't cold and cigar-etty but a bit cigary and lovely soap.

Out of an awkward silence she said, 'It's ever so lovely. Can I telephone then please? For the taxi?'

'Yes, we'll do that for you,' Johnny said heartily. 'But we are going to give you a glass of champagne . . .'

'While I wait for the taxi?' She felt a bit shy and odd now.

'While you wait for the taxi, yes. You see, you said that you felt like a bubble and you should be full of bubbles.'

'Full of something,' Andy sniggered.

'Do shut up, you'll spoil everything.'

Iris smiled at Richard, grateful.

'Come and look at the view,' he said, leading her to a window. 'Aren't we high up? Crumbs, the eighth floor, isn't it?' He pushed the window up and she leant out, seeing beyond the Dorchester across Park Lane to the park itself. Perhaps that was Kensington Palace over there in the distance to the left.

'Isn't it wonderful?' she said. He was leaning out with her. 'Fancy living so close to all this.'

People walking in the park were insects. Nearer, crossing the road, they became the size of children and below her in the narrow street, just one person walking, almost normal except for being shortened. 'Hallo,' she called gaily, but the walker continued, oblivious of her presence above.

'Ouch!' He head banged forward, grazing her forehead on the brick. 'That hurts. Lift it please. LIFT IT PLEASE,' she shouted. 'It hurts.' The window had fallen on her back, trapping her, her body and her arms. Why didn't they lift it? It didn't only hurt, it was uncomfortable. She kicked her legs. They must see that even if they had forgotten her, or hadn't noticed.

She was two separate people.

Out here she was cold and dizzy with an ache across her chest, but this part was free, alone in the air above Park Lane. Inside the flat her other half was warm, but men were looking at her waiting their turn. They had released her legs, which had been held wide apart, because she had stopped kicking and struggling. It was too painful and too late. The second man hurt not only inside her body where he was pushing and pushing, but her stomach hurt too where he was grabbing what little flesh there was. Part of the pain was the picture she had of them – looking. They were looking at a piece of body, not herself, not her face, not her smile. And she had been wrong about something so important. They didn't like her.

This one was taking longer, or had she missed it happening, had someone else started? She tried to kick again but as her body moved it happened. Perhaps moving made it happen. Would it be over quicker if she kept moving? The next one didn't touch her, just pushed it in. It would be different for him, he couldn't know, not now, what agony it was, how painful. Only the first man knew she was a virgin.

'Cor, Iris, you don't half stink.' Sam ducked but her fist connected. 'Blimey, that hurt.' He rubbed his chin. 'That's what they call an upper-cut, Iris. Bloody hell, it hurts. Bloody hell.'

'Don't swear,' she said automatically, putting her hand on his jaw. 'Nothing wrong with you, rude little sod.'

'Don't *you* swear. And say you're sorry then.' She was looking at him all different.

'What's up, Iris?'

'Mind your own bloody business.'

'All I said was . . .'

'And don't say it again, short arse.'

Hurt, he turned to the door. He was short, shortish anyway, but she never, ever, not Iris, ever said that. Always cheered him up. Plenty of time, years, she said, for you to catch up. And if it turned out that you were a bit, well, not so tall, it never did Alan Ladd or Billy Butlin any harm. He closed the door and shouted through it, 'Anyhow, you *do* stink.'

The kitchen was cold, the boiler out. She could go down to the big communal cellars and get some coke, nick some from number six, they always had plenty. But it would take too long to heat the water. The little bathroom was freezing. Her dad had stuck strips of newspaper round the edge of the window but it didn't do much good and now they couldn't open it so it was cold and smelly. The Lysol didn't really kill the other smell. Under the window, next to the toilet hung more newspaper cut into squares and hanging on a string. Horrible. She thought of the nice white stuff, all soft, that other people had – rich people.

Shivering, she turned the bath tap on, the hot one. Might as well try, she didn't know when the boiler had gone out. Better lukewarm than bloody freezing. She felt the water. The chill was off as her mother would say, but not far off. The towel wasn't wet but felt like it from the dank cold. 'Sam!' she shouted up the hall. 'Sam!'

'What?' He shuffled down, stopping short of her reach. Poor little sod, his face was scarlet where she'd struck him.

'Look, I can't explain, but I'm sorry, sort of. You shouldn't have said that . . . what you did say, and I shouldn't have either, said what I did. All right?'

His little face looked up at her with a false jaunty

confidence. 'No, it ain't all right. 'Cause you was right. I am a short arse . . . and you do stink.' He was out of range when she raised her hand but she didn't reach out to hit him, her hand covered her mouth stopping it. Stopping it from making the noise that was inside her that would become a howl that, if let go, would become awful crying. Her hand was pushing back all the pain and tears . . . Quickly she slammed the bathroom door.

The bath was nearly full. She felt the water – the chill was definitely back on.

'Iris, Iris.' Sam tapped on the door. 'What did you want then?'

'Would you light the oven and warm the towel for me, love?' She opened the door and handed it out.

'You'll catch your death having a cold bath.'

'You sound like Mum.'

'As long as I don't look like her. What's that, Iris?'

There was a long, red mark, red and bluish like a bruise, spread across her chest.

'Nothing, love.'

'It's a big nothing.' He took the towel into the kitchen.

Lovely and warm, he held the towel inside the oven hoping the gas wouldn't run out. If it did, Iris would have to cough up a shilling for the meter. The heat was making the oven smell of last week's joint. When Iris dried herself would she smell of roast lamb? Better any old how than what she smelled of when she came in.

He'd do his homework now his hands were warm. Much easier. Easier to hold the pencil.

'Sam, Sam, quick now. I'm getting out.'

The mark was awful, and peculiar. A straight line, about two inches across the top of her chest things.

'Get out. Stop looking.' She rubbed herself hard, roughly.

'Oh Christ all bloody mighty. That's them. Go and talk to them, will you. I don't want them to know I've had a cold bath. She'll start asking questions.'

'I'll say you're having an up and a downer.'

Their voices could be heard through the heavy front door. 'Use the key on the string, Florrie.'

'I don't want people knowing it's there.'

'Everyone knows it's there, woman. Everyone's got one.'

Sam got to the front door before the row could get to, 'Nice night out I must say. You! You going to treat me? Some hope. Oh, yes, you buy me half a shandy, you pay for half a shandy – then, oh yes, then *I* pay for your next three pints.'

His mother's voice could be heard hissing, 'Keep your voice down please. I'll get mine out. Ssh, please, Bill. I don't want to be thought the class of person who . . . Oh, Sam, thanks.' She shut her big black handbag sharply with an aggressive click. 'Your father's lost his key as usual and somehow or other, I'm to blame.' She trotted up the hall to the bathroom, her heavy high-heeled shoes clattering on the uncarpeted wood floor. 'Ooh, I'm dying to go.'

'Won't be a sec,' Iris called.

'You'd better not. I'm bursting.' Her mother waited at the door. 'We both want to go. Your father's had a skinful.'

'Bloody fast. Pubs only been opened an hour.' She opened the bathroom door. 'Here you are, Mum.'

Her mother eyed her suspiciously, forgetting her bursting bladder. 'What are you doing here anyway?'

'I live here, remember?'

'Don't start, Iris. Don't get her going.' Her father spoke without looking at her and walked into his bedroom slamming the door.

'No, Dad. No, please don't.' She yelled.

'Don't what, for Chrissakes?'

'He's pissing out the window, isn't he?'

Florrie shrugged. 'If he can't wait . . . Anyhow, I've got to go too, all right?'

'Pissing out of the window. It's disgusting.'

'Don't go on, Iris, please don't.'

Sam took her hand, pulling her into the kitchen. 'Let's put the radiogram on. You make something nice for all our suppers, Dad'll go back to the pub after, Mum'll listen to *Have A Go* and we can sit in your room and play "wishing".' He waited. 'Yes?'

She smiled. 'You're a baby, a big baby. Here.' She took some coins from her purse. 'Put all these in the meters, electric and gas.'

'Cor, Iris. That's smashing. Give us a wish then, go on.'

She stared out of the window above the big white kitchen sink at the walls of dingy brick with rancid yellow weeds poking out of the cracks. 'Wishes? Well, to start off with, I wish I was dead, then, I wish I'd never been born.'

Disappointed, he could tell there was no talking her round.

Sam put the money in the meters in the hall. Where had she got it, the money? Not just these shillings, but that bundle he'd seen in her handbag when she got out the purse. A huge bundle. Big white fivers. Sitting on his narrow bed in the hall where he'd been banished four years ago when Iris got her monthlies – she had to have a room to herself, she'd said, 'I'm a woman' – he tried to work it all out.

She thought she'd been woken up by the clatter of dustbin lids out in the back alley. Cats were investigating the remains of last night's fish suppers from the chippy down the road and the tantalizing smell of empty sardine and pilchard tins. But it was her back, her neck, her stomach and most of all her vagina that had done the waking. It was all a jumble of pain and aching and soreness. Her breasts, which had been pressed between the window and sill, had the same pounding pain as her head and that still felt as if it was hanging, as it had done over the street. Every part of her body had been affected by the assault. As she sat up, her head was dizzy again and the sickness returned. The stiffness in her neck made it agony just to straighten up. She stood, trying to stretch, but unbalanced and lay down again.

The fear and shame of touching herself had been instilled by her mother. 'Always keep it clean.' *It.* As if *it* was a pet mouse kept in a cage like Sam once had. 'Don't touch down below. It's not right.' 'How am I supposed to keep it clean then?' 'Don't touch when it isn't necessary, Miss Clever Clogs.' She touched now, carefully. It was swollen and tender like a giant bruise. The whole area was swollen. Her fingers gently pressing back the sore flesh couldn't find the bones, the tender skin was torn in places and, as she examined her fingers, was, she could see, bleeding. The official word for *it* was vagina. She knew that from the dictionary. When they were about twelve or thirteen, three of them from school had hung over the big dictionary in the library, squealing delightedly at all the rude words in it. Bust, chest, even . . . breast . . . was in there; bum, behind, arse, but best of all had been Mavis Atkinson's information that 'down below', your 'private parts', had a name: vergina. It had taken some tracking down because of the spelling. They had been sidetracked by Mary O'Reilly who, being a Roman Catholic, of all things, said it was something to do with the Virgin Mary. So time had been wasted on VIRGINIA, then more time going up the cul-de-sac of VEGETABLE, but after trying VOG and only finding VOGUE, useless, they had a go at VU – very worthwhile because they'd happened on VULVA. Terrific! An extra! Last attempt was VAG, and there it was, VAGINA, next to VAGARY and VAGABOND. It was a much nicer way of putting it, vagina, than Mum's 'front passage' which only made you think that girls had a wee in a corridor. VAGINA though was a bit of a let-down after the frankness of VULVA: The area immediately surrounding the clitoris and the openings of the urethra and vagina in females.

VAGINA: The tube which connects the uterus to the vulva in female mammals. The problem was we weren't sure if we were mammals.

What was she touching now, that hurt so much? Not her vagina – it hadn't been used like that, something soft and pretty, it was her cunt.

Chapter Ten

It was such a pretty place, Le Routier; from across the street it looked like a house: scrubbed steps, freshly Brassoed knob and knocker, pink and white flowers in the window-boxes. Too early for customers. But waiters and cleaners and cooks would be in there, hoovering, polishing, laying the starched tablecloths, twisting big napkins into clever shapes. Glasses shining. Knives and forks lined up. It would be warm in there and smelling nice from the flowers and food being started.

No, she couldn't go there. Maybe not ever again, and definitely not yet. Not tomorrow night as asked by Patrick to be with him and people from abroad. Only three times she'd been out since. Once with Patrick to a new French café, where the owners sat with them at a table covered in a red check cloth with candles stuck in bottles and the menu was written on a blackboard hanging on the wall. Patrick said it was amusing and he'd get all of society to come, and even the cook sat with them after dinner. It was free so it was nice not having to be obliged and Patrick didn't have to be obliged either because he was going to do them a favour.

The next time out was to Les A and she couldn't go through with it. All the men looked like them and though they weren't, had they been told? Were they sniggering, thinking about a window and half a naked body and legs being held apart – so she pretended to go to the toilet and left. The third time was the easiest, just cocktails at an embassy. Russia, or somewhere near, she'd gone in case Nick would be there as a foreign office person, but there was no sign of him.

If only – if only, someone to tell.

She didn't want to go on to dinner even though it was a Russian restaurant and should be safe, so she took the tube to West Hampstead, on the Bakerloo line, and walked the rest of the way. Nice anyway to be tired enough to sleep.

There was an early customer, somebody opened the door, as if by magic, the customer had been seen approaching the restaurant from inside, just as she had seen him from outside. He'd wait in the bar for his friends, you could tell that by all the red veins showing in his face.

It was a waiter who'd opened the door, smart, neat and clean in his black and white.

Better go now before she drew attention to herself. Better safe than sorry.

Best then would be to have a word with Patrick. Since New Year's Eve he'd been a tiny bit different. Friendly – in a normal proper way, that was it. And quite kind. Even though there was something behind it, the nice front was real.

Given that the cash from Steve would run out, and

given that she couldn't live on the unreliable coffee-bar money, let alone give Mum two quid a week as well as the occasional help to her dad, she had to do something. And she mustn't touch the other money, in case.

Lie down in a warm clean room with a hundred thousand rose petals pressed against 'it', that's what she'd like.

Long term was all planned – in her head: go to see nice films where the actresses spoke properly, be ever so careful with her make-up, not talk in company till she'd got the hang of what was being said and get the right kind of newspaper. Basically the papers were rather dull and needed a lot of getting through in the reading, but quite a lot of the news stuff sank in surprisingly. When her voice was more all right, her sentences as well as the sound, after a while what with that and knowing news stories and looking more day to day ordinary, maybe Nick would introduce her to better people like some in the country and a man would fall in love with her and stick to her through thick and thin in spite of his parents not being pleased.

She was lolling sideways on the bench, her weight on her left hip and shoulder, it still hurt but not as much as it did lying on her back and worse still sitting up. Six weeks gone and the pains only going slowly, and nothing had changed. Mum and Dad hadn't noticed the careful way she was walking and sitting and if Sam guessed anything he wasn't saying. He might well have put two and two together, he was all keen on reading about sex and talking smutty with his friends, and then he had noticed the smell, at his age he no doubt recognized it.

Shut up, shut up, don't think. Humming 'Some Day I'll Find You', she stood up. Parks didn't appeal to her, too gloomy, but squares like this had a bit more of interest. Not too much green or sun-stealing trees, but houses, cars, people. Kids and prams, the postman, horse and cart selling coal, visitors ringing the bells and banging the knockers, those who lived here with their keys. The dustmen, one or two taxis, two girls abreast on bicycles, wobbling and giggling. Cats, all sly, coming and going silently and secret as if they were invisible. Dogs pushy and barking but frightened by the smaller cats. It would be empty, the square, nothing going on for twenty minutes, then: two old ladies carrying net bags bulging with shopping, a mother with a whining toddler, three men walking confidently to the Queen's Elm round the corner. Don't think. 'Some day I'll find you, moonlight behind you.' A ball bounced ahead chased by two boys. And then all quiet again and the square empty.

The future was such a long way ahead, at least next year, and how was she going to put it to Patrick? She wasn't up for going out with those who fancied her straightforward and wanted the usual. But if that MP was still up for the rubber skirt business or anyone else like that who had some out of the way idea that didn't involve doing it, she was game, only it would be nice if it included dinner and dancing. No. Hopeless. Couldn't be the MP, Nick would kill her and that would put paid to her new life however many times she read the *Telegraph* or listened to Anna Neagle or Margaret Lockwood.

Not much hope of it working anyway. It stood to reason, young men who could go out at night for a good time didn't do sex enough to get bored with it and want something peculiar. Older men who were married and used to doing it a lot whenever they felt like it had to do their things in secret in the afternoon and weren't on for dinner and a dance. Pity there was no one to talk to.

On the top floor of the house opposite the window was wide open and a man was looking out, maybe he was an artist and wanted to paint her, after all this was Chelsea. He waved. Had he seen her sitting on the bench holding herself for protection against the hard wood? She sprinted away.

Not wanting to go home, delaying, putting it off, she stayed on the bus for another three stops. If it wasn't possible to go to her other lovely life and home made her feel cold and sick, where then? Where? Nowhere. Home it had to be. The telephone was there. The wonderful black machine with wires that disappeared into the plug in the wall. Those wires must run all over the place, everywhere in the world, though the phone worked even in the air with no wires. Right now her body was probably walking through conversations. It might even be walking through a voice talking to her mum, somebody might be saying, 'Hello, may I speak to Miss Winston please?' And her mum would say, 'Iris is out, this is her mother, can I take a message?' And it would still happen, they would hear each other in spite of her body walking through the words.

'I already said no, for all the calls you get it's a waste of money. Don't start, Iris, I know: your money, not mine. Well, all I can say is, for what this telephone costs I could give my family something decent to eat every night of the week, go to the pictures once a week and not have to keep one pot of tea going all day. Not much to ask. After all I done for you and your brother. And your father. I've kept this family together, you'll never know what I've been through, keep it to myself I do . . .'

'If only,' Iris muttered.

'What?'

'Nothing.'

'I could have been someone, a secretary, an assistant to a man in business – a big shot . . . What's the matter with you? White, you are, very funny looking. Where are you going?'

'Lie down. I got up early.'

'Oh, here, there was a message, got it muddled up with yesterday when there was none. Two in fact. Today that is. All nicely written down. Nice voice, not one of your usuals. Denis?'

'I don't know. Was it Denis?'

'No. Peter, yes, definitely.'

'For Christ's sake, Mum, make up your mind.'

'I have. Peter.'

'What's his number?'

'He didn't give it. Don't look at me like that.' Offended, she pointed to the scrap of paper and stump of pencil lying next to the telephone. 'If he gave it, it would have been on there. You ought to know his number if he's a friend and if you don't know it you shouldn't phone him.' She frowned, thinking. 'Oh yes, beg pardon, and a woman this morning, ordinary sounding, said it was fine. As arranged.'

It was an address in Bethnal Green. Old flats with stone steps and outside landings. Kids were playing on the big space set between the three blocks and the road. They were everywhere, shrieking and running and skipping, singing and crying and playing ball up against the walls. Number eleven was opened by a cosy little woman with mousy hair done up in a straggly bun.

'Come in, come in love. Hope you don't mind cats.' There were quite a lot if you did, at a quick count, six. 'Come into the back lounge quick, dear, in case the boys get back on time for their dinner.'

Iris could smell the dinner, nice, some kind of stew.

'I've got three boys, all in work,' the woman said proudly.

In the lounge the curtains were closed and the light was on, one naked bulb hanging over a narrow divan. There were two mattresses on the divan covered in a rubber sheet and against the wall was a bowl, a kettle and a pile of clothes.

'You brought the money did you, dear? I have to

have it first. You look nice and trustworthy but some, well, I do it and then they say, "I haven't got any money." Not much I can do after that,' she laughed.

'Here.' Iris handed over the seventy-five pounds.

'Thank you, dear.' She rolled it up and put it in an old tobacco jar on the mantelpiece. 'And I can see you brought your towels, good girl. You undress to your waist, lie on your towel facing the wall with your knees up to your chest and I'll just give my hands a nice wash.'

It was Auntie Reeny who'd put her on to this place. Iris remembered just before the end of the war all the whispering and crying with Mum, Auntie Reeny and Gran. Her husband was due back from the war, he'd been away two years and Auntie Reeny was three months gone. She hadn't done anything about it in case he got killed but as he was definitely coming home she had to be fixed up. Very nice she'd been about it, gave her the address, didn't say a word.

'Right, dear. Would you like a gin?'

'No thanks.' She faced the wall, her eyes tightly shut, thinking about a beautiful story from a film. It was in Vienna in olden days. Couples dancing the waltz in a big beautiful ballroom. The ladies had huge skirts, wide and full, silk and lace, white, so clean they must be new. Little feet doing neat steps and bodies moving and swaying and bending. Men looking down at the faces of their partners with true love, and nobody bumping into each other. Lovely music: 'In green Vienna woods one day we wandered through the live long day the breezes blow the branches sway . . .' And candlelight and mirrors so the ballroom was even bigger . . .

'Sit up, dear.'

'Is that it?' Not as bad as she thought.

'Not really. See, I don't think I can do much for you. I can't do anything because of the state you're in. You took on too many, dear, for a kid of your age. What you want to do when you're better . . .'

'What? Why can't you, I can't have it . . .'

'No, no, no.' The woman tried to soothe her. 'You won't be having it, that pregnancy won't last. Now you listen to me. Money isn't worth it. Get yourself a nice older man to keep you. Married. He won't be able to get away so much, or stay the night, or be so vigorous. Or find yourself a couple of foreign business men, occasional visitors.'

Funny, Iris thought. It wasn't unlike the advice Bobby gave her.

'You haven't been on the game long, have you dear?'

'I'm not. It was, they . . .'

The woman interrupted. 'All right. None of my business, but take the advice of one who knows. Don't go to the police. They'll think you're a brass anyway and you'll be wrote down.'

'I wasn't going to.'

'No, dear. That will sort itself out, down below. Go to a doctor if it doesn't mend but give it time, and it don't look to me as if you'll be carrying much longer. If you dress yourself and push off sharpish you'll be gone before my boys get here.'

From the open landing Iris could see 'her boys' coming up the stone steps. Late forties, early fifties; heavy, balding. They smiled sympathetically and nodded passing on the steps. They must know from experience. A pale face and a bag big enough for towels. Well might they smile – their mum had kept the money.

It wouldn't do to tell Mum and Dad about the flat, not yet. Sam had to know if he was going to cover up for her. Not that they'd notice. Mum had complained about her not going out and being in the way, and without saying much you could tell they were both worried lest she stopped giving them the cash they were getting used to. She'd asked him how long could she have it. 'Everything is transitory,' he had said. Later on she had looked that up. It meant that the flat was hers not forever. Number sixty-seven Three Kings Yard, Mayfair. Only two rooms, that's what Patrick had said. Only! It wasn't only two rooms because that didn't include the little kitchen and bathroom. And both all fitted. Kitchen with electric cooker, modern sink, and lovely fridge that made ice. Bathroom with a heater – and fitted carpet. Fitted carpet everywhere. Beige, lots of beige; curtains and sofa and bedhead. It was a sweet little place. Near Claridges and Grosvenor Square – bit too near Le Routier, but who knows, she might get used to it. Time heals.

It was a good day when the rain made her bump into

Patrick. It was all to be taken slow, her move up in life, and she wasn't going to need taxi money, leave it to him. Going out last night had been dead easy. An American film star, nobody she'd heard of, but he must be a big-timer, he was making a film here and they flew him in on purpose for it which must have cost a fortune. Dinner was at a restaurant new to her, where actors and film stars went and all sorts to do with show business. They weren't alone, table for two, others to do with the film were there, ten altogether, laughing and talking, drinking cocktails, telling stories which were funny about people who were famous as if they were anybodies, going back and forth to other people at other tables – like a party. Choose what you like off the menu, money no object. Jedd looked like the hero type of film star with big cheekbones and jawbones and very very white teeth.

When it all broke up because some were working, shooting, next day at six o'clock in the morning, she went on with Jedd and another couple to dance in a place on the edge of Soho near Tottenham Court Road. It was ever so small and smoky and sophisticated. Dark red and gold and very low lighting. There was a trio playing all the latest things, they were thin and short which was just as well considering the size of the room. When her eyes got used to the smoke and the gloom she decided the musicians were either children or midgets, extremely good idea in the circumstances. Most of the time Jedd sat talking to the other woman who was attractive in a mature sort of way, and she danced with the man. Not much chatting, on account of what the trio lacked in size they made up for with noise. They turned out to be the sort of foreigners who come short in size. They dropped her back to Three Kings Yard at three a.m. No taxi money!

Late in the morning she walked up to the Express Dairy and got everything for breakfast, it was fun all right but peculiar too. In spite of the busy streets it felt a bit lonely. But when Jedd called and asked her round to drinks at his place she cheered up no end, then Sam rang and that was nice too, it made her feel busy. The man from last week, Peter, had left a messge again, this time Sam got his number and it was all very interesting till he said that Peter said to remind her he was someone to do with Le Routier – or Le Rooters as Sam put it. Were any of *them* called Peter? No. Couldn't be sure though. The telephone number wasn't anywhere posh: RED-cliffe, which was near Earls Court. Perhaps it would pop into her head when she wasn't thinking about it.

If it was only drinks at six maybe she should nip home after, put in an appearance and pick up her two good blouses. The service flat where Jedd was staying wasn't far from Three Kings Yard, near enough to walk. On the way over quite a few men gave her the eye, it was the snug navy blue jumper and new uplift bra that did it, not to mention the straight skirt and high heels which made her take small teetering steps. There was a doorman standing outside the building which had been difficult to find, the number being on a small brass plate which the man's body concealed. He was dressed in a good dark grey suit, the only way you could tell he worked there was the cap trimmed with a discreet bit of gold braid. But he guarded the door like a policeman on duty outside a bank.

'Mr Royston isn't in,' he said.

Charming! No sorry madame, or anything. To the question, 'Do you know when he'll be back?' he said, 'No.' The way he was eyeing her, cold and snooty, anyone would think she was on the game. What now? Stand out there? Through the windows flanking the front door she could see a reception desk, the lift, a long leather sofa and a low glass-topped table with a vase of salmon pink artificial flowers, magazines and a big ashtray.

'Mr Royston was expecting me at six o'clock but as he is delayed I will wait for him.' The best Anna Neagle she could do, with a touch of Loretta Young.

Begrudgingly he opened the door; when she sat down he positioned himself behind the reception desk and looked above her head at the opposite wall.

After two cigarettes and flicking through the most boring magazines she had ever come across in her entire life, all about the countryside and old furniture, she was willing to give up and go home – or wherever – to the flat.

One quite well dressed woman had gone out and two very properly dressed men had come in, wearing the sort of suits that made the doorman's clothes look like what they were – a working man's best.

She tried to sit up gracefully, not easy in this low sofa wearing a tight calf-length skirt. Placing her knees to one side she levered herself up, not very dignified, but at least the silent porter hadn't got a look up her skirt.

'Perhaps you would be kind enough to tell Mr Royston when he returns that Miss Winston couldn't wait any longer.'

He didn't open the door, just stood back, looking at her, his head cocked on one side.

Once again on the way back, taking silly little steps like a fat toddler, she was getting the glad eye. This skirt was only going to be worn from now on getting in and out of taxis and being there, wherever it was.

Right. Now what? Go home? Sitting here in the nice beige room, all warm, wasn't this it? Her nice new life? Better than freezing smelly Kilburn. Not that it was Mum's fault, she did her share of scouring and scrubbing. While she was living here she ought to pop over every so often and do a bit, turn a room out. She shifted her position in the armchair, uncomfortable, aware still of the tears and bruises slow to mend.

If only . . . If this had happened – Three Kings Yard – before . . . what happened, it would have been nicer, even nicer, but now . . . well. In olden days it would have been really fun to go right now to Les A or even Le Routier, say hello to the doorman all confident, go to the toilet, have a look in the bar, click with someone in a group, have a drink. She could have gone for a stroll all around, kept her eyes open for a taxi or car arriving with someone she knew, latch on and be set for the evening. Not now. She was more frightened than in the war. And frightened of friends more than strangers. And it was all her own fault, as Nick said, she'd been asking for it, little did he know what she'd got. Playing with fire, she had got burnt. Another 'if only' was Nick: if only he didn't have to do his foreign office work in other countries, she could talk it all through with him, well, not all perhaps. Bobby was no good because Patrick didn't want her mixing with him, 'Not good enough for you,' he said. She had just made up her mind to get the bus and go home, get a bit of credit, when the telephone rang. Waiting for the three rings so she wouldn't look too eager, she picked up. 'Hello, Mayfair four-two-nine . . .'

'Oh, hi, Eileen?' It was him, Jedd. Bloody cheek.

'No, I'm afraid you have the wrong number.' Eileen. Bloody cheek.

'Gee, I'm certainly sorry. It sure sounds like you.'

'Well, it ain't – isn't, my name is Miss Winston, Iris Winston.' Not often these days she did ain'ts for isn'ts, but crikey who wouldn't, 'Eileen' on top of not turning up.

'Of course! Iris! Oh, my Lord. Please forgive me, baby. Iris, of course.'

She didn't say anything, she wasn't going to help him out. Shit.

'Look, hey, honey, did we have a date or something? A plan?'

'I understood it to be a cocktail party.' She said it all haughty like.

'Yeah, that's what I thought. See, honey, I'm still here right now, at the studio. And I want you to know, very sincerely, that I truly regret letting you down, young lady. So, this is what I propose.'

What he had proposed was ever so much better than drinks in that block of flats. But half past six! Never been up so early, and no breakfast. The train to Elstree, chugging slowly out of the station, its wheels squeaking, the engine puffing and moaning like her auntie who had asthma, sounded as tired as she felt. Not true, not any more. No, she was awake now, excited. She looked shyly at the three other girls in the compartment all chattering, whispering, yawning, adjusting stockings and checking the seams, wiping the corners of their thickly lipsticked mouths, squaring shoulders and pushing out chests in tight jumpers. One by one they examined their faces in the reflective glass covering an advertisement for SUN AND SEA IN SHANKLIN, laughing, twittering, disturbing their hair with spiky fingers. Fluttering like birds. Occasionally one of them would glance at her then turn away, ignoring her little smile. These must be actresses too and they didn't look bad considering. After all, if they were regular actresses it meant they had to get up at five o'clock every morning. Still, thirty bob wasn't bad, and more if you did anything special, like speak. And what a lark – being in a film with Jedd Royston! One of the girls was wearing false eyelashes, you could tell, there was a definite difference between the two layers. Should she have put on more make-up? Braving the girls' quick scornful appraisals, she examined herself in SUN AND SEA IN SHANKLIN. All right, not bad, natural-looking; but she couldn't tell if that was a shadow under her left eye or a sandcastle from the picture. The film took place in olden times in Rome, Jedd said, and young ladies were required to loll and wander around. What sort of make-up was worn in olden Rome? She'd seen *Cleopatra* with Claudette Colbert, really lovely eye stuff, but that was olden Egypt and couldn't be the same.

Not only the girls in her compartment got off at Elstree but all down the platform girls were walking to the exit sign. There were all sorts: blondes, brunettes, redheads; tall, short, some as old as twenty-five, even thirty. So whatever people looked like in Rome in those days there was plenty here to choose from. The girls in the compartment had disappeared, blending in with the others on their way out. Very handy this crowd, now she didn't need anybody to be nice or helpful she could just follow and copy.

The film studio was a big let-down, on the outside at any rate, buildings that were no different from factories or warehouses. Then they all went in single file through a sort of prefab Nissen hut where a man with a clipboard was taking names. She tagged on behind a couple of girls who were a bit quieter than the others, and more dull in a nice way.

As they stood in the queue, whispering, she could

hear names of people Bobby almost knew; Larry and Vivien, Gladys someone, old Vic. Names that had been on good luck telegrams in the dressing-room at Bobby's show. Back-stage. She'd been back-stage, so put that in your pipe and smoke it! Behind her it was all dirty talk.

'I let him put two fingers in.'

'Not very generous, mean cow.'

'Two fingers would be lost inside you.'

'If I want him to treat me like a lady, I've got to behave like one. I'm not letting him come inside me till he's taken me out proper and spent some money on me.'

It was nearly coming up to her turn. A couple up in front were giving their names, the man gave them a sort of not very nice smile and slapped their bums. Cheek. He'd better not try that on with her. Then the two right in front gave their names and mentioned an agency. They got a quiet nod and a wave through.

'Iris Winston.'

'Yes?' he said impatiently. 'Iris Winston,' he tapped the clipboard with his pencil. 'From?'

She couldn't answer that. Stoke Newington was the answer but that wouldn't do. Running a finger down a very long list, he said, 'No Iris here of any kind, Winston or otherwise.'

'Well, I spoke to Jedd, Mr Royston, last night and he said I was to be here at half past seven.' She yawned, it made her feel tired just saying it.

He eyed her up and down with more interest now. 'Tired are you? Keep you up, did he? All right, Iris, my little flower, ever been an extra before? No, don't tell me. OK. Follow that lot and when you get to

Wardrobe tell them you're in the Forum bath scenes. Next. Oh it's you, Jeanie, hope you haven't been at the garlic again.'

'I aim to please,' Jeanie simpered.

The man put his hand in his trouser pocket and jiggled it. 'So do I, young ladies are usually pleased with my aim.'

The woman in Wardrobe was shaking her head. 'I don't see you in a towel, no point; I won't be able to pad your bust. Turn round, darling.'

Obediently, Iris turned slowly. She was wearing her best underwear, which matched, all bought at the same time. Extravagant! Off-white silk; bra, knickers and suspender belt. Not her best stockings though. The bra didn't do anything for her but it felt nice, looked nice. The other girls were dressed, dressing or half naked, some being pinned into long dresses and some into short towels. One little group were talking about her, 'Jedd's piece,' she heard, then from the back of the room someone called, 'Give her something she can get out of quickly.' Ha, bloody ha, silly cow. But she laughed, show them she didn't care.

The women gently lifted her hair. 'No, you must be a Roman lady. Make-up will be pleased with your hair. All the wigs they have been sent look like poodles' hair.'

'Are you sure, miss? The man at the gate definitely said the bath scenes.'

The kid was nervous, anxious to please, not her idea of anybody's 'piece', it must have come from Mike, what did he know about her to say that. 'My husband doesn't always know what's best.'

She must have been ready for hours. Sewn into her Roman dress by a little old lady with cold fingers, so short she couldn't reach her shoulders. But she'd knelt to help her and Carol the wardrobe lady had given her a nice smile. How anybody as kind, and pretty too, could be married to that groping, rude pig at the gate – well, it was probably something to do with the war, a shortage of men who hadn't been killed.

Upstairs, a few flights above the dressing-rooms, in the extras' make-up room, her hair had been curled a bit on top with very hot tongs which nearly burnt her forehead, it made her fringe into a big sort of sausage, the rest was left quite nice and a bit wavy. If this was what Roman ladies looked like in BC it wasn't that much different from Rosalind Russell and Joan Crawford in 1940. The make-up was the quickest and nastiest anyone could possibly imagine: thick as thick yellowy-beige pancake, powder as coarse as flour and her eye-brows and lashes plastered in sticky mascara that turned into dry stiff clumps. It was done to everybody whatever they looked like. When she went to the toilet, girls were carefully altering their faces. Some taking off, some adding. She wiped away the stuff on her eyebrows and with a safety pin separated the glued-together lashes.

Now here she was on the floor, on the set, and after hanging around for ages and ages something was happen-ing at last. Quite a few of the Roman ladies had been brought down and there were a lot of Roman gentlemen too. The forum bath towel girls had come down earlier. No one had said what was going on, she didn't even know what time it was. No watches, they'd been told. The set was absolutely enormous and quite nice. Lots of columns and arches and big cushions, most likely for lolling, and long tables and large candles and through the biggest arch were the baths, which were like a cross between the Turkish baths at the Dorchester Hotel and East Finchley swimming-pool. As the girls weren't friendly she tried standing next to some Roman gentlemen to see if she could find out anything. All she learned, apart from the fact that the canteen was cheap but awful, was that this was a party scene, which she'd already guessed. Then an assistant was moving her around as if she was deaf and dumb and on skates. Someone was shouting instructions, and people got into positions. The assistant looked at her for the first time. 'OK?' he said. 'Got it?'

'Got what, please?'

'Oh, Christ! Weren't you listening?'

'Beg pardon.'

'This is a rehearsal – SILENCE PLEASE.'

In the middle of the set now filled, flooded with a light stronger than she'd ever known, brighter even than the searchlights that took away the night during the war, was the camera. Around it in pools of shade people stood. A few sat in chairs like upright deckchairs on the beach.

The assistant took hold of her arm. 'All right, sweetheart,' he spat. 'Let's go through it.' Pushing her none too gently, he said, 'On the word ACTION you count three; one, two, three, right? Then you walk slowly towards this pillar, where this gentleman . . .' a Roman dressed man stepped out of a group and joined them '. . . will escort you smiling and talking, *not* so we can hear you, to pass behind Miss LeSage and Mr Morepath who will be there in front of the camera, and off towards the baths. *Do you understand?*'

'Yes. Thank you.'

'I'll see her through it, Gordon.' The Roman man gave her a nice encouraging wink.

'If either of you fuck up this shot I will kill you both.'

'You are only a second assistant, Gordie, not Nero.'

'First positions, please!'

She hurried back to the foot of the cream circular staircase and got in place.

'QUIET PLEASE. This is a take.'

Somebody shouted something about a red light. A young man stepped in front of the camera and banged something.

'QUIET . . . Action!'

One – two – three, she counted carefully. Slowly she walked towards the column, her feet slapping the floor in her loose thonged sandals. The man stepped out of his group and joined her but walking much faster. 'You are too slow,' he mouthed.

'I was told to go slow,' she replied in a tiny breathy whisper.

'Cut – CUT.'

'What is it, sound?'

'She spoke when she was under the boom, the extra, I could hear her speak, sorry and all that.'

'First positions everyone.'

Gordon grabbed her arm, pulling her over to the camera. 'You are walking like a fucking geisha girl, and you . . .' he turned to her partner 'are mincing like a fucking poof.'

'Takes one to know one, dearie.'

One of the men in the chairs beckoned her over. She recognized him from her night out at the actors' restaurant, he was a friend of Jedd's.

'Oh, hello. What are you doing here?' she said.

'I'm, er, David Miller . . .' He laughed. 'I'm always here. You see, I'm the director.' The others sitting near him joined in the laughter, but only sucking up to him, she could tell. 'And you are Iris, right? A friend of Mr Royston?'

'Yes, that's right.'

'OK. What's wrong with your sandals? Too big? Wardrobe!' he shouted. 'They'll strap them round your ankles, and you, sir,' he turned to her partner, 'stride out, lengthen your step and look at Iris as if she's the world's most alluring sodomite or catamite – whatever your taste is.'

'Sodomite will do nicely, Mr Miller.'

'OK. Let's go again . . . and Iris,' he called after her, 'don't speak, just smile, you have a lovely smile.'

The rest of the morning had been much easier. Nothing special on her own. All she had to do was mingle with other Romans at the fountain, laugh and eat some grapes, murmur without being heard and bow when the head Roman walked in. All this was with Ken, her partner, who was very nice and knew Bobby quite well. No surprise considering he was usually a dancer as well as being queer.

Now everybody was at lunch, or most were, Ken hadn't asked her, nor had anybody else, and here she was, up since five o'clock, bloody well worn out, sitting in the hot smelly dressing-room and nowhere to lie down and have a kip. There were places, dressing-rooms, where you could lie down, she knew that because some of the girls had paired off with assistants of some kind and a person called a stunt arranger. Ken said the way to get more work was to do it with useful people. For instance, the girl who stood in while they were fixing the lights so June LeSage could have a sit down was only five foot two inches with light brown hair, whereas June LeSage was five foot six inches and dark. Make-up had to give her a wig and Wardrobe very high heels. So, Ken said she must be doing it with someone useful. Perhaps they were using Jedd's dressing-room, he wasn't working today, his call had been changed. Ken showed her the call sheet. He wasn't down for tomorrow either – Roman ladies were, so, would she be asked?

She woke up as the girls started coming back after lunch. Sleeping with her head pillowed on her handbag had left a big red mark on her cheek. It would have to be dealt with in the toilet, too many people, assistants to this and that kept popping in and out, like spies for the Make-up department, and she wasn't going back there to get turned into an advertisement for 'before'. Although in those magazine transformations 'after' wasn't always better anyway.

Back on the set with her face done over she felt a bit more confident, it was all just about the same as the stuff in the morning only now nobody was bothering about her she could get a good look. How anybody understood everything, exactly what was what – well, you'd have to be Professor Joad. And why were they all so bad? Everybody, absolutely the whole lot of them kept getting it wrong, over and over and over again they did the same thing. Only little bits were changed, a light brighter, the camera nearer, the actors louder, and a bossy woman was stopping and criticizing all the time, 'a hand in the wrong position', 'a word wrong', 'a curl out of place', 'his toga crooked'. If she was that director she'd sack every man jack of them. People were getting irritable and tired and the noise kept rising; chatting, rustling of papers, men walking high up on the iron girders, others ignoring the red light and opening doors. The whole studio seemed to sigh with relief together when the tea-trolleys appeared. Hungry, first food of the day, she took a handful of biscuits and two pieces of ginger cake.

'How do you eat all that and stay so nice and slim?' A Roman lady holding a water biscuit smiled at her.

'Oh thanks. Well, I didn't have any breakfast, see, or lunch.'

'Too long a day for a diet like that. You don't want to faint. Take a tip from me. When the trolley comes round in the morning take a bacon roll and keep it for lunch. Free, see?'

'Yes, I will . . . oops.' The ginger cake was crumbling on her dress.

'And don't eat anything in the morning or afternoon that takes your make-up off and buggers up your frock.'

Iris smiled gratefully. 'Thanks ever so, that's really kind of you.'

Mike pushed his way through the crowd still queuing at the tea trolley. 'All right, let's see; you, you, you and you.' He rounded up a few extras including her and took them back on the set, putting them right near the camera. Winking at them all he said, 'That means, ladies, that you will all be on call tomorrow, we will never finish this tonight.' He gave a funny look to the nice lady who'd tagged along with them.

'Don't you give me the heave-ho, Mike. I'm with my mate here, Iris.' She giggled, a bit too coy for a woman who wasn't a girl.

At half past six, after quite a lot of takes all on the same bit and everybody getting ratty – the last time the clapper-boy held up the board he'd said, 'As The Romans Do. Scene seventeen. Take twenty-three' – somebody shouted, 'Cut. Kill the red light.' Then someone else shouted even louder, 'Strike the . . .' something she couldn't hear, but she could tell that was it because the two big heavy doors were opened and the whole lot of people were streaming off the set and making more noise than she'd heard all day. Then Mike took her elbow and led her aside, away from the crowd. 'Listen, love, you'd make a very good stand-in for June LeSage; you've got the same colouring, a bit younger, yes, but not too much personality. What do you think?'

Frightened, she shrank back feeling the padded wall.

'Go on, Iris, she works a lot, could be a steady job.'

'I couldn't,' she stammered.

'Why not? It was Carol's idea.'

'Carol?' Christ, she thought, who was that – somebody who organized all the dressing-rooms for sexual intercourse in the dinner break?

'You met her this morning. My wife. Carol. Wardrobe.'

'Wardrobe, oh, yes.' Still she hesitated.

'Why not?' he persisted.

'Can I think about it, please?'

He shrugged. 'Don't do me any favours, and here . . .' he fumbled in his pocket, reminding her of his crude gesture this morning, 'Mr Royston left a message with his driver. Lucky girl, he's taking you home.'

She brightened up. 'I don't believe it. Oh, how wonderful, how absolutely smashing! I'm so tired!'

'Yeah, well, get an early night. You're called first thing. Seven o'clock in Make-up.'

Sitting in the back of the car she was glad the driver had another girl sitting next to him, she was too tired to talk. Now she could just enjoy the treat. Door to door service. And tomorrow Ken could put her straight about whether or not it would be safe to stand in for June LeSage. It would be nice to have a career. A regular job that wasn't too regular. Specially if the flat got transitory early.

On the outskirts of Hendon the driver dropped the girl off.

'Sorry about that, miss, only a short diversion.'

Oh yes? Pull the other one. She knew it was out of line, him taking that girl. Not part of the job. Nevertheless she smiled sweetly at him in the driving mirror. 'Quite all right.'

'Thank you, miss.'

She rested her head on the back of the seat again, ready to doze off.

'And don't you worry, miss, I'll have you at Mr Royston's in ten to fifteen minutes. A few back doubles; down West End Lane, Abbey Road, Lisson Grove, through the park . . .'

She sat up quickly snapping awake. 'Mr Royston's?' Alarm made her voice shaky.

'Yes, miss, straight there, he said. I was to take you directly to his apartment, as he called it.'

Slumped in the corner, looking out of the window with little interest at the shops, not a patch on Regent Street, she wondered what they were doing at home, which was so near, and what she and Jedd would be doing tonight. Only a drink would be nice. Not like her, not wanting to go out for a good time, but these filming hours were bloody.

'Here we are, miss.' He jumped out smartly and opened her door with a flourish.

The same foul rotten porter was there holding the door open but only enough for a starving cat to get through. 'Madame?' The stupid sod was guarding the entrance as if it was Cartier's, but the driver was lovely.

'Madame is expected by Mr Royston. Good-night, Miss Winston, I will see you at the studio in the morning.'

His flat was a bit like hers, smarter and even more modern, but not much bigger.

'I've made a batch of dry martinis, okay, honey?'

Dry martinis could mean two things: the flavoured winy stuff or loads of gin with so little martini in it it was hardly worth bothering. Not waiting for a yes, no, or kiss my arse, he handed her a glass, which she could tell from the colour was the loads of gin sort.

'Cheers.' He clinked glasses very carefully so as not to spill.

'Cheers.' No point in telling him it was not done to clink, men didn't like being told anything. She sat up straight in the armchair facing him, he was perched on the arm of a sofa. The electric fire was on, one of the elements spitting as if it was about to go. For the life of her she couldn't think of anything to chat about, it had been such a long day. 'Oh, Jedd, thanks ever so for putting me up for the filming. Really nice of you. Yes, I did enjoy it.'

He finished his dry martini and filled the glass from a little jug sitting in a bowl of ice. 'You are welcome, honey. More?' He offered the jug.

'No thanks. Actually, I'm working tomorrow, filming, I mean.'

He was relieved, she could tell. 'Oh, great, early night, right?'

She nodded and smiled, she was relieved too.

'Well, let's see now, Iris, honey bunny.' He slid down off the arm into the comfort of the sofa. 'You are European,' he wagged his finger at her as if she'd just been cheeky. 'And I am American.' He took an olive from a bowl on the bamboo coffee table and dropped it into his glass, raising the level dangerously. Before it spilt he drank a little, fished out the olive, ate it and licked his fingers. 'And that means that our cultures are basically different. Right?'

Strictly speaking she was English not European, which meant French, Italian and Spanish; and a few other places as well.

He continued, 'We Americans are simple folk with no sophistication, none of your kind of old world background going way back to the ribald days of the Holy Roman Empire, the subtleties of Macchiavelli, the Borgias, Marie-Antoinette. You know what I mean?'

She was only sipping her drink but it was hard concentrating because it was going into a stomach that was empty except for the cake at tea-time.

'That fire sure smells funny.' He jumped as it spat.

'One of the elements is about to go, that's all.'

'Yeah, right. Is it safe?'

'Oh, yes.' Should she join in, say something about history? 'You don't have kings and queens neither.' She offered this as a continuation of his theme, not as a nugget of conversation.

'So true, so true. You. You Europeans, as I said, are a sophisticated race with sophisticated tastes. You are open to . . . things, to experiments. In all departments. Yeah. Yes sir! You are worldly wise – free from Baptist shackles.'

Something was coming, he was getting to it – but what? Discreetly she checked the door and the position of her handbag. She held her drink taking tiny sips; if he attacked her she could smash the glass in his face. With a bit of luck it wouldn't be necessary; they wouldn't thank her at the studio.

'I'm expecting a call at . . .' Pushing up the cuff of his red and white striped shirt he looked at his watch. 'OK. It's half past eight, so it's half past twelve in LA.'

'Oh, yes,' she said politely.

'What I have in mind, young lady, is something naughty, OK? Something down and dirty. I would like you to tie me up prior to urinating on me.'

She choked delicately into the small-stemmed, vee-shaped glass.

'I knew you were the gal for me when Patrick told me you didn't put out, but anything else goes.' Undoing the buttons of his dark grey cashmere jacket he did a little dance to the bedroom door. 'Like the song says, anything goes.' He looked over his shoulder, grinning boyishly. 'I guess you save your pussy for your boyfriend.'

Trying delay tactics, she put down her glass and said brightly, 'Who's calling you from LA then?'

'My fiancée.'

'Oh, that's nice, you're engaged.'

'Here, look.' He beckoned her over to the bedroom. 'This is her, my Lila.' He pointed to a photograph in a leather frame of a blonde with a bust so big it must have been at least size 40 and a double D cup.

He winked at her, doing the boyish grin again. 'It's not the sort of thing you could ask the young lady you're about to marry to do.'

She looked again at the photograph. It was of the sort of young lady you could ask to do anything.

The last tie, quite nice, pink and grey striped silk, had just been knotted carefully around his ankles when the phone rang. She felt like a nurse as she picked up the receiver and tucked it under his chin. It had worked. Taking her time, she had obediently tied his wrists together and strapped them with a real crocodile leather belt to the brass rail of the bed head. It was difficult, being scared, her hands weren't working proper. He'd agreed not to take his clothes off yet, accepting her promise that she would undress him – slowly. He was talking all lovey-dovey.

'Hi, Lila sweetie, how's my little girl?' But gesturing to her to untie his hands and wait in the other room.

She nodded sweetly, pretending not to understand and gestured back with a little wave and a tender smile.

As she pressed the button for the lift her hand was trembling. The porter wasn't there, if he'd knocked off for the night Jedd Royston was going to have a good long rest. So. What now. It was only ten to nine, where should she go? Not the flat. Not the one in Three Kings Yard. Because that was somewhere that a girl – young lady – honey – could stay only so long as the honey who didn't put out accepted that anything goes – except for it. Right. Get the make-up and enough clothes for tomorrow but not so much that Mum would notice, then a taxi to Kilburn. And tomorrow after the filming get the rest. It was daft to be so shaky; if all the dinner and dancing, meet at Les A for a drink was over, well, that Mike and his wife, Wardrobe, said she could be a stand-in. That was something. It *was* over. Patrick wouldn't put up with her doing nothing. When the flat had been suggested there'd been no two ways about it. It was hers, no rent, just as long as certain things were done. The 'things' were uncertain really because he hadn't said what. Now she knew what, and she hadn't earned the right to stay there. 'Immaculate, untarnished, that's what you are,' he said. 'And that intrigues certain men. They will like soiling you.' Little did he know she'd been 'tarnished' five times. He said everything so politely and sort of light-hearted. 'It would be easy – nothing to worry about – less than a kiss.'

Her few bits and bobs for tonight and tomorrow fitted into a big brown carrier-bag. The telephone rang and rang but that sound had lost its lovely excitement and promise. She definitely wasn't going to answer, she wasn't up to being told off, not all tired and trembling.

The shakes had come on after writing the note to Jedd. Dead clever it had been. 'Felt awful when your girlfriend rang. (She didn't know how to spell fiancée.) Hope you understand. Don't worry. Won't mention it at studio. Or anywhere.' She hadn't signed it. Because why? *He* knew who it was from and nobody else need know. And 'won't mention it' meant she could if he got nasty.

The taxi was warm and smelled of cigars; nice and luxurious. Not much more of this though, whatever a stand-in got it wouldn't be taxi-money. The taxi took the same way going out as the studio driver had coming in. It was quite different, though, at night, the shops themselves dark and the flats above all lit up. Lots of foreigners lived round here, the sort of people who went to the coffee-bar, bus conductors used to shout, 'British West Hampstead' when they got to the stop at Fortune Green Road. Nearly there. Not far. Who'd have thought that Kilburn could ever be a welcome sight.

'Are you all right?' She was scrabbling in the gutter for the dropped change.

'Yes, thanks. Here . . .'

The driver looked at the coins lying in the palm of his hand. 'It's too much, here.' He took out a shilling.

'No, no, go on.' She pushed his hand away. 'There's your tip to take into account.'

'It's still too much, specially for a kid like you. Go on. Take it back.' He smiled. 'Give it to your mum.'

Only ten o'clock but they were all in bed. It wasn't cold but a hot water bottle would be comfy and while the kettle was boiling she'd wash her face and get all the muck off. What a come down. Cold dank bathroom. No hot water. No heated towel-rail. No heated towel.

Sam had left a note by the phone: CALL IRIS. BOBBY RANG URJENT.

She set the big alarm for six a.m. and wound it up. Bobby would have to stay 'urjent' till tomorrow night.

At the studio she figured it all out, learning enough yesterday to make it work today. Mike checked her in as if she was a regular. Carol, Wardrobe, took a bit of time dressing her, there were fewer girls down today, made sure everything looked nice. She put her own make-up on, pretending in the busy room that someone else had done it and waving vaguely in the direction of two make-up men crouched intently over girls who'd seemed pretty on the train but now looked like brand new dolls. At the tea break eating three egg and bacon sandwiches made the shaking go away a bit, although it got the usual reaction from people seeing her eat. 'Oh, you do actually put food into your mouth, Miss Skinny.' Then when lunchtime came, as Mike told her to, she took a tray of ham salad to Miss LeSage's dressing-room and had a chat while she ate. The actress kept giving her long looks all through them talking, even comparing faces with her in the brightly lit mirror. It was fairly clear that she was older than Iris but much more beautiful – well, beautiful – and Iris was only . . . Iris.

All day no one said anything about Jedd, even the man who was the director, he just said, 'Hi, Iris, how'yre doing?' Nothing about *him.* So perhaps everything was going to be all right.

The nearest bus stop for Three Kings Yard was on the corner of Davies Street and Oxford Street. Two carrier-bags would be enough for the rest of the stuff then a taxi home. The last taxi! The men standing outside number sixty-seven were straining to see inside the garage, standing on tip-toes with their heads up close to the dusty windows. Waste of time, no cars had been in there, for the last two weeks anyway. They didn't notice or hear her till she put the key in the lock, it was the big heavy one for the street door and the Yale key for the flat. Then all four of them crowded round her, came too close, hid her from the street. Her scream was stifled not by a hand over her mouth but by a thumb on her windpipe. The key was turned, the door shoved open, and half pushed half carried she was bundled up the stairs. Screaming didn't work, it made a peculiar husky empty sound, anyway the men were singing loud enough to drown her, as if they were drunk. But they weren't, they were sober and efficient.

Singing, 'Ta-ra-ra-boom-de-ay, ta-ra-ra-boom-de-ay.' Till they got to the top of the stairs.

'Where's the key to this door?' The pale man with shaggy ginger eyebrows flicked his finger against her throat.

'Must've dropped it,' she croaked. He flicked her throat again. 'On the stairs,' she added quickly. 'Or outside.'

One of them backed down the stairs on his hands and knees, feeling the carpet. 'Got it.' He eyed her viciously, blaming her for his undignified search.

'Sorry.'

Fear had taken away her breath, and 'Please don't please don't' came out all strangled. The old pain from the rape had started, everywhere; her back, her stomach where one of the men had dug his fingers in, while he was inside her, and between her legs. What seemed to be the main man was talking, questioning. Questions? Did that mean they weren't going to rape her? Dear God, let it be a mistake, dear God let it not be me they want.

'How much do you give Mr Courtney? Does he get it all and pay you? Where's your book? Do you deal as well as use? Where's your diary? Do the punters pay you or him?' He stopped. One of the others took it up.

'Where did you meet him? Does he set you up with Specials? How many tricks do you turn a week?'

'No. No, you got the wrong person. I'm not – that.' She tried to clear her throat but it hurt, like as if she'd swallowed a hairbrush. The older man started again, slow and sarcastic.

'Miss Winston, we need your help,' he said politely. 'And in exchange for that help we are going to help you.' He took a piece of paper, official looking, from his top pocket and held it out – they were policemen. 'You tell us about your relationship with Mr Courtney – and his friends – and we will see what we can do to take care of you.'

Care, Iris thought, a little of their 'care' went a long way.

'Try to keep you out of the papers, difficult of course with your illustrious boyfriend.'

Mr Courtney, she'd only just twigged, that was Patrick. Putting her hand to her throat she said with what she hoped was a sad, plucky little smile, 'I'll certainly do what I can to help you.'

He was surprised. 'Oh, right. Jones, take this down.'

'Only . . .' she whispered painfully.

'Yes,' he snapped.

'I don't know what you're talking about.' There couldn't be any proof. She wasn't a tart. Of course, the MP had given her some money, expenses you could call that, but Jedd had given her nothing.

'I don't take kindly to being fucked around, lady, so spit it out.' Except for the 'fucked' the line came straight out of one of those films where the private detective wore a white mac. Keeping her hand on her throat and swallowing to ease the soreness, she said, 'This flat belongs, I believe, to either Mr Courtney or a friend, I don't know. He said I could use it for a couple of weeks while I was filming. Otherwise he's just a casual acquaintance.'

They surrounded her again, all four of them. Too near, she felt faint. 'I was just going to take my stuff home, see?' She pointed to the two carrier-bags dropped in the corner.

'Let me tell you again. Explain. Last time, right? Last warning.' The one standing behind her was tall, his breath was lifting her hair like a hand-held dryer. The vicious one who found the key was putting his gloves on. Perhaps that meant they would go soon.

'What I want is dates, venues, names, how much

money changed hands, and if you can't remember make it up fast. I want a statement. Now. Or do you want to come down to the station? Eighteen, aren't you? I'll have to call your mum and dad. Is he still in hock to Chancery Lane, dear?'

'That isn't a crime,' she muttered.

He nodded. Behind her the man suddenly twisted her arms up to her shoulders. The one on her left grabbed her head and held it rigid, then the one wearing the gloves forced her mouth open and pushed one gloved finger down her throat. He stepped back sharply, avoiding the sick that spewed over her face and body.

'I'm trying to be understanding.' The head policeman withdrew a couple of inches from the smell of vomit. 'I've got a daughter your age.'

So fucking what, she thought. Everybody's got a daughter my age. Every bleeding taxi-driver, copper, managing director, doorman – didn't stop them trying to get in her knickers.

He repeated. 'I am trying to be understanding but I am getting just a bit impatient.'

It was difficult to speak, her arms were still trapped behind her back and the sick was drying on her mouth like gum.

Smirking at the others, he said, 'Or perhaps you would like to speak to your lawyer.'

Lawyers? Nobody she knew had a lawyer. Well, Nick probably did, you had to be rich or somebody to have a lawyer. A big shot. The younger man went to the window, shoved it open with his shoulder and threw the gloves down to the pavement.

'I would like to call somebody, please.'

He was eyeing her now all kind of sly, probably thought he was on to something. 'Yes, why not, dear. Give me the number?'

Should she? There wasn't anyone else. He might not be able to help, or want to, but he was the only chance. And he had said she should.

'Give me the number.'

Half past seven, where would he be, try the office.

'Trafalgar 4492.'

He dialled slowly and waited, frowning. 'Oh, what's the name?' he said. Before she could reply, she could just hear a voice say, 'Hello.' The policeman was still frowning, pursing his lips, shifting his weight uneasily. 'Ah, good evening. This is Detective Inspector Appleshaw speaking. I have a . . . oh, so sorry . . . sorry to disturb, I didn't . . . well, there's a young woman here, she is . . . I'm here with . . . yes, of course, Iris Winston. Under suspicion . . .'

Iris wondered what was up, he was pale and smiling anxiously into the receiver.

'Yes, sir, yes sir, sorry sir. Nothing wrong, sir. I'll do my best. Sorry for wasting your time. Would you like a word? Yes, sir. I'll tell her, sir. Thank you.'

He arranged his features into a 'nice old uncle' face. 'Naughty girl. Why didn't you tell us you were a friend of Mr Brown's?'

The man behind her released her arms. She pitched forward on to the floor.

Chapter Eleven

'I'M SURPRISED THEY are allowed to do that.' She bounced on the bed, pleased to have a listener for her story. Not all her story, that wouldn't be sensible. Or safe.

'For heaven's sake, Iris, sit on the chair. Do you have to bounce? I am supposed to be an invalid.'

'I'm so sorry.'

Sitting in the armchair, she crossed her legs under her.

'My God, you can do the lotus position. And whatever happened to "beg pardon"?'

'Oh, I'm a quick learner, anyway how can the police – *the police* – do something like that to Bobby? And me?'

'*The* police don't. *Those* policemen do. Bobby is homosexual, his sexuality is against the law. In fact so is yours.'

'Not true.'

'You take money for sexual favours.'

'Not really.'

'Really. Just because you don't actually fuck doesn't mean you are any more than a virginal tart.' Seeing her pale little face wince he softened. 'In their eyes anyway. And that's what they needed, you see, to get Patrick, evidence from a young girl he was pimping for. A victim, and all the better if she was taking drugs, he supplied them to others, why not you.'

She unfolded her legs and sat up primly in the armchair.

'I don't take drugs, and I only smoke to be sociable.'

'God knows why they are getting at him, Patrick Courteney isn't the only posh pimp pusher around. Maybe he wouldn't co-operate, pay silence money – or give silence favours. You know what I mean? Keep quiet about people under police protection, or police themselves.'

'It wasn't that,' she said.

'Oh?' He was interested now. 'What then?'

'Don't know,' she shrugged. She did, but she wasn't going to tell.

'Did he ever ask you to marry him?'

'Patrick?'

'Yes. He was always intrigued by you.'

Iris thought about it. 'I don't think so.'

'But you don't know?'

'Well, now you come to mention it . . . maybe that's what he meant. Oh, poor love, I hope I didn't hurt his feelings.'

'What did he say? What did you say?'

Whatever was said, not to recognize a proposal of marriage was *very* hurtful, he thought and laughed. 'Go on.'

'Something about living in a cold country, not many people, all pure and private and I said I was too young to fancy that and he wasn't quite old enough to retire, a few more years left, and when he did heat was supposed to be better for old bones.'

'Charming. He will no doubt marry his princess . . .'

'Princess Margaret?' She shot out of the chair and winced with pain, forget about it for five minutes, remember it for an hour.

'Of course not. He's had a friend for some time, a princess, as you would put it from foreign parts.'

'Dusky?'

'Wonderful, Iris, you never let me down, what a typical bloody working-class word.'

'No. Excuse me, Nick. You might be wrong this time. *Dusky* is how *Picturegoer* describes Miss Dorothy Lamour in a film where she comes from very far away.'

'Thank you. I stand corrected. I should defer to the language of *Picturegoer*.'

He sipped his barley water and replaced the glass on the elegant walnut lowboy which served as a bedside table. 'Most of his pimping was quite innocuous; girls for parties at Les A, well-connected young women as dinner-party fill-ins, participants in rather sedate après-lunch orgies, that sort of thing.'

Making an effort to control her trembling hands, her panic, she got up and said, 'I'll pull these curtains a bit, let the sun in, it's colder outside than it looks. This is a lovely room, if you've got to have malaria at least you've got a big bed and a nice view and a lovely mother to look after you. And help, servants. She was extremely pleasant to me, very kind. I like the big wide stairs and the way the doors shut firm but quiet. "It's good of you to come," she said. Doesn't she look young, must be the country air. "He likes to see friends," she said. Though my mum looks quite young even in the London air and she's about the same age as you.' Her hands were shaking, she pressed the palms together as if in prayer but they sprang apart still fluttering.

A door was slammed downstairs and the barking of dogs released into the garden could be heard under the window.

'I'm glad you don't let your dogs into the bedroom, it isn't hygienic. Cats are different partly because they're smaller. And they clean themselves. Funny their tongues are so pink considering all the dirt they have to lick off. This idea of having small carpets on top of big ones – I like that. Thank you so much, Nick, for telling your mother that I'm a friend.'

He was surprised that in spite of her evident distress she wasn't crying.

On a sigh into the silence she said, 'If I could be bothered to think about it I suppose I would wish I was dead.'

'I think I prefer you bouncing.'

She sat at the foot of the bed hoping that he'd say something, like 'What's the matter, what's happened, tell me all about it.' But he wasn't up for that and fair dos, he'd got enough on his plate what with malaria and Bobby probably going to prison for doing it in Leicester Square underground toilet, even though it was with a policeman. And then him being one himself all this must make him feel a bit nervy. Much worse for him than Bobby if he got caught. Imagine the headlines in that Sunday paper the *News of the World* that had all the dirty stories in it: FOREIGN OFFICE POOF FOUND AT IT IN LAV.

'Good girl, you're smiling.' He turned on his side, pulling the blankets up to his chin, and closed his eyes. Closing her off. 'You've got out of it lightly. Leave Patrick and all that behind you. Nasty as the incident was, well, treat it as a warning, don't you think?'

She hadn't got out of it all that lightly; it was nastier than nasty.

'Yes. Put it all in the past. Dead and done with.' She spoke softly in case he slept. 'I've got what looks like a regular job, part-time stand-in at the studios and twice I've been out with someone I like – only *like*,' she added hastily. 'A man you would like, I think, well, you probably know him in a way. Not rich or posh but not, not a – not bad. The pictures, a trattoria and saw me home.'

He was pretending now, but he would soon be asleep. Pity, because he wouldn't mind hearing about Peter, or Pierre as he was known in his working life.

The first time they were to have dinner before going to the pictures. Not Le Routier, it wouldn't do for staff to take someone out to a meal where they worked, she knew that, and Lyons' Corner House wouldn't be his style, he was a cut above. It might be a Kardomah coffee house, there was one in the Kings Road where they served a mixture of high-tea things; like baked beans on toast or poached eggs, and full meals, roast pork, toad in the hole, that sort of thing. They met outside the tube station, he'd already bought the tickets to Piccadilly Circus. The restaurant was in a little back street near St Martin's Lane. Quite nice. Spaghetti bolognese, then an interesting ice-cream, tutti-frutti. Red wine in a jug, all right but not what she was used to, but generous of him, it was a bigger treat considering he was only a waiter. The waiters here were jolly, lots of 'Bella Signorina', and generous with the grated cheese. They all called Peter 'Piero' because he'd worked there once. The table had a sensible red cloth on it (didn't show any spilt wine) and a bottle turned into a lamp with a red shade. If she'd been in love with Peter it definitely would have been romantic, but the peculiar thing was that she felt awkward. Yet he was more right, more suitable than the rich spoilt silly boys, or Nick and Bobby, or the maharajah, or, well, Steve Brown and . . . Oh Christ, the strange men who wanted sad and stupid things.

The film was not particularly interesting in itself, but it was special because the screen was huge – going sideways – and was very much in some ways like her film, specially to do with the clothes. He had seen her all the way home, walking to Oxford Circus through a bit of Soho, dingy on an evening lit with late summer light, the smell of urine, where dossers and drunks had pissed in narrow alleys, mixed with California Poppy cologne worn by the tarts. As they cut through Berwick Street market the smell changed to mouldering vegetables, nobody had swept up the discarded outer leaves of cabbages or washed away the slime of old spinach and lettuce.

Turning left at Great Marlborough Street then right at Liberty's, old-fashioned but quite interesting, into Regent Street was much nicer. Cleaner, and busier with people who had a purpose; not loitering and keeping an eye open for a pick-up or a sucker. Until they got on the bus it had been easy talking. There were things to see and remark on.

A couple of the girls had given cheeky looks to Peter, but only teasing. He pointed out a pub famous for writers and painters. Greengrocers were pushing their barrows to Covent Garden and one offered to give them a lift! But on the bus it was like being alone. She sat by the window but couldn't look out, that would be rude. They had to talk about something but the usual bits and pieces of chat had been used up in the café. And she didn't know where she was with him, what he wanted. With some of the Mayfair crowd it was straightforward, they wanted you flirting and being all girly and shutting up when they were talking serious. Others needed you listening, and agreeing and 'I'll have the same as you.' There was dancing and getting them home safe when they were drunk, all of which passed the time nicely. Nick said he liked her being herself, but there wasn't any 'herself' even with him, because he only wanted the funny ignorant plucky Iris. This Peter lay half-way between the might-have-been boyfriends in Kilburn and the rich nobs he'd seen her with at Le Routier. It was a cheek in a way for him to call her, a customer, and a mystery as to where he'd got her number. She wasn't going to ask, couldn't force herself, it brought it all back. And he didn't volunteer anything except for what he said on the telephone. 'I was concerned. You stopped coming into the restaurant; they haven't been in either.'

Peter introduced a couple of subjects. So did she. But they all faded away, the thread of the conversation breaking, and it was a relief to get to West End Lane where they got off. The streets were dark, he held her arm guiding and protecting. Saying goodnight, he kissed her cheek and said very matter of factly, 'I'm still concerned, Iris, and I want to see you again. Next time I'll borrow my dad's van and we'll go over the river. Sunday.' It wasn't a request, it was what was going to happen.

Nick was really asleep now. The room had changed, the sun setting behind the trees threw leafy shadows on the walls. One turned his clean white pilllows black and hid his face. At the bottom of the stairs she could hear a wireless playing behind one of the closed doors. Would it be polite to tell them she was going, or would it look like she was cadging a lift to the station? Mrs Wytham had told her off for not calling when she got to Cricklade, they always sent a car for guests, she said. It was half past six, a difficult time. Everything was leading up to dinner for these sort of people. Nick's mother might not actually be doing the cooking but maybe telling them what to do. And the gardener who was the person to pick guests up might well have knocked off for the night. No. Better just go.

A little rush of cold air as she opened the heavy door

reminded her of the jacket that Mrs Wytham had taken from her. What a bloody fool she was. Now the door might bang as she closed it and draw attention to the fact that she was going to leave without saying goodbye and without her jacket.

'Oh, it's you, Iris, isn't it?'

'Yes, hope I didn't . . .'

'I'm Nora. If you hang on a teeny mo, I'll get the car keys. Did you have a coat?'

'Yes. A jacket, red, a jigger coat, three-quarter length.'

'Excellent, first class. I will know precisely what I am looking for.' She was one of Nick's secretaries, the country one, and did stuff for Katherine, as she called Mrs Wytham, when not too busy.

Sitting in the car at the station waiting for the London train she learnt that Katherine always had a lie down in the late afternoon. Nick's father only appeared at meal times. They had sold the big house; how big was it? This one wasn't exactly small. Nick had got as far as he could go in the foreign office because he was a silly boy. (How silly did that make his boss, who liked having lunch with young girls who had no knickers on.) Nora's husband had been killed during the war. She used the flat over the stables which was 'too wonderfully handy'. Katherine had said Iris should come down any time to visit Nick.

'What a relief! That's what she said, my dear. You see it could have been another silly boy, they never grow up, you know. Like Peter Pan.'

When the train came she didn't want to leave the car or Nora. But she shook hands properly and said, 'Thank you very much for driving me. And honestly to tell the truth I tried to slip away so as not to be a bother, but I'm really glad I didn't because I enjoyed your talking.'

Nora remained on the platform as the train chugged away. Iris waved till she and the station were out of sight.

It wasn't as bad as it could be, considering. There were a couple of new people and places now instead of her old lovely new life. And Nick would be a part of them, though she would only ever be on the edge of his life; whatever Nora or Mrs Wytham might say. The little trips up to town and lovely food in warm clean restaurants and dancing and compliments and the lark of getting out of the taxi home and keeping the cash, that was over and done with after what both Steve and Bobby had said. But – one door opens as another slams in your face! The new job was definite to start off with. Eight weeks June LeSage's film would take and she would be her stand-in all the time. It could be very boring indeed, and up really early too. A lot of the time she was only a sort of servant, getting her tea in the morning, taking her lunch to the dressing-room unless she was invited to the studio restaurant by a high-up producer or director, but Miss LeSage didn't like that. Lunch break was for lying down, learning her lines and not mucking up her make-up. One of Iris's other unofficial duties was reporting to Make-up and Hair about Miss LeSage's mood so they were prepared. Even Carol Wardrobe liked to know when she had the curse because she put on weight and blamed the clothes. The job wasn't every day and if she didn't work she didn't get paid, but Carol said if she did well June would give her a good tip at the end and always ask for her. And Carol was a new friend, she definitely liked her. 'I am going to protect you from all the one-eyed snakes on the set,' she laughed and hugged her.

Peter had got his father's old van and they were parked in a pretty old street facing the river in Barnes. It was like a village, little lanes, a duck pond, but better for being on the edge of London.

It was all right after all. Two drinks in the pub, she bought the second round so as not to take advantage, and now they were sheltering from the rain and laughing all companionable. The picnic had been got from Le Routier last night. At the end of the week the waiters were given all sorts of things that wouldn't last, and he being the head waiter along with the wine waiter got the pickings. In the laughing and the friendliness and the food he asked about them, Johnnie Pilsherd and his party, and was there any reason for him to be worried.

'I didn't like it, Iris. You were happy enough, your lovely smile when they gave you a flying angel, but that crowd, well . . .'

'Well?'

'They can be . . . not just spoilt rich kids and jaded old married roués, but, you know, vicious. It would be a change, a lark, to take something for nothing, what they might normally actually pay for.'

She felt sick, but he looked sick.

'Normal,' he sighed. 'God help us.'

She was looking through the rain-smeared windscreen at the river, they were both a dreary grey. If she could tell him absolutely everything the knot under her ribs and chest might go. With the words all the bruises and rotten secrets and fear would come out, like being sick only it wouldn't burn. But the long talk with Patrick had made the secrets permanent. The danger that he was in for knowing too much about some big shot in the police could spread. 'Friends of friends in peril,' he said. Though Steve thought it was even-stephened by what the police knew about Patrick. Anyway she wasn't going to blab about the MP or Jedd or any of those things.

'You all right? I don't want to push you, Iris, but a problem shared is a problem halved.'

Not in this case she thought. If I tell you the problem would be doubled. He wanted to pat her shoulder, stroke her hair, keep her warm. She was like a cat that needed a saucer of milk, a warm lap, and a gentle hand reassuring her.

'You see, most of the people who go to the restaurant and other places and clubs are straightforward, young singles, some aristos, married couples, self-made businessmen. Rich? Yes. But not out of the ordinary. That day I don't think you were really aware of what was going on. They were talking and sniggering about you. Seeing you with someone like Bébé, alone, well . . . you would be tarred with the same brush.'

'Someone like Bébé?'

'Yes. You see, it puts a "for sale" sign on you too.'

Uncomfortable, he switched on the windscreen wipers. 'I asked her about you, she gave me your number. She was worried too.'

That tall, dark-haired, beautifully dressed woman Bébé; not a girl out for a good time, more of a call-girl.

'It was odd, you know, no sign of you or the stag party. Johnnie Pilsherd was off on his honeymoon, of course, but the others . . .' He was kind, talking gently, stroking her hand. Maybe that part she could tell him, just that bit. 'One day I saw you across the street from the restaurant, staring. Very pale, walking slowly, your hands on your stomach. I thought you might be ill.'

'Something did happen.' She took her hand away, crossing her arms and hunching her shoulders. 'They . . . took me . . . they . . . somewhere opposite . . .'

'Go on, love. One of them?'

All right. She relaxed her arms. *One* of them, make it *one*, if that's all he could take. The truth, five, might put him off.

'Yes. One of them . . .' And she explained what had happened in the flat. With the window.

'Who was it, Iris, which one? Bastard, bastard.' He was more than angry, his hand gripping the gear shift like it was a cosh.

'I don't know,' she whispered. What she didn't know was which one was first and which one didn't.

When the rain stopped and lights across the river were lit they went back to the pub. They sat at a table with an old woman who was nursing a half pint of Guinness, both hands holding the glass protectively.

'Two whisky macs to warm us up and I'll take you home.'

'Right,' she nodded. 'Right.'

The old woman sipped her Guinness and replaced it on the dark wood table stained with a thousand rings from wet beer tankards. She hadn't replied when Peter said, 'Anyone sitting here?' A bit deaf, probably. Her eyes were sort of milky, a bit blind too, poor cow.

Iris could see Peter detach himself from the crowd at the bar; he was carrying two whisky glasses – and something else. Half a pint of Guinness. She smiled across the room at him.

Part Two

1965

Chapter Twelve

This part of London hadn't started to come up in the world, not like Kilburn, or bits of it anyway. The people who lived in their old flat called it West Hampstead now. And up the road the real West Hampstead-dwellers dropped the 'West' from their address to smarten it up – nothing so smart as Hampstead. Funny that it hadn't happened here, tasteful developments by the water. Not that there was much water to be seen. The canal was a dark, greyish yellow, the water thick with disintegrating rubbish. What wouldn't disintegrate floated on the surface; puffs of dirty white pieces of plastic crates. Jutting out of the water here and there were old prams, the occasional child's bike and unrecognizable pieces of rusty iron. She stopped on a bend of the towpath to examine the mysterious shape of a construction that could, she thought, be a half-submerged sewing-machine. But why would anyone throw it away, and how did they get it here? Still the same thing could be said for the prams and bikes.

The air was sour from the stagnant water and its contents. Even the greenery smelt putrid, the weeds limp and heavy with dust-coated slime. On the opposite side of the bank the surface was disturbed for a moment. A rat? A frog? Sickening, a little clump of plastic wasn't the usual discarded wrapping from sandwiches, it was used condoms clinging together. Did the contents of the condoms get muddled with the frog spawn? How confusing for the tadpoles. On the rough path here and there were plastic bottles and broken glass. The bottles had traces of HP brown sauce, tomato ketchup and salad cream. The broken glass bore no traces of its one-time contents. The beer had all gone down the throats of the drinkers and, having drunk the light ale, they had no intention of carrying the bottles further.

She took the rickety wooden bridge in two long leaps. The barge was moored under a particularly nasty tree, grey-black, humped with not many branches, the trunk still showing signs of an attempt to set it on fire. When Sam had bought the barge a couple of years ago, he had traded it in, or that's what he said, though what he gave in return she hadn't been told. Now of course, she had guessed, perhaps had always known. It had been green and red and yellow, clean and bright, a little corker. She loved it. But within a week of getting it up here from the canal over in Maida Vale, it had been painted brown and dark grey. No sign remained of the pride of the previous owners. The name too had been changed, many times. 'Maid of Chiswick' had become 'Maid of Wood' but the joke got too much attention. What was it today? Carefully painted in a darker brown than the boat and barely decipherable, it said, 'The Barge'.

His old bike was tied to the roof along with broken deckchairs and a rusty old kitchen sink. An effort to appear like any other working-class barge dweller.

The narrow tin chimney was puffing out smoke like a steam train. She could smell the smoke, a tarry scent, nearly drowning the reek of the fetid canal. A long, heavy stick was lying behind the tree, no accident. Sam left it there for visitors to use as a knocker.

'Coming,' Sam called.

She could hear some scuffling and a woman's laugh. Oh Christ! Had he been at it?

He poked his head out of the aft hatch door. 'Lovely surprise, Iris. Come on in, my friend Annie's dropped in for a coffee but she's off now, aren't you, Annie?' He put up a strong muscular arm to help her down into the saloon.

A pretty young woman was trying to release her curly, red hair caught round a button on the sweater she was pulling on.

'Hi, nice to meet you, Iris. It's hot in here, ain't it?'

'Don't go on my account.' Poor girl, embarrassed and being thrown out.

'She's got to go anyway, haven't you, Annie?'

'Well . . .'

He brushed aside her hesitation. 'She's due at work at half past eleven. Don't want to lose your job, do you? She's the main attraction at Café Chiswick.'

The girl tidied her hair in the little mirror over the galley sink. 'Yes, all right, I suppose.' She looked pathetically over her shoulder as she climbed the steps. 'Drop in tomorrow, shall I, Sammy?'

'Not tomorrow, no. I'll give you a bell, OK?' He pulled the hatch shut with a heavy clang. He noticed her little frown. 'Yeah, I changed it, steel lasts longer than wood. Here . . .' He held his arms out. 'Give us a hug.'

'I should think your Annie's done you all right in that department.'

His back was broad, his arms and shoulders strong with every muscle clearly defined. When at the age of eighteen he was still only five foot six, he had given up any hope of growing and joined a boxing club. He soon became, rather self-consciously, the sort of tough guy people didn't mess with.

'You know, Sam, you look a bit like a young James Cagney.'

'That's not what the girls say, they think I look like Marlon Brando.' He hunched his shoulders and narrowed his eyes. 'I coulda bin a contender.'

She laughed. 'Not bad. So Annie is one of many then? No one special yet?'

'They are all special, Iris. I'm not an animal. But there's safety in numbers, see?'

'Safety? From what?'

'A semi-detached in Felpham with a telly in the lounge and a Vauxhall in the garage.'

'Better than your old Vespa. Shouldn't think that's any good for pulling birds, no one would give it a second look.'

He pressed the plunger down on the pot of coffee. 'Exactly. Just what I want. And I get enough crumpet, thanks, without a Jag, or whatever.'

'Thanks.' She took the coffee. 'What about kids, Sam? Don't you want to keep the Winston name going?'

'Fuck that for a start. Anyway, when are you and Peter going to get down to it? I'd make a better uncle than a dad.'

She felt her face redden and touched her cheeks.

'What's up, love?' He took the cup and saucer from her. 'Your hand's shaking.'

'I'd forgotten. Christ, I'm really ashamed. That's why I came here. I didn't want to ring you, I wanted to tell you in person.'

'What is it? Peter? Has he had an accident? What? Iris, for Christ's sake, what?' He pulled her to her feet shaking her.

'No, no, nothing like that. Nothing bad.'

He let her go. She sat, hands folded in her lap, calm now.

Christ, she could rile him. He loved her but she was off on some other planet most of the time, out of touch. It was easier dealing with his shit-heads. 'Sorry I shook you, Iris, love. Go on, spit it out.'

'It's just that Peter and I had a talk last night.'

'Yes?'

'About the future.'

'Yes?'

'Don't know how to say it . . . how to explain.'

'Just say it, please Iris, tell it me straight. OK? No fancy words.'

'He is leaving me. He has met somebody else. He wants to marry her and go to America. We had an offer, a while ago, to run a sort of restaurant club in New York – and that's what he wants to do.' She said all this flatly, as if reciting a shopping list.

'When did this happen, love?'

'Oh, it's been going on for some time,' she shrugged.

'And you knew?'

'Yes.' She smiled her pretty crooked smile.

'It's hard to believe you're pushing thirty.' He didn't mean it as a compliment. 'You know you still look like Audrey Hepburn.'

'She's older than me.'

'You know what I mean.' He sighed, impatient with her. 'Well, at least you'll get alimony, if he's the guilty party.'

'Oh, no, that's not fair. He asked me and I said I honestly didn't mind.'

Sam looked out of the porthole; a huge piece of wood, probably a telephone pole, was wedged in the static green sludge.

'Poor bugger,' he said softly. 'You'll have to tell Mum and Dad.'

'Why? We never see them bar Christmas and not then now we do Christmas dinners and things. No, I won't bother unless they ask direct.'

After coffee they sat unspeaking in the neat cosy barge, quiet except for the old squawk of ducks and the distant shouts of children on the new council estate. There wasn't any more to say unless she told him everything and let the whole thing unravel.

He took her silence as a prelude to departure. 'Give me your mug,' he said, taking it from her hand. 'You'd better be off, lots to do, right?'

She did not want to leave. It was a question of keeping quiet about having to see Artie till she knew exactly what he wanted. The same sort of thing had happened when

Mrs Brown died, and the message was the same: don't go to the funeral, the brothers will be in touch. Only now it was Steve who was dead. And there were two brothers left. The message had been delivered by the corner shop where they bought their newspapers. It was a newsagent, tobacconist and bookie, and a supplier of 'rubber goods for the weekend'. It was difficult to figure out what he'd died of, certainly not what the papers said. Unexpected cardiac arrest. Not that they weren't saying some sort of truth. Unexpected? Of course it was. Healthy man in his thirties. Cardiac arrest? All that meant was his heart stopped, and however he died his heart stopped.

'You'll be lonely, girl.'

'Not really, I've got a business to run. I'm always with people. Phoning, visiting, planning, shopping, cooking, driving around. It's all done with people.'

'You're a success, you and Peter.'

'I'll be a success on my own. I won't take on so much, that's all. And Bobby's a big help.'

'One of your faggots.'

She shrugged. 'So what.'

'There's room here, Iris, remember that, if it all gets too hard for you. That cupboard folds out into a bed.'

'Falls out, more likely. No, don't be daft. I'm all right, but thanks.'

He watched her till the bend in the canal took her away.

*

She was wearing sunglasses, lots of make-up, white ivory foundation, dark grey eye-shadow, two coats of black mascara and lipstick the colour of her own anaemic pink mouth. Her dress was shorter and tighter than usual and her shoes had the highest of stiletto heels. She had got herself up like this so as not to look conspicuous. Anyone seeing her slip through the back street entrance to the club would think she was one of the girls. Three sturdy young men waiting just inside the door nodded a greeting, and silently ushered her upstairs.

'Get out, you two, and wait in the hall.'

They left, still silent, unsurprised by the unseen decrease in their number.

Artie tried to sit casually on the edge of the large partners' desk, but the tightness of his silk trousers stretched to breaking point over his fat thighs gave him no manoeuvrability. 'Right.' He changed his position, leaning against the wall, his thumbs pushed into the silver chain belt of the trousers in imitation of his late brother. 'There's been a little misunderstanding. We wanted to help him. Sam. Your bruvver. See? We give him the manor including Willesden. Safe, very safe. Because, er, because, yes! us bruvvers had an eye out for him, see? Now. He don't seem to realize that he had the whole . . . the whole . . . the . . . what's the word?'

'I don't know, Artie.'

'Don't know? Course you know, *I* know – when I know. Franchise! But. He was only doing grass and that was not unbeknownst to us. Then we very sadly find out, and, what's more, it comes to us on the vine, that our business competitors are dealing everythink else.'

Interesting, she thought, the surviving brothers still with the old accent: muvver, bruvver, anythink.

Like a thought reader Artie continued, 'But Steve, cut above us, nice talker, says leave him be, on account of you. Anyway and in any case he's been treated noble, handsome. And. We sold it now Steve has passed over. And that's fucking that.'

Tired of leaning against the wall, uncomfortable, he sat in one of the straight-backed chairs placed in a row in the centre of the room. 'Would you like to sit down, Iris, go on, 'ere, sit down.' He patted the chair next to him. 'You won't catch anyfink.' He screwed up his eyes staring at her as she sat in the offered seat. ''Ere, I remember you now. You were fond of Mum, weren't you?'

'Yes.'

'Yes. She was pinning her hopes on you. Yes.' He looked vacantly round the cold airless room. 'Dead now.'

'Yes, I know. I'm so sorry.' She decided against her instinct to pat his hand, he might take it as an invitation.

'Long time ago. Our Steve had just come home. He didn't mind going down. It was his duty, as my big bruvver Vernon explained. Two years. Some months off for good behaviour. Good behaviour! Do me a favour. Not that I'm saying anythink against it. Deterrent, is that the word?'

She nodded.

'Yes, deterrent, right. But, for who? Definitely not for a married man is prison. Nudge nudge, wink, wink, know what I mean? So – what was I saying? Oh, yes, well, Steve said – what was I saying?'

'You-are-not-against-prison.' She said it slowly and distinctly.

'No, that wasn't what I was saying. It was Steve, he got in touch with the best, sorted out all. All, that's all.' His head was jerking back and forth, but suddenly he stamped his right foot and jumped to his feet, crossing to the desk. 'I hope you didn't take it as a personal affront my brother not fucking you?'

'Oh no, not at all.'

'Do you smoke?' He held out a silver cigarette case and took a cigarette from it putting it in his mouth.

'No thanks,' she said. 'I gave it up.'

'Right.' He took the unlit cigarette out of his mouth and stubbed it out carefully on a dirty saucer. He was staring at her again, puzzled, and rubbing the dry flaky skin of his forehead. Examining his nails, long and beautifully manicured, he said resentfully, 'I've got dandruff of the fucking face.'

The three men tramped down the stairs ahead of her then stood back, letting her open the door herself. With a little smile, she said, 'Thanks, you two.'

Not a smile, not a titter. It would be nice to know she'd never have to see them again. Or the brothers.

Round the front of the club it looked a bit more swish than in olden days. The décor had been modernized but the girls were still there, the hostesses. No black pianist entertaining, a cabaret now that was supposed to be political satire to keep up with the fashion. As Nick said, 'Satire and suck offs, a heady mixture.' Anyway, satire? A couple of jokes about sending Wilson into space instead of the Russians and calling Edward Heath, the new Tory leader, the blasted Heath. Then it was back to dirty jokes: 'My girlfriend's skirt is so short when she bends over you can see what she had for breakfast. *She* drives a mini, *I* drive a maxi (groping his crotch).' She'd only been there once, by mistake. The name had been changed and when she got there with Peter it had been too late to back out.

Years ago, after all the trouble with the police, back and forth, sorting it out with Patrick, before she and Peter got married, Steve had said, 'You steer clear of us but we'll always keep an eye on you and yours. Any trouble we'll sort it out, you needn't know how. You and yours.' Yours had meant Sam. Lovely way to help, thank you very much, turning your little brother into a drug-dealer. The anxiety she felt had shown.

He was so smart, Steve, he could read anyone – well, maybe not the person who killed him. He had sussed she didn't want him having anything to do with Sam. Not angry though, sarcastic.

'Take my word for it, Iris, what you've got in mind is out of line. I don't shit on my own doorstep.'

Sam would have to be told soon, immediately, or the new lot would turn him over, do him an injury.

He'd better take the barge out of Goat's Wharf. Get it all the way up the Grand Union Canal through Harlesden and Paddington Cuttings, dreary and dirty, beyond the much nicer Little Venice. Round the canal by Regent's Park Zoo and settle somewhere like Eagle's Wharf or even Limehouse. Paint it red and green again, the normal barge colours. Tomorrow. She'd go tomorrow morning. Now, being in Soho, it would be fun to get dinner. Everything they liked, all their favourites. At the smoked fish shop in Old Compton Street they were surprised to see her dressed to the nines but she ignored it. 'I'm shopping for us, not work, just a nice dinner.' They picked out the best smoked trout and gave her a lemon on the house.

A few doors along there was a tatty shop selling ADULT MAGAZINES, next to it through a half-open door you could see rickety stairs covered in threadbare carpet. Above the doorbell was a sign, LOVELY MODEL THREE FLOORS UP. The poor sods who visited her would be too tired to do anything by the time they got there. And why lovely model? Why not lovely bus conductress – or lovely cook?

In Berwick Street market, Spud, her favourite costermonger, offered her his biggest and best cucumber with the usual exaggerated leer, which she accepted. Over the road at Randall and Aubin she chose a rôti de veau made from a rolled breast of veal which she would unroll and line with thyme and zest of lemon. Finally at Roche she got some of the French beans flown in that morning and a perfect smelly Epoisse. 'Here, Madame Wimbourne, some beautiful cerises, sweet, perfect for a clafoutis.' Good idea, have one tonight, as a rehearsal, and if it was reasonably simple, it would be useful for a dinner party. Cherry tart for people who liked straightforward English food, clafoutis for the francophiles. Right, all done. A taxi, and she would be back with plenty of time to cook.

Their flat was in the basement, a bit dark, but a garden more than compensated. A huge kitchen and a tiny sitting-room, the wrong way round for most people but perfect for them because of the catering business. Peter would be gone in a week and this weekend they were doing a dinner, a cocktail party and a Sunday brunch, so this evening together alone would be nice and cosy.

'Peter,' she called, 'my hands are full.' The door opened so quickly he must have seen her get out of the taxi. His face was all sad and angry at the same time and he didn't say hello, just stood aside to let her in.

'I'm not late am I? What's the matter?'

She knew what was up the minute she saw Sam. He was sitting at the kitchen table, his head in his hands. Neither of them took the shopping bags or offered to help when she hesitated, not liking to plonk them down in front of Sam. Instead she heaved them awkwardly on to the chopping block.

'I can explain,' she said. Sam looked up, waiting. She was waiting too. She couldn't explain. Given time she could sort it all out. Yes. And it would all be all right. It wasn't that bad now if they would leave her be. One of the shopping bags toppled on its side, the bag of cherries fell out and one by one they rolled on to the marble pastry slab. Some fell on the floor. She bent to pick them up, relieved to have a distraction.

Again, neither her brother nor her husband helped her.

'Sod the cherries, Iris,' Sam said quietly. 'Get up, get on with it. There's no hiding behind lies.'

She left the cherries on the floor, so juicy that some had split in the fall. What a pity. Would the dark pulp stain the white squares of lino? Sod's law of course, none had splattered on the black squares. Sam was still sitting at the table but looking up at her now, frowning, biting the inside of his cheek, eyeing her with distaste. Peter was on the other side of the room by the big sink, one hand resting on a tap, his look went past her to the cork board where all their future work was pinned. It was eerie. It was like a photograph. Or as if a film had suddenly stopped in the middle of a scene and nobody knew what would happen when it started again. Would Sam move and pick up the cherries? Would Peter turn the tap on and fill a glass with water? And she, what would she do?

It was Peter who spoke, twisting the tap on and off. 'I haven't got another woman, a girlfriend, you know that, Iris. Why tell a lie about something like that?' The water, running and stopping, running and stopping, drowned some of his words. Then Sam stood up and put his hands on her shoulders. He was no less threatening for being a bit shorter. He shook her, not hard, but enough to put her on her guard. A touch of the James Cagneys.

'Or is it you, Iris, are you sending Peter to America to let him get the new job going while you hang around here with a fancy man?' He put his forefingers in the funny bit just inside the shoulder and gave her a sharp jab. 'What are you done up like this for? Tight skirt, stilettos, your face covered in muck. Been with him today, have you? All this . . .' He waved at the shopping. 'All for a nice cosy dinner with your hubby to save your conscience before you shove him off? Keep him going? Right? Too fucking right. Keep the position of wife open in case your bloke doesn't come up trumps.'

'Leave her alone,' Peter said, splashing himself with a sudden vicious turn of the tap.

'For Christ's sake, Peter, turn that bloody thing off. And she's my sister, don't forget, as well as your wife.'

'That wasn't where I was today.' She quickly told them the story about Artie Brown and the club and the bodyguards and then explained about the changeover in protection now that Steve was dead. Peter took his hand off the tap, scratched his forehead, examined his fingernails and laughed. 'Dandruff of the face.'

'You worry, Iris, when there's no need.' Sam was a bit more relaxed but still suspicious. 'I always knew Steve was keeping an eye out for me, as far as any local villains were concerned I was a no go area. But he didn't put me in the business. I drifted into it really. Musicians, the youth club, connections, do someone a favour, and, well, there you are. I never meant to make a life's work of it.'

'Oh, oh, that's wonderful, Sam.'

She smiled at Peter and back at Sam and around the kitchen as if it was filled with approving admirers. 'Not my fault then? Nothing to do with me. Oh, good.' She laughed gaily. 'Sometimes I think everything's my fault. I feel like a pie that everyone's got a finger in. You know what I mean.' It was ticking along nicely, the whole atmosphere nearly normal. Maybe starting the dinner would add to that. Busy and ordinary. A bit of a chat while rolling the veal. Her head down concentrating. Measuring the flour, making a well to add the beaten eggs and milk. The smell of vanilla was comforting and using a wooden spoon, well, that too was all part of a domestic picture that men liked. June LeSage had tipped her off about all that. Her husband was a seldom-employed theatre director who sneered at the way she earned her money – the money that kept them. The more she worked, the longer the days, the greater need he had for June to be his wife, or housewife. She would get home, put on a nice gingham apron, sprinkle some flour on a worktop, put a wooden spoon in a bowl, then heat up a tin of baked beans.

'Very dainty, Iris, very nice. You got a nice way of putting things, but it doesn't quite wash, not with Peter and me. We know you, see, that's what you do, talk a lot saying nothing. Or you don't talk. Right. So you were at the Browns' today sorting it out. Only for me? For your little brother? I think not.' Sam picked up one of the cherries, pulled off the stalk and threw it in the air catching it in his mouth. Iris waited. He was puckering his mouth ready to spit it out. At her? No, he opened the French doors to the garden and spat it out sharply like a bullet. Peter wasn't saying much. Scared? Keeping his counsel, waiting. She tidied up the shopping, placing it neatly on the work surfaces, in order, ready for use.

'Of course there was something else. Some things,

actually. But Artie didn't say anything else so not to worry, right?' Her apron was blue and white stripes with large front pockets with the name of their company embroidered in red on them, FULL COURSE. She wouldn't need the wooden spoon just yet but she put it out ready. 'Peter, love, can you rinse and dry the thyme for me, please?' Her smile took in both of them. 'And I'll light the oven.'

'What things?' Sam took the matches from her and lit the oven.

'Steve was always doing something or other. He sorted out Dad's money-lender in Chancery Lane. Something to do with compound interest. Extortion, Steve said it was, a bit rich coming from him. Mum called it daylight robbery. A fat lot of good it did in the end. The man wouldn't lend Dad money after that so he went to that woman in Northampton Street near the Angel. She was worse, and what's more her brother was a bailiff. Furniture went in and out of that flat in Kilburn like there was a revolving door, they even took the cooker once.' Re-rolling the piece of veal and tying it with string, she placed the pan on a rack in the oven.

'And? What other stuff was he up to with my little sister?'

'Would you like a drink, the two of you? I suppose you're staying for dinner, Sam?'

'Yes, stay.' Peter didn't say please, but he was pleading, Sam could see that. Christ, maybe there really was something up between the two of them. 'We would like you to stay, go on, she's a terrific cook now.' He took some potatoes to the sink and started peeling them. 'I taught her all she knows but now she could teach me a thing or two. Right, Iris?'

She concentrated on cracking the eggs on the side of a bowl and tipping in the contents. 'Oh, I don't know.'

'She could teach us both a thing or two. Women, see, Peter, they're the snakes in the grass. They've got enough venom to see us all off into the wide beyond.'

'Charming.' Her shiny dark hair fell forward as she bent over the batter mixture, working on it with the wooden spoon. Fucking lovely, her brother, whom she had tried to keep an eye on all her life – nice way to speak. They could both take a fucking running jump. Her face was hot, red from effort and anger.

'All right, Pete, fine. It looks like it's going to be a good meal.' Sam looked around the kitchen. 'Beer in the fridge?' He took out two bottles of Worthington, opened them both and poured them simultaneously in two glasses. 'Here you are then, matey, cheers.'

The kitchen smells were a blend of lemon and thyme wafting from the oven, vanilla from the mixing bowl and a little whiff of yeast from the bottles of beer. Sam was still looking at her like she was a bit of dirt. Why should she take the can back, get blamed, for nothing but sorting things out.

'I wouldn't mind a glass of wine, thanks for asking, when I've finished this clafoutis. And why don't you both sit down and if you've got nothing better to do, Peter, why don't you lay the table. And while you're at it tell Sam about borrowing two thousand quid from Steve Brown to get the business going.'

He was startled, turning round with a bottle of white Rioja half-opened. 'You knew? I thought that was between Steve and me.'

The mandoline was making neat thin round slices of the potatoes ready for sautéeing. 'Nothing was between Steve and you, or between Steve and Sam, or between Steve and Dad. Steve owed *me*, not any of you. Steve's mum died thinking we would get married and because of that she didn't get to know he was a poof and because of that *Steve owed me*.' She dropped the potatoes into a bowl of cold water to wait for the last-minute cooking. 'So Steve checked with me that it was on the up and up, our business, that it was all right by me for you to have the cash. Here, there's a bit of smoked trout to nibble on while we wait for the veal.'

The trout had been placed on an oval plate, cut into thin strips with brown bread and butter and a jar of horseradish sauce.

'Ta.' Sam ate a bit and washed it down with some beer. 'Lucky sod, Pete, you're on to a nice one. The other Browns won't know about the two thousand, no, that debt died with Steve.'

They settled down at the table, had another couple of beers, chatted. Cricket, whose team was doing the best. All based on where they lived: Sam supported Middlesex because he'd lived near Lord's. Peter supported Surrey having lived near the Oval. The Beatles, great boys, good they got the MBE, bad that some people said they were 'nincompoops' and returned their medals. Peter finished opening the wine but didn't give her a glass. Forgot. Absolutely typical. Bloody marvellous. Dad fucks up their entire lives with his debts; poor old Dad. Peter borrows money from a gangster, someone known for his violence, for Grievous Bodily Harm, Demanding Money with Menaces; Oh, all right, lucky you, now he's dead. Peter was smirking, pleased with himself. They'd forgotten about her, Iris, the venomous snake-woman. Roll up, roll up, come and see the human python. He'd turned against her, Sam, because she'd interfered with the cosy picture he had: Iris and Peter – Till Death Us Do Part – Lovely Young Couple – Making Their Way – Doing Well – They Can Afford Kids Now – He's Lovely to Her – She's Lovely to Him – Good Business – Nice With It. It all meant more freedom for him if Iris, his smashing sister, toed the line. But was a happy ending ever on the cards, even with someone you loved? Not yet anyway, or not with Peter.

The kitchen was a bit too warm now. The beans sat in the steamer nearly ready, the potatoes were spitting in the hot oil adding to the heat. She took off her apron, wished she'd had a chance to change.

Peter looked up. 'You hot? Have a glass of water. Oh, I forgot your wine.'

'Don't worry now, this is nearly ready.'

'Right.'

Neat and quick, he cleared the table and laid it. Drained the beans and sharpened the carving knife. He was taller than her, a bit heavy round the middle but nice-looking. A reliable type. You would think. But she had never been able to really suss him, and never sure what he wanted. After ten years he was an unclear figure, not part of the foreground. In the beginning she was that bright vivid teenager, her accent showing, making her a possibility as a girlfriend even though as a waiter he served her food, called for taxis and accepted her escort's tips. After he'd heard an edited version of the rape she became a victim to be protected, his feelings expanded to love – ah, poor little Iris – and to the ultimate protection of marriage.

The balance changed with the opening of Full Course. She learnt fast, both the cooking and organization, and though he was better as the front person with all the smiles and chat, they became partners and equals. And she had protected him then, let him think Steve had lent the money to his abilities instead of to his wife. In memoriam. Steve's mum.

'What?'

'I just said it was ready.'

'I do know that, Peter, I bloody cooked it.'

Sam put another chair at the table. 'Always day-dreaming, my sister.'

'I am perfectly able to think of two things at the same time. I've always got at least two things going on in my head, practical stuff and wishes; I turned out to be just like Mum. Let's get on with it. And don't eat too quickly, Sam, after all the work put in.'

*

It was always like this, all of life: threats and unease, then in no time 'Hello, how are you, pass the salt.' And nice easy chatting back and forth. They'd all had a good laugh about the lord who lived and travelled in a gypsy caravan with his wife and mistress, 'living the simple life', he said. Which included all the cooking done by caterers like themselves wherever they were, all the laundry taken away and delivered fresh and nice to the next stop and a local riding stable grooming and caring for the horse. But they'd got on all right, he was a laugh and interesting and knew the whole thing was daft really. He played the guitar too and knew rock and roll people.

Then, clearing the plates, 'See, I told you she's good, isn't she?' from Peter.

'Better than good, bloody marvellous,' from Sam. And, 'That cherry whatsit smells all right.'

She dropped a plate.

'Ho, ho, ho, too much wine, I thought you were looking a bit red.'

And she shouted. Screamed. 'I haven't had any wine, nobody gave me any.'

The men were surprised. 'Calm down,' Peter said. 'Just as well you didn't drink . . .' and he gave Sam a look, pointing to his stomach.

'And not only did I not get any wine which you didn't notice, but if you knew anything about me at all you would know I haven't got my period. It finished yesterday.' She banged the clafoutis on the table. 'Sitting here both of you, calm as calm, calling me a viper, that's what you did, Sam.'

'I never, I called you a snake.'

'You fucking arsehole, a viper is a snake. You still called me a viper even though you didn't actually specify which snake.'

'If you don't stop crashing those dessert plates down, Iris, we'll have another breakage.' Peter pushed the plates away from her. 'What's up with you?'

'I've been cooking and eating and you've been eating and drinking and chatting and I've been putting in my two cents' worth and it's all been lovey-dovey, but any minute now . . .' She hung her head. 'I'm all in, I'm tired, look at me, I haven't even got out of my glad rags.'

'Shall I go?' Sam was disappointed to miss the tart but hysterical women weren't anything he ever wanted to deal with. None of his girlfriends ever got the chance, they were out first sign of a mood.

'No, don't go, mate. Finish your dinner and we'll sort it out, won't we, Iris? Right? Sort it out later?'

'Funny that. When I came in with all the shopping you two were like thunder. *I* had told a dreadful lie. *I* was a two-timing, nasty little piece of work. It never occurred to you, Sam, that I might have been telling the truth. OK, all right, I wasn't, but I wasn't far off.' She handed round the plates holding them carefully to control the little shake of her right hand. 'Now you don't feel like talking about it, after torturing me for two hours' waiting.'

Both Peter and Sam picked up their spoons awkwardly, the smell of the tart was difficult to resist, but did that make them insensitive? Pathetic they looked, the pair of them, Iris picked up her spoon too. 'Oh, go on, get on with it, eat it.'

It was her fault too, all this waiting. Cooking and making the atmosphere nice. It only postponed the trouble. 'I don't want to let you down, Peter, and honestly it's more than likely understandable, but I saw that photo. I was very hurt.'

Sam finished his pudding, pushed the plate away and smiled. 'Listen, love, you don't want to worry about a sexy photo. Poor old Pete. You going to accuse him of having it off, just because you find a bit of naughty in his wallet?'

'I haven't finished yet. And how many bits of naughty have you got in your wallet?'

'None. But that's different.'

'What's the difference, what's the difference?'

'I'm not married.'

'Can I say something before this gets out of hand? I do not have any photographs of naked women. I do not have any pornographic stuff at all.' Peter didn't shout, he was hoping to clear it all up somehow later when they were alone.

'It was about six weeks ago,' Iris said. 'Round about the time Frank Stamp started talking to us about the club in New York. I'd done a few days on a film at Elstree, special extra, almost a little part. Three pretty girls in a backstage scene, that sort of thing.'

'Bloody show-business. I've never liked you doing that.'

'Honestly, Sam, standing in for June LeSage and a few days' extra work is hardly show-business. And a bloody sight more decent than selling marijuana.'

'Please don't, you two, it's not like you. You always

got on. It's important, family.' Peter put his hands out and patted them both. 'You're tired, Iris, you get ready for bed. I'll clear away and then we'll talk it through.'

Neither of them moved. Sam didn't leave. He needed to stand up for his sister *and* protect his brother-in-law from unreasonable female behaviour.

'I brought the photo home. It had been taken by the stills photographer. An episode of *The Saint.* The three of us in minis, Pam, really lovely natural blonde, two kids though you'd never know. Jackie, terrific long legs, dimples, a dancer. And me. I showed it to you and left it on the dresser somewhere. Next day I saw it thrown away in the rubbish. I was a bit hurt and fished it out. Lo and behold! There was Pam, there was me but Jackie had been cut out.'

'That's a bit strong, mate. Look, I'm off. You don't want to end a good marriage because of one photo though, Iris.'

The Vespa was kicked into life and Sam chugged away towards his barge and a welcome solitary bachelor night.

'I didn't do anything about it, you know.' They cleared away together, sharing the washing and wiping up. 'This clafoutis's all right cold too.'

She stuffed another bit in her mouth. 'It was my pride, too, that was hurt. Here, give me that cloth, I'll do the glasses, you never get them quite right.'

'Bit of a cheek, Iris, considering I taught you how to do them.'

'Well, you know what they say: the pupil often outshines the master.'

It had all settled down, lost its threat, they would be in bed soon. A cuddle, maybe even make love. He stroked her hair. 'The funny thing is, she looks a bit like you.'

She didn't mind that much, not really. It gave her the little bit of freedom she needed.

It could all turn out all right whatever came of it. Peter had gone to New York but not for ever. If the job was all it was cracked up to be she could go over too and see if they could make a go of it together; themselves as well as the club. And they had got on OK, the last few days, working well, him being terrific at all the handing round, the out front bit and the food too had been a big success. All their chats had been about 'when we' implying they had a future. Making love a bit more than usual, he had been nice and considerate as always but passionate with it. Deep down one of the troubles was that even after all these years he still treated her body carefully as the subject of a rape. And that was probably where the photo of Jackie came in. She did look like her, but she was an Iris who hadn't been raped.

Now the party in Oxfordshire was coming up and that was another reason to stay on alone. Nothing was likely to happen but if he recognized her and said anything it would be easier without Peter. It was bloody peculiar how she was almost looking forward to it. And he couldn't have any idea. And he might not even remember. Like most of their dos, it was booked ahead; except for music-business parties people usually allowed at least a few weeks. First off it had been discussed on the phone; what, where, how much, then confirmed in writing. Then accepted in writing. A charity dinner. Mrs Robert Bucklebury. Call me Vivienne, she said. She and Peter had *Who's Who* and *Debrett* so they didn't get titles or awards wrong, very important in their business. Churchmen were very tricky with their reverends and very reverends and not reverend at all. And they'd been caught out with the Honourables, too, it seemed that they only used it on writing paper. He was there in both, her husband, only esquire, but the house was named after the village where they lived. No house in London, he didn't need it with all his clubs. She was there in his bit as *née* Upton. It hadn't rung a bell or not a loud one until Vivienne Bucklebury had suggested meeting for tea or a drink at the Dorchester to finalize arrangements. 'You can usually park quite easily round there, South Audley Street, for instance, I've never had any problem, my brother had a flat once near there.'

She didn't want to face South Audley Street or that little square or Stanhope Gate or the street opposite the front of the Dorchester. Even when she'd been staying in Three Kings Yard it had been possible to avoid it by taking a long way round. The couple of times she'd been back to Les A the taxi had gone through Shepherd Market or up Hamilton Place from Piccadilly. Today, after getting special bits and pieces at Jacksons and

Fortnum and Masons and coffee from the Algerian Coffee Stores in Old Compton Street, she parked the van in the old bombsite off Greek Street, got a bus in Oxford Street to Marble Arch and then walked down to the side door of the Dorchester which was the entrance to the bar. Really, there were memories all over London so she might as well get used to it. Or try. Right here next to the hotel, this small block of flats was where Beastie Baldwin had planned to deflower her, one of his many attempts. They had walked up to have a drink at the Dorchester after everywhere else had closed. In the group was a couple who were staying there so were allowed to drink after hours. Beastie, poor fat old thing, had tried to get her up to his flat promising her a look at television, as if she didn't know that it stopped well before midnight. Bloody cheek. You had to laugh though, who did he think he could get, just for a look at TV. Give him his due though, he was always offering her hundreds for her virginity. Anyway there was no problem because he got stuck in the revolving door where she left him and joined the others in the hotel lounge. It had ended up as one of those lovely nights like in a film. Three Americans said they would take her home at about five o'clock in the morning and asked the taxi to show them some sights on the way. He did all the usual, Piccadilly Circus, the inner and outer circle of Regent's Park, Burlington Arcade, up Haverstock Hill to the top of Hampstead Heath where they saw the sun come up, on to Highgate where Dick Whittington had been, then back to Kilburn. And saying goodbye the older man had said 'Thank you' to her, as if she'd done anything except have a lovely time, and given her a dollar note, like a pound note only it wasn't *a* dollar note, it was a hundred dollars. 'A souvenir of a great evening,' he said. Not that she'd kept it as a souvenir. At the bank it turned into twenty pounds.

There was no doorman in a top hat at this entrance but the minute you pushed the door open there was someone there to help you.

'Mrs Bucklebury? She is in the corner, miss.' By rights, he should have called her madam, he should have noticed her wedding ring, and she was dressed like a businesswoman in grey and white. It was showing your knees, it either made you older or younger.

'Hello, you must be Iris. How are you, do sit down, did you manage to park?' Nice table against the wall where they could see the whole room as well as each other and easy to catch the waiter's eye, which she did. 'What would you like to drink, Iris? Or is it too early for you? I'm having a Bloody Mary because the vodka will perk me up and the tomato juice is a food really, isn't it, like soup, and that will keep me going till dinner which won't be till heaven knows when. Do I look a bit pink?' She patted her cheeks. They were a bit flushed.

'A little,' Iris smiled. 'Not much.'

She was a pretty woman, short straight blonde hair tucked behind her ears but her eyebrows were black so either the hair was dyed or the eyebrows over-mascara'd. 'I tried to cover the pink with make-up, don't want to look like a healthy country bumpkin, but I was too shiny – I've been downstairs, you see. Ah, here he is with my

Bloody Mary. Do you ever go downstairs? It's the best in London. So, what have you decided?'

This was all too lovely to be careful. Half-way between the old Iris wanting to buy her good time with a 'refreshing pretty little scrubber' performance and the new Iris – 'people like me are accepted today'. The basic performance was the same though: what you see is what you get, no bullshit. 'Dry martini, please. Like you, Vivienne, the alcohol will perk me up and the olive will keep me going till dinner.' She got a laugh from Vivienne and even the waiter smiled.

'I will bring madam two olives.'

'Two olives, I'll put on weight. Did you have a Turkish bath then, downstairs?'

'Yes. Wonderful, aren't they? And those women, huge, like giant-size nannies, who scrub you clean and hose you down, delicious. Years ago, before I was married, I would eat and drink too much, sweat it out here, then sleep it off at my brother's flat over the road in Deanery Street.'

So. There it was. Definite. My brother's flat over the road in Deanery Street. Someone that day, Andrew, Johnnie Pilsherd? had made a joke outside, 'we are taking you up to UPTON'. That's what it said on a little bit of varnished wood above the top bell.

'This dinner is for Michael.'

Iris crumbled the crisp as she put it in her mouth. 'Michael?'

'My brother. It's his charity, his wife died of cancer.'

'Oh, Mrs Bucklebury, Vivienne, I'm so sorry.'

'Thank you, dear. And I was wondering . . .'

Iris knew what was coming, they all tried it on.

'. . . Ah, here's your dry martini – make sure it's dry enough before I send him away.'

'Perfect.' Just a sip till this was sorted out.

'You see, Iris, we try very hard to give as much money as possible to the charity.'

'Yes, always a good idea. Nice of the waiter to bring us all these olives and things.'

'And although you do have an excellent reputation . . .'

'Thanks, it was the Riselys who recommended us, wasn't it, we did a picnic for them at Henley Regatta.'

'Yes, they were quite pleased but if your husband isn't going to be available . . .'

'Oh, lord, don't you worry about that, Bobby works with me a lot, as much as Peter, my husband. People absolutely love him, he might even be persuaded to sing.' Try and stop him! Anyway, she wasn't going to help her out. She was going to have to ask – nicely.

'Basically, I want to ask you to do me a favour, and do Cancer Relief a favour too.' The woman smiled, a practised, warm but tragic smile. 'Would you cut your fee by ten per cent?'

'No. I am sorry, Vivienne.' She too had a practised smile for this sort of thing: deep regret and sincerity. 'You see, when you told me initially what the evening was in aid of I reduced my fee immediately. But I do mean *my* fee. I can't get the food for nothing and if I asked the staff to take a cut in salary they might well say, "Fine, if you can get ten per cent off my rent."' Now she was going to have a good swig of her martini.

'Oh dear. Charity really does begin at home. Nothing you can do? Not even a few pennies?' Now the smile was a tight little 'Oh you've let me down what a sad world' sort of thing.

'I've got an idea,' Iris said brightly. 'Why don't we substitute pork for veal?' This was so usual, this kind of bargaining, that they normally built in an extra ten per cent to take off, like antique dealers, but she wasn't going to do it for this woman whose brother's flat she was raped in.

'Oh no, that wouldn't do. You can't cut corners with things like that. Right. Practical things. There's a maids' and utility room off the kitchen, used to be the dairy, where you can all change. The Aga will be stoked up . . .'

'And I will be bringing a small camping stove just in case.'

'Is that extra, Iris?' It was said a bit sarcastic but with a bit of a twinkle too, she wasn't bad. 'These are the dimensions of the dining-room, hall and morning-room. You don't want another martini do you? I shouldn't have any more, or waste any more time, they'll be expecting me.'

'No, thank you.' She looked around for the waiter. The man at the bar was eyeing her more openly now, no doubt on to his third or fourth whisky. If she sat at the bar with him, listened to his rambling pointless chat and let him exhale the foul breath from his unfed but alcohol-laden stomach he would probably give her a measly ten bob for her taxi home. As the waiter laid the bill in the centre of the table, Iris waved away Vivienne's offer of 'Split it?' Cheaper to pay for two drinks than knock off ten per cent.

'See you on the twenty-third then. Telephone if you have any questions. 'Bye, Iris. I'm glad we met.'

'Oh, Vivienne, will your *younger* brother be there?'

A funny cross little look darkened her 'goodbye' smile. Her ownership questioned, a relationship she didn't know about. Iris knew all about that brother-sister ownership and protection racket.

'Richard? Oh no.'

Chapter Thirteen

'Did you get the money?'

'That was it, the ultimate, utter degradation,' she laughed. 'That's what I said to myself, "Don't take it, Iris. If you do, you are the tart they think you are. Leave it and you're only a scrubber." But had I left that odd sum – 83 pounds all you had on you or in your flat I suppose – maybe your char would have taken it. Pathetic. I took it. Just as well. It paid for the abortion. Bad luck wasn't it, getting up the duff on my first date, my first rape.'

He winced.

'Am I upsetting you?' She resurrected her old accent. 'Beg pardon. Did you think I was a tart then, mister?'

'Not quite. A call-girl, perhaps, or someone like Bébé. Don't forget, I didn't see your face, or hardly.'

'Had you seen my face what would you have known? Would you have called the police, ruined Johnny's wedding? I think not.'

He didn't look like his brother, Richard. A resemblance, but not enough to have made her guess. It had been his voice. Hearing it in the large, beautifully fitted Aga and pine-filled kitchen, the faintness had come on. Steadying herself on the decorative but useless butcher's block table, she heard the voice again. 'I want to thank everybody concerned for the magnificent food. My aim is to steal the cook.'

'That's Iris. She's the creative boss, we're just her slaves.'

And then she had looked at him.

Michael examined her face. It was so pale, grey, as it had been when he saw her yesterday in Vivienne's kitchen. 'I'm so sorry about all this.'

Was that what he had said then? What had he seen when he arrived in his lovely flat in Park Lane? A semi-naked woman. A semi-woman actually because half of her was trapped outside the window. The fifth man had been banging her faster and faster. Literally banging, her knees hitting the wall inside, her breasts forced against the window-sill. But he had stopped suddenly and, for a few minutes, she had simply hung there, her legs shaking. Then somebody had tidied her skirt and lifted the window. She was frightened when she turned, hardly able to stand, the blood from the blow to her forehead had dried. The mascara running from her early tears, that had dried too. She was overwhelmingly conscious of her smell, their smell; of what was inside her. She didn't want to lift her head. It would have been painfully difficult it was so stiff, but to see anybody who had seen her – like that – was impossible.

'I'm so sorry about all this.'

What a peculiar thing to say, especially in a posh voice. You see a bruised, bloody-faced young woman who has been raped in your flat by five men – one to go – the day before the consecration of the marriage of one of them and all you've got to say is, 'I'm so sorry about all this.'

'They have all gone, you know.'

She didn't look up.

'Would you like *me* to go?'

She nodded.

'Yes, of course. I understand. Er, have a . . . well . . . use the bathroom if you wish and, let's see, I won't be back for, say, a couple of hours.'

Have a bath? Not possible. What if one of them came back? But screaming at the pain, she had 'used' some of his eau-de-cologne to mask the smell, wiped herself with a towel which she threw away in the park and, walking away from the lovely flat, the Dorchester, Le Routier, South Audley Street, everywhere she had been that day, she got a taxi at Marble Arch all the way home.

'Are you all right?' He knew she had been remembering.

'Sure. Cold, that's all. What were you doing there yesterday? At the do?'

'It was a fund-raising party for a charity I'm involved in. Vivienne, my sister, organized it for me.'

'I know that, I did the cooking, remember. One of those parties where it costs you five hundred pounds for dinner for two and you might sit next to a star.'

'Very good dinner.'

'Thanks.' She wasn't faint any more and she didn't feel shy, just awkward. Trapped again. 'Well, that's that then. I'm off. I don't know why you wanted to talk. It's upset us both. No use crying over spilt milk, as my mother would say.' She rose and picked up her handbag. 'Goodbye.'

He put a restraining hand out but she shrank from him sharply.

'Seeing me disturbed you, I know . . .'

'Very observant.'

'. . . but if I don't ask questions – you know we can talk about something else.'

'I don't much like being with people outside of work.'

'People? Everybody? Or do you need to avoid me?'

'No, I get bored, can't be bothered, and I don't have to. Quite a few clients, customers, ask me to things, show friendliness, but I can't skip along easily with the conversation. No mutual terms of reference, I believe it's called. There was a time when I tried to bone up on stuff and bridge the gap. But it isn't a gap, it's a bloody great chasm. What did me in was quoting something from a lovely poem and being sneered at. My friend Nick was always saying, "They are not long, the days of wine and roses." It was supposed to be a warning to me,' she laughed. 'I didn't know at first what the fuck he was talking about. Then I bought a book of poetry that it was in, and there was another poem by the same poet. I thought it was romantic and bitter. I had discovered it for myself, no one told me.

'Then one day I was trying to do my best at a party

we'd cooked for; a really nice couple who insisted I came out of the kitchen and joined them. There was quite an interesting chat going on about love, and if it's gone, make do with being fond and that could become love, you know the sort of thing. Eros can become Agape but not the other way round someone said. And then an older man said you can come an awful cropper if you start a new love, making do before the old passion has gone. So, I quoted from my poem, "Last night, ah yesternight, betwixt her lips and mine there fell thy shadow, Cynara . . .", and this man who I had quite liked, interesting, corrected my pronunciation, "*Chy*-nara", he said curtly, looking at me as if I was a twit. Big slap in the face. They all went on talking, so did I though I felt a bit wobbly, and we got on to all the other stuff of love; romance, romantic art, music. They mentioned pieces I didn't know then, obvious now. *Tristan and Isolde*, the barcarolle from *The Tales of Hoffmann*, the slow bit before Hymn of Joy, Mozart's twenty-first, a bit of Brahms, you know the sort of thing. So, I put my two pence in and said "The Warsaw Concerto".' She laughed at the memory. 'Shock! Horror! You'd have thought I'd said, "Bollocks to the Queen Mother." I went back to the kitchen.'

'Did you always want to better yourself?'

She was a prickly little thing, the tone was quite venomous, not just defensive.

'No. I wanted to have a good time, that's all.'

Still standing above him and staring at him, she was making him nervous.

'What you said about not seeing me properly that day . . . if so, how did you know it was me yesterday in your sister's kitchen?'

He thought of the photograph. Richard, Johnny P., the twins Jilly and Milly, Mark Hunter, and Nick Wytham standing next to a girl with his arm around her. He had dropped in on Richard clearing out his service flat in St James's, a dull anonymous place.

'I'm throwing away my past.' He threw a pile of photographs on the floor barely glancing at them.

Michael had picked them up, tidiness being the main reason and a little idle curiosity. 'You don't want this? It's Miranda, looking very pretty.' It was also of the Huttons, Jessie and Paul. 'Surely you don't want to chuck away photographs of your fiancée?'

Richard took it, gave it a quick glance and threw it back on the pile. 'It's also of Jessie and I'm not to keep photographs of girls Miranda knows I've had.'

The next photograph was Johnny P. and the twins, whom everybody had had either separately or together. Rather young they had been, fourteen, well he had been young then too. He pushed away a little stab of guilt.

'Who's the beautiful girl with Nicholas? Have you had her?' It was a lively piquant face. Dark, heavy fringe, blown up a little by the wind, wide eyes and an enchanting huge smile.

His brother laughed quietly. 'I'm ashamed to say I have. You shouldn't need to ask.' He sniggered, riffling through the pile of photographs. 'Here is the reverse, the negative one might say.'

This photograph was taken from behind. Richard and Johnny P hadn't got their arms round the twins as it had seemed, they were lifting their skirts to show them naked from the waist down. Nick Wytham's hand wasn't around the girl's waist, it was holding her skirt down protectively. You might have thought he was stroking her behind if he hadn't been a pansy.

'What are you thinking about? How did you recognize me?'

'I saw, some years ago, a photograph of you.'

'What do you mean?' She sat down, frightened. This sort of man was nice enough on the surface as most were, but he was after all the brother of one of them, and tarred by the same brush as Mum would say.

'It was a lovely photograph of you with Nick Wytham.'

'Oh yes?' She relaxed a bit, lifted her cup of coffee but put it down again. It was too full with her hand like this.

'Taken in the country. You were smiling.'

'Oh, that's all right then.'

So it wasn't something that could pop up from the past. Not a photo taken with her not knowing. There had been occasions that had made her uneasy, Bébé and the dress for a start, she'd been a right ninny about that.

It must have been a two-way mirror and her starkers and Bébé touching her tits. Christ. How stupid.

'This wasn't a good idea, Iris, meeting in a public place.'

'Quite right. I'm hard put not to throw my coffee at you. But to tell the truth, let's see, what I would like is, well, to talk about it with somebody who knows. Do you understand?'

This couldn't be right. It was a small square or maybe more a courtyard, with a big beautiful house facing you. Three storeys and little attic windows at the top, probably maids' quarters, and stone steps leading up to a door. On either side of the courtyard were lower versions of the house, only two storeys and attics. Even though he'd said it wouldn't look like somewhere you could go in, and taking that into account, this didn't have any recognizable entrance. There was nothing that made it clear that this led to a block of flats – he might call it chambers or rooms but that was private posh language – and yet it should because it was where he'd said, opposite Fortnum and Masons and the bookshop. He had asked her.

'Come to my place,' he said. 'You can relax there. Cry, shout, talk, whatever.'

Fat chance of relaxing when you couldn't even tell what or where it was. The nearest she'd felt like this was in Oxford at Nick's beautiful old college. Even though he was with her there was a certainty that you were trespassing and intruding. Not just in the building and the grounds but into the lives of very special people with habits, patterns of life, clothes, food, words that were all private and mysterious. And not available to outsiders, which must have been deliberate. But when an outsider got something wrong it pissed them off and you were good for a laugh. Now, what they *should* be feeling, that private few, was satisfaction because you'd just proved you didn't belong and their group was exclusive. Which basically must be the whole idea. Right. She had decided.

She was going to walk in a square. Up Piccadilly to the Circus, left up Regent Street. Passing Swan and Edgars she'd have a quick look at the windows. Left at Vigo Street which led into Burlington Gardens and left at Bond Street, which had some nice jewellery and handbag shops but too many art shops. The whole area was full of art shops, she didn't know how they all made money. And there was that shop that only sold amber. Only amber. Necklaces and brooches and earrings, the gloomiest jewellery you could ever imagine. Did anybody anywhere ever say, 'I'd love a nice bit of amber'? Left again back into Piccadilly and if she hadn't plucked up enough courage to cross the little yard she was going to the phone box at Green Park tube station and ring him.

Just up Vigo Street, opposite Savile Row, full of gentlemen's tailors, and ordinary men's too like pop stars and actors, she stopped. There, next to a pretty house with bow windows like a sweet shop in an olden days film, there were wrought iron railings round a black door, very discreet and secretive. She had never ever noticed it in all her days of cutting through from Soho to St James's. This must be the back door of the Albany, so where she had been hesitating in Piccadilly near the Royal Academy must be the front entrance – however much it didn't look like it.

She nipped down Burlington Arcade, busy with tourists wearing clothes that looked as if they'd come straight out of the shop windows, and humming with the sound of American accents. This was the voice Peter heard every day now. They were all so pleased to be there, it was official, in an American magazine: London was *the* city. Oohs and ahs, and 'Oh my God will you look at that.' *That* could be the gas lamps, a very mini mini-skirt, cashmere or tartan. Tartan kilts, tartan scarves, tartan socks, tartan handbags; tartan every bloody thing. 'Look at that cute girl with the long braid, isn't her coat just darling.' That was her, Iris. She had a long braid, a plait, hanging down her back and her coat was definitely darling: fine cotton corduroy in a sort of ginger colour with a little imitation fox collar. It was short, above her knees. The woman walking behind her thought she was cute, not a boring old married cook.

There, outside what she now knew definitely was the Albany, he was waiting.

'There you are, I thought I saw you from the lobby, but when I came out you had vanished.'

'Oh, what a relief. I couldn't figure it out so I went for a walk and then I found the back door and I did figure it out.'

Inside it felt even more like the Oxford college except

that the porter wore a top hat. There were tiles on the floor of the corridor which made the place feel even chillier than it was, and boards with inscriptions were stuck high up on the walls, too high for her to read. They looked like things in churches: SACRED TO THE MEMORY OF, could these be memorials to people who had lived there? Nick used to say, when he was having a go at her, that she was fossilized in the needs of her class. What about his class? His and this Michael's? Wanting to live in a block of flats that was a cross between school and a church.

'You are not going to sit down?'

Her face was tense, her lips pressed together. 'I don't think so. No. Not yet, I can't. I can't . . . just . . . sit down. I hadn't expected . . .'

The room was different, bigger, the ceiling higher, longer windows, but other things were the same. She remembered a sofa in a faded pinkish patterned material. That leather armchair had definitely been there, lined and cracked but comfy looking. Some pictures on the wall, they were the same. And the lamp by the window, blue and white, converted from something, that had been there too. And the smell. Nice warm smell. Smoke, not cigarettes, good cigars. And his cologne.

'What is it, Iris, you look desperate?'

'I'm daft, it didn't occur to me . . . new flat, new furniture, I thought.'

'I'm so sorry, it was crass of me . . .'

'For Christ's sake stop saying I'm so sorry – what the fuck do you say when you tread on someone's foot?'

His cologne was softer than most men's lemony sharp smells. Peter's was a gentleman's one, he was proud of knowing about it: Trumpers. Citrusy and clean. This one was like a dry flower, both the sharpness and sweetness were hidden. And it was only just there, drifting, something left behind. She knew it well. She had poured it into a cupped hand and rubbed it on the inside of her thighs to take away the other smell and screamed. Even her thighs had been chafed and torn.

'Would you like something? Or would you prefer to go?' His instincts were useless. He wanted to hold her, warm her, take away that old, pinched look, but she could misinterpret the gesture and fly away.

'No, no – I can't go. I'll be all right in a minute.'

'Coffee?'

'Yes. Good idea, thanks.'

'Or tea? Perhaps you would prefer tea with lots of sugar?'

'Don't be so bleeding condescending. I would like coffee. And I hope it's decent. I get my coffee, *beans*, in Soho.'

'The Algerian Coffee Company?'

'Yes.'

'So do I. Much better than Fortnums or Jacksons.'

'Yes, well, good,' she said truculently.

He wanted to laugh, it was absurd. Defending her

taste in coffee, renouncing any working-class taste for tea.

'Here, look, I'm sorry. I keep welling up with remembering feelings and then just want to lash out, hit, scratch my face, and you going on like that about tea and coffee just sets me off. Because, see, it's all in a big lump like a ball of string and I don't think about it in the order it happened. Sometimes I'm in bed at home in Kilburn, in my mind you know, and the pain and ache is there, and not only of their raping. I mean not only in that bit of my body.' She had picked up a cushion, holding it against her breasts. 'But where the window was trapping me against the window-sill. Funny. Come to think of it that mark was still there after the torn skin had healed.' Her foot lightly tapped a tapestry stool sitting under the window. 'Nice view of the garden you've got here. Don't worry, I'm not going to kick this out of the window.'

He smiled. 'I am more worried that you might scratch your face.'

Ignoring this she said, 'In that awful memory, all joined up together, is them carrying me up high, down the street, them laughing, me laughing, and people in the street smiling, envious of us all young and happy.'

He struggled to speak, to say something that could help. Helplessly he said, 'My poor girl,' and touched her, just a hand on her shoulder.

'It's all right. I'm OK. What about that coffee? Do you think I'd better help you, seeing as how I'm so fussy?'

★

She stepped away from the kitchen, stunned. 'You know you really take the cake. I can't believe it. Honestly. You had that flat, only *just* off Park Lane, can't get much better than that, a penthouse. Lovely bathroom, hot, and properly fitted.'

'Yes, nice flat, I agree.' What on earth was enraging her?

'Properly fitted?'

'Exactly.'

She remembered Nick's lesson. 'You had a nice lavatory, wash basin, *and* a bath, all in the same room. I mean to say, even we, the Winstons, had that in Kilburn, except it was cold and damp, and hot water only once a week when we lit the boiler. And what have you got here? You've got a . . . a . . .' Outraged, she faced him accusingly. 'A bath in the kitchen! It's so unnecessary. Anyone would think you were Irish.'

'No, no, if I was Irish there would be coal in the bath.'

'I'm serious. You know, we have a matching toilet suite in Fulham.'

'This is quite interesting.' She was holding her coffee with her right hand; on the left hand was a large fawn glove, its pair lay on the table.

'Better than scratching your lovely face.'

'Do you think it's lovely? Really?' The little glance at him was both shy and sly. 'Anyway, the feeling's gone. I don't want to scratch any more. And I don't think I would have.'

'I wasn't taking any chance.'

The feel of his gloves warm from the radiator had been shocking and very nice, sweet. She hadn't been scratching her face but pulling at it, rubbing the skin on her chin, smoothing away the lines on her forehead. He had put the gloves on making a joke about boxing but serious.

'Michael?'

'Yes? More coffee?'

'No, not coffee.'

'What then?'

'I'd like to ask you a question.' It would be wonderful if the answer was yes, it would mean something. He must be quite old now. Older than her but not old enough to be her father. Somewhere in between. Forty-five? In his forties anyway. He was still exceptionally nice-looking in a not very remarkable way: brownish hair, firm mouth, blue eyes with rather a lot of lines round them. Not much hair on the face like some older men. He was posh, but in a way that was dealable with. 'You know, you're a bit like Nick.'

'Well, I'm not sure that I'm pleased about that. After all he is . . .'

'Oh, I can tell you're not queer, and I expect you're a bit younger, but there's something.'

'Do you keep in touch with him, Mr Wytham, my double?'

'Not really. Christmas cards, that's all. He has asked me to go there and stay with him and Hadrian, but if I could get away and have a holiday, go abroad, I don't think I'd, well, I should say we, anyway, Morocco wouldn't come first. Bobby goes, tells me all the news.'

'You are examining me rather carefully. Looking for any signs of my resemblance to an ageing homosexual?'

Her staring wasn't rude or bad-mannered quite, but it did make him feel like an object.

'When people go away I don't seem to think about them very much. No, I was noticing on your face that you don't have much of that hair that men of your age have, you know, coming out of your nose and ears. And eyebrows like daddy-long-legs.'

'Thank you, Iris, very much. I suppose that is a compliment?'

'Sure.' She shrugged, dismissing it.

'What was the question you wanted to ask?'

'Oh yes. Well, you must promise to tell the truth. It doesn't matter. I'd just like to know.' She slid her right hand inside the glove to join the warm left hand. 'Did you talk to your brother and Johnnie P. or the others? Did you tell them off? Did you tell your brother he was a criminal, disgusting? Did you punch him? Hit him? Knock him down?'

His nice healthy skin was turning red.

'No.'

'I like the idea of someone standing up for me. You could have thought, "that poor girl", and defended her.' She was on her feet. 'After the act, I know, but to let it go? That was a gang-bang, a rape, on a virgin – and I was seventeen.'

His eyes were shut, and he was shaking his head. 'Please don't,' he said. 'I'm so sorry.'

'Your brother and his mates went to a slap-up wedding the next day that took place in a church. And you must have been there. Joining in. Singing hymns. Even if you thought I was a tart . . . Oh, bloody hell, I know I was asking for trouble, was a bit of a cock-teaser . . .' She threw the glove at him and shouted, 'How much did you pay for that picture over there, the engraving, the Rape of somebody or other, how much? When you look at it do you admire it, are you pleased with it? I don't suppose it makes you think though.' She was sobbing without tears. The telephone was ringing. 'Excuse me, I'll get rid of this.' He answered it in the bedroom.

When he returned he saw with relief that she had gone.

Listening carefully – Peter always spoke quickly on the phone from New York, thinking of the cost – she tried to work out if he really did want her to go over there. Ten days. Including her birthday. Special cheap flights. See if she liked it, he obviously did. No big decisions straight away, put a toe in the water. Have a good time, see the city. Work a couple of nights at the restaurant, see how she felt. He wanted to know about new work, the list was stuck on the wall next to the telephone. The glove was there too, hanging on a hook on the dresser. Three things had come up this week; two dinners and one buffet lunch. Yes, Bobby was available for all of them, she could manage. He thought TWA was the cheapest, find out soon. It sounds lovely, a good idea.

''Bye. I love you too. 'Bye, 'bye.'

One of the dinners had been booked last night. Dancing at Mick-Macks with Bobby, eating sandwiches and drinking whisky sours after they had catered a very formal cocktail party, which was tiring and dull. They got a lot of attention on the floor, it was too crowded to do real dancing but they managed to do a sort of jumping on the spot dance waving their arms. People near them copied and it spread till everyone was doing it. Laughing and exhausted, four people joined them at their little table. They were to do with music, rock and roll, a drummer and a manager from a well-known group, whose name she couldn't remember. The girlfriends were gorgeous; tall, slim, long straight blonde hair, big sexy mouths. The club was so packed they were huddled together, sharing drinks and cigarettes; one of the girls said Iris ought to be a model so she told them what she did and they asked her to do a dinner for them at their house in Cheyne Row. With them all being so close together and having to shout above the noise and the music it felt like you were having a good time even if you weren't. It justified having a night out if you got work from it. Not the sort of thing Peter enjoyed. Quite right. It was tiring if you were trying to build up a business. All this, thinking round in circles. If she was going to New York, and face it, she had to, there was stuff to organize. Call about flight, *now*. Book Bobby and the cooks from EAT-IN, *now*. She took the glove off the dresser. It had absorbed the smells from her kitchen, vanilla, saffron, cumin, orange and rosewater had drowned the smell of what she now knew was jasmine and stephanotis. After looking round Floris in Jermyn Street her nose had found his scent. It was intriguing the mixture of fear and pleasure it produced. She hadn't heard back from him. There was a message on the answering service when she got home that day. 'Mr Upton called to see you got home safely.' So she had called him and got his answering service. 'Please tell Mr Upton that Mrs Wimbourne got home safely.' Did he think Mrs Wimbourne was cold and formal? A bit 'keep your distance'. Would 'Iris is home and says thanks' have been better and kept the door open?

Preparing as much as she could for tomorrow. Rolling the pastry, grating cheese, making mayonnaise, it was usually very calming. That and the radio. And working out how it would all go, thinking ahead, anticipating, being ready for anything that could go wrong. But she couldn't get rid of all the anxiety that had been dug up by the visit to his place, and how she had left. In the middle of 'I could've gone to the police, matey', the phone rang. He answered it in his bedroom and closed the door. Embarrassing and insulting, what made him think she wanted to listen? She stood in the corner of the room as far from the bedroom as possible. He had been on the phone for six minutes when she left. Bloody rude. You can always ring someone back. The porter was very polite, a smile. 'Good day, miss,' as he opened the door. She noticed the glove in her handbag when she went to pay for her ticket on the bus.

It didn't have to be a life-long friendship but there

were things left to say. What would be handy, what she would like, was to see him a bit, the odd occasion. Have dinner, have a chat. Let him have a turn to talk. His grown-up children. His wife, and her being dead. Friends. And who was it on the phone that she should be shut out at such a moment? If it was possible, because he knew so much, to explain about how the other things gave her nightmares in the day. To call him again wouldn't be right. It wasn't her turn. Never a good idea to grovel when you needed something.

She wiped down the surfaces, cleaning up the floor, the olive oil, the juice from the chopped tomatoes. The nutmeg grater was put back on its hook and all the implements put in to soak. With her hands clean she took out a large brown envelope and wrote 'Michael Upton, esq., BY HAND' on it. On a plain white card she wrote 'Sorry I took this, my right hand didn't know what my left hand was doing. I will be in New York for ten days from the thirtieth. Iris.' Couple of laughs there: BY HAND especially. Dignified message from a successful businesswoman who travelled. Not bad. Should she put a little drop of his scent on the glove or was it better to let it go home smelling of its visit to her kitchen? She put it in the envelope and sealed it. If she left right now she would be at the Albany at half past nine. He would be eating, dining out maybe.

The underground from Parsons Green got her to Green Park with a change at Earls Court in half an hour. She watched from across Piccadilly trying to figure out if she could see his flat and got so nervous she nearly ran away. Again the porter was friendly and polite. 'Mr Upton is away, miss, but I'll make sure he gets it.' As usual she thought she was dressed more to earn a 'madam' in her black coat and grey and white silk scarf. Put on deliberately so that if she saw him she would be all busy and breathless, 'Late for dinner, do excuse me,' she'd say. Two men entered the lobby from the long covered walkway through the garden, they both raised their hats. One of them wasn't even wearing one. Automatic old-fashioned manners.

Bobby absolutely didn't understand her at all but then he didn't know half the truth of the story. No point now in upsetting him. He was different since that time in prison; jolly on top, same old Bobby Brighton, but watchful and sad under it.

'You don't particularly want to go to New York? Do me a favour, you've always been a real goer, Iris, first one at a party – last one to leave.'

'I'm older now.'

'You were older last week when we were out dancing, you hardly sat down and you even smoked a joint.'

'I did not, I stuck it in my mouth to be polite as they were passing it round, and as the smoke in the room was mainly marijuana, taking one puff wouldn't have made much difference.'

'Oh, yes?'

'That party is the week I get back, just the two of us they want, can't think why, hard work.'

'Trust, that's what it is. Sex, drugs, and rock and roll and we'll keep our mouths shut.' He compared his two pieces of paper. 'I never thought I'd start a list with fifty bunches of spring onions and a box of squid. It used to be a bottle of Scotch and a packet of condoms.'

'This is nice isn't it?' She rubbed his shoulder on the way to the sink. 'You see, New York is an interruption, I can't afford the time with good parties coming in.'

'That's rubbish. And you keep saying me, me, me, and I, I, I, as if Peter wasn't coming back.'

'No. Right. He might not. It suits him, he's getting on well. Marvellous, I think, making a go of it in a foreign country. I admire that.'

Bobby took off his glasses and shook them at her. 'You are the most pathetic bitch I've ever known. You only ever had one good thing happen to you and you talk about it as if it was nothing, a brief fling, nice but unimportant.'

She sniffed and quickly opened the oven door, removing slices of bread. 'Just in time.' Her rolling pin was ready for crumbling the baked bread into crumbs.

He raised his voice. 'A decent man married you when you were a right little scrubber on the slippery slopes to a knocking shop in Soho. You had no friends, no career, no interests. No life outside sleazy dates set up by Patrick.'

'And a few with a vicious criminal pervert set up by you,' she said with a little smile.

'Look at you, you don't even care that I'm slagging you off.'

'I just wish you could have a row and get on with the work as well.' There were only two small parties while she was away, but good smart ones, and she wanted every detail settled.

He put his glasses back on and bent over the lists again. 'He gave you all this, he started the business, saw you weren't a bad cook, sent you to the Cordon Bleu School. He changed your entire life.'

Oh God, he was a bit like Sam. People who hadn't got it in their lives felt safe in the security of yours.

'I don't know, Bobby, I did my fair bit for him. Kept my job as a stand-in to help out. And *his* business was started with a loan from a friend of *mine*.'

He mumbled something that she could only just hear, but it included 'ungrateful cunt'.

'What did you say, dear?'

'I was reading off the list, checking. Honestly, I don't know why you've asked me to do these parties, fancy putting down "Don't forget salt and pepper." You don't trust me.'

'I do it myself,' she protested. 'You can forget the most obvious things. I was doing a dinner in Surrey once, boeuf en croûte. I took everything – everything – except the boeuf!'

'You'd never keep it going, love, him in America, you here.'

'Oh, yes I would. He's been there for over two months now and I've kept it going.'

'Not the fucking business, I'm talking about the marriage.'

She switched on the television set. 'Do you mind,

Bobby? Only I love *Ready Steady Go*, you can shout at me above the music.'

'I will.'

She moved around the kitchen, still working, singing, 'Just a walkin' down the street singing dooh wah diddy diddy dum diddy do'.

'Look, you've been married a long time, haven't you?'

'Yes. Eleven, twelve years, I think.'

'Charming, you don't even know. All I can say is everybody gets a bit bored after a while but it's better than . . .'

'Exactly how long, Bobby, was your longest monogamous relationship?'

'Three weeks. But I'm a poof, and I've never met Mr Right.'

'Neither have I.'

Chopping and grating and whisking, the music was making her do it all too fast. She pushed her fringe out of her eyes. 'I don't know, Bobby, I don't know. All I know is my hand is shaking again like it used to and I want to go out dancing but I like doing the food and I do love Peter. I remember it all but not as if I was there. Especially my twenties, and now they're gone soon. I can't hardly imagine going anywhere, especially New York.'

She put down her whisk and wiped her hands. 'My mum thought that olive oil was a medicine because you could get it at the chemist's. Just as well I got a recipe book or I might have used cod liver oil, it's cheaper. How many cods do you need to get out their livers and extract the oil, do you think?'

He took her in his arms. 'Don't say any more. I'll open a bottle of wine and make us an omelette and a salad. You turn up the sound – look, it's the Searchers – and dance. Go there. Give it a chance. OK?'

It was terrific at the airport. She wore her dark glasses with thick tortoiseshell frames, her nineteen-forties French film-star beret and the white trench coat, very casually belted. People were looking at her. She didn't smile once, not at anybody. They were probably thinking: what is this mysterious woman – a spy? She had taken up being this character when she started driving and had to wear glasses. For the lessons and the test she wore her clear ones but the second she passed she only wore the dark glasses. Even at night. Or in the rain. She had to admit that glasses were a *big* help in catching buses and going to the pictures. Once on the plane with glasses off and coat folded away her mystery vanished, or if anyone was looking at her she couldn't see. Hours and hours. Time to think things through. And sleep a bit. He must think it would work out if he didn't mind them spending money on her going over for a look. He knew *he* liked it, and three months was long enough to weigh the ups and downs. New York together. And if not: home and a successful business. Either way she'd be all right. Lucky. She could remember clear as clear Mum saying, 'It's about time you pulled yourself together and faced facts, what you've got to do, Iris, my girl, is find someone and settle down, you can't leave it all to luck.'

It was just before her eighteenth birthday. Facing facts would take longer than finding someone.

There was absolutely no reason to get into a state. Ten days would be plenty, time enough anyway. Then if there was no message, that was that. It wasn't a crush like on film stars when she was a kid. For once there was someone, if it worked out, who could be a bit of a friend. A man who knew a lot about her and perhaps could be told more. Then between Bobby who had known Steve and all that, and Sam who was from earlier days and home, there would be no need for worrying about things being found out because they would all be known, even if not to the same person. Though it would be a risk telling Michael Upton about the Patrick stuff. Why did he call to see if she was home safely and then not again? Was the home-safely call timed, like her returning the glove, knowing she wouldn't be home? Never mind. Not for now, anyway. Bobby had been told not to answer the phone and not to let the cook, Clarissa, answer it either. The service would pick up and take messages and she would telephone every day and collect them. If by chance Michael called while she was away a man's voice might put him off.

No Peter at the airport, he had said he couldn't, but she'd half hoped. In the crowd getting off the plane someone said the bus to New York was as fast as a taxi, and as her fifty pound limit wouldn't go far she got in the queue for the bus. More of a milling than an orderly line. The peculiar thing was that though people spoke English she hadn't reckoned on so many accents and not always being able to understand. But at least everybody was helpful with the bus and her big suitcase. The customs and immigration people had been nice too. 'Welcome, young lady, enjoy your visit,' that was after they'd seen her return ticket and fifty pounds' worth of dollars.

From the bus station she took a yellow cab. It was the most terrific fun to think that it wasn't eight o'clock but only three, she'd been given five hours as a present! The taxi driver talked a lot, told her everywhere she should go, same as everyone else had said: Staten Island Ferry, Empire State Building, Greenwich Village, Central Park Zoo. It was hot and the air was thick as if you could hold it in your hands, like a clear fog.

He dropped her as instructed at the corner of Seventy-first Street and Columbus Avenue, outside the cleaners where the key would be.

'Careful now. Have a great vacation, but this ain't a real good neighbourhood, a lotta spicks here.'

The man at the cleaners was Italian and all sweet and helpful, he carried her case to the brownstone round the corner where the apartment was. So far all she'd heard about rude New Yorkers was rubbish.

The flat was small but very pretty. All checks and stripes. And a terrace big enough to sit and eat out on, with lots of pots filled with bright plants, mainly geraniums in reds and pinks and oranges. One bedroom, one living-room, kitchenette and bathroom. Absolutely smashing wardrobes, all built in, one like a little room.

Peter hadn't brought much with him so she had plenty of room, even in the bathroom only his toothbrush and toothpowder. It was a bit stuffy and hot. She tried to open the French windows to the terrace but they were either stuck or locked, she made do with the window in the bedroom. He hadn't left a note, so she'd unpack, put everything away, and wait for him to phone. And have a shower, that's what you did in America.

It was strong and powerful, nothing like the pathetic dribbles she'd come across in England. Because of the humidity she finished off with it cold, turned on full blast, it was like being attacked by icy needles. He ought to call any minute now. He knew the time of the plane and how long it took to get in to the city. Made-up, hair brushed and plaited, absolutely ready to dress and go out, she didn't know what to do with the waiting time. The bed was neatly made, coverlet in place, pillows arranged just so, some of them were for decoration, embroidered and lace-trimmed. Lying down wouldn't work, her brain might remember it was five hours later and go to sleep. What she would like was a walk up to the end of the street, have a look at Central Park, and then come back down Seventy-second Street which was supposed to be full of shops, but what if he called? Sod it. It was five o'clock, if he hadn't called by – let's say – six, she would call him. Now would be the right time for his work, after lunch and before cocktails, the cocktail hour. Cocktails in New York. A dry martini. No, Americans all knew exactly what they wanted, a Beefeater dry martini, up, with a twist. Neat, no ice, with a twist of lemon.

It was seven o'clock when the ringing of the

telephone woke her up from a half sleep, her body slumped on the sofa.

'Yes, darling, everything is fine . . . right . . . I'm ready now, waiting . . . of course I want to, I'm not that tired.'

Wearing her glasses, she checked herself in the long mirror in the bathroom. Fine. But she must remember to clean the bath. Or was there a cleaner?

It was quite a discreet entrance to the club. Stone pillars, flowers in tubs, a grey and white awning, luxurious but not flashy. A small brass plate was set in the wall by the door engraved with a stamp, no name. The owner's name was Frank Stamp. Not a name she'd ever believed in. After all, bit of a coincidence, frank meant stamps. She half expected Peter to be inside holding menus, like at Le Routier, but naturally he wasn't because he was the manager.

'This way, Mrs Wimbourne-Smith.'

Bloody hell, Peter might have warned her. Thank God he hadn't elevated her to the peerage. She was shown to a little table by the bar.

'Your husband tells me you like champagne.' The barman was carrying a bottle wrapped in a linen napkin and a flute-shaped glass.

'I do, but as this is my first time in New York I'd like a cocktail, a Beefeater dry martini, up, with a twist, please.'

'Certainly.'

He was pleased to be making a proper drink, she

could tell. He put some crushed ice into a silver cocktail shaker, poured at least a triple measure of gin in it and with an eye-dropper extracted a tiny amount from a bottle of dry Vermouth and let one drop fall into the gin. He put the top on the cocktail shaker and shook it gently with one hand, taking a vee-shaped classic martini glass from the ice-box with the other. He poured the martini into the glass and twisted the finest sliver of lemon peel over the cocktail to release the tiniest amount of oil, then put it into the glass.

'Madam.' He put it on the table in front of her and stepped back, waiting.

She was laughing. 'I've never seen anything like it, you are an artist.' She sipped carefully. 'Perfect. Better than the Ritz. The best.'

'Hey, that's great, it's great to be appreciated.'

There were the usual nuts, crisps, olives, on the table. All of them very good. What was she supposed to do? Drink and wait? Where was he, he knew she hated being in bars and restaurants on her own. She'd put her watch forward to New York time, it was nine o'clock. Only nine? She'd been here for twenty minutes. And it was two a.m. in England. In Fulham.

Don't get ratty, Iris, you don't know why he's kept you waiting. Waiting on my own, for Christ's sake. He works hard here, he told you. The barman brought the rest of the martini to the table. She let him top her up, it would be well diluted by now. What she wanted was to stand in a dignified way and walk slowly out of the room, as if that had always been her plan. Sure, no surprise. Fly to New York, go to an apartment, unpack, have a shower. Get a cab to a club that was managed by her husband who she hadn't seen for two months. Drink two dry martinis and piss off.

'Hello, there you are, Iris.' His arm was around her, helping her up. Helping her too helpfully.

'Peter! There *you* are! Sit down, darling. Where did you think I was?'

She gave him a tight, bright little smile. He sat down, anxious; his eyes flickered around the room, noticing the barman watching, he nodded briefly.

'Peter, long time no see. It's me, see. Iris.'

'Have you had a lot to drink? Did you drink a lot of champagne?' He turned and faced her.

'Hello, Peter, it's nice to see you. No, I did not drink a lot of champagne, I had one excellent Beefeater dry martini, up, with a twist. And don't treat me as if I'm mad or drunk.' She patted his cheek. 'You look good, you've got a bit of a tan.'

'You must be tired,' he said, pulling her firmly to her feet.

'I-am-not-tired. What I am is hungry. And cold. You should do something about the air-conditioning here, it's boiling outside and freezing inside. 'Bye, 'bye,' she waved to the barman. 'Thank you.'

'People expect it.'

'Oh, yes.'

As they walked through the little foyer women were draping jackets or little stoles over their shoulders.

'Where are we going, Peter? What about dinner?'

He relaxed as they turned the corner into Lexington Avenue.

'There's a very good deli on the corner, they do great sandwiches. You'll see, American sandwiches are a meal in themselves. And you can get another dry martini.'

They ran out of conversation after exhausting the flight, the greatness of the pastrami sandwich, and the lethal quality of the martinis because of the high alcoholic content of the gin. They had spoken weekly on the telephone, there was no catching up to do.

'When did we become Mr and Mrs Wimbourne-Smith?'

'You know what they're like, double-barrelled names, it adds a touch of class.'

'You might have warned me.'

'Sorry, yes. I just got used to it.'

The room was full. People eating huge, stacked-high sandwiches like hers, or coffee and cheesecake. Some with beer, smoking. On every table there was bread and jars of different pickles. If you sat at a table out of sight you could make a coffee or a beer last and make yourself a free pickle sandwich. She could see a young couple doing just that. And laughing, their faces close together.

'Why aren't you eating?'

'Look, I've got to get back.'

'What's the matter?'

'Nothing. You're tired. I eat at the club, later.'

'It's like hypnosis, if you go on saying "You're tired, you're tired, you're tired," I *will* be tired.'

'Let it go, Iris, please.'

She nodded politely.

'There's an after the theatre crowd comes in for supper.'

'And you ought to be there?'

'Yuh. I'll pay and put you in a cab.'

There were mints and toothpicks to help yourself to at the desk. She looked back at the young couple, their foreheads were pressed together over a glass with two straws in it. The mints would be their free dessert.

They skirted a big hole in the sidewalk protected by a sign DIG WE MUST FOR GROWING NEW YORK.

'Are they making apartments underground?'

'Come on, the light's green.' He took her hand. 'No, that's Con Ed, electricity cables.' On the other side he let her hand go. 'We'll get a cab going uptown on Madison. Do you need some dollars?'

She put one hand on her hip and held the other out. 'Sure, honey, that'll cost you twenty-five bucks, OK?'

No laugh, no smile. He gave her the money and slammed the door. He was watching the cab join the stream of traffic but when the lights changed and held it up, he turned and hurried away. It wasn't a mystery, he was working hard, and she would have to fit in.

It was still close in the apartment, in spite of leaving the bedroom window open. These French windows weren't stuck, they were locked. From the flat upstairs a little light spilt on to the terrace and the windows in the back of the houses opposite added more. Those pots out there had been watered, there were splashes of water all round them. Somebody upstairs must be doing it, regularly, they were flourishing. Climbing up bamboo sticks, cascading over the sides of the pots, creeping up the trellis, it was lovely. She leaned out of the bedroom window as far as she could, twisting her neck to see the apartment above. There was someone leaning out of the window, smoking.

'Hello. Hello up there,' she called.

'Oh, my God! Wow! You gave me a shock.'

'Sorry. I just arrived. This afternoon. From England. I want to say thank you. You've been watering the plants, haven't you?'

'Yuh. I hated to see them die, nobody's been looking after them.'

'Thanks. Do you know how to unlock those long windows?'

'Well, Chris – it's Chris's apartment, she's in LA for a while – she used to leave the key on the ledge above the window.'

'Hello!'

'There you are. Welcome to New York.'

'How do you do, my name's Iris.'

'Hi, I'm Nadia.'

'How did you reach those tubs at the back?'

'I used a water-pistol.'

'Fantastic! I don't know why my husband didn't know about the key – he's terrific with our garden in London.'

'I didn't know it was rented yet, haven't seen him around or . . .'

'Well, he's working long hours. And I think he might stay overnight at work sometimes.'

'Anything you need to know, I'm your girl. Best breakfast is Nate 'n Eds on Columbus at Seventy-third. Hope you're happy here. Come up for a drink, sometime, OK? Goodnight, Iris. See you.'

The smell of the scented geraniums and something else she recognized nearly drowned the city smell of dustbins, cars and cooking. Maybe only her imagination but all the different cafés, bars and restaurants she had seen added their own flavours: Chinese, Yiddish, Italian, French, and American burgers. Little drifts of different music mingled with sporadic birdsong. The birds were bamboozled by street-lamps into believing in eternal day. Car horns and the screech of brakes faded as she shut and locked the long windows. She put on her glasses and examined the bath, it wasn't dirty, it was dust the shower had disturbed.

The front door closing woke her. He had shut it with care and crept round the apartment with care too as he prepared for bed, but her sleep was shallow enough to be disturbed by a change of air. When he was in bed, turned away from her, asleep, she checked the time, four-thirty a.m.

Nate 'n Eds was like rush hour on the tube. Eating breakfast out wasn't just for the rich or idle, or tourists. There were mothers with babies and schoolchildren, students, old men, very old ladies, workmen. Ordinary people. Eggs: poached, fried, boiled or scrambled whizzed past. Stacks of pancakes, jugs of melted butter and maple syrup. Toast of every description. Sausages, sausage patties and every cereal ever made in individual little boxes. She wanted to join in, her choice of wholewheat toast, orange juice and coffee changed as the waitress stood there, pen poised over her pad.

'Yes, honey?'

She copied the order from the man in the booth behind her. 'Coffee, o.j., bacon, eggs over easy, rye toast, and hold the butter, please.' It sounded utterly daft in her English accent but the waitress said, 'Coming up.'

When it did, 'hold the butter' meant *no* butter, so she wouldn't do that again, it was terrific but tomorrow, o.j., coffee and wholewheat would be enough!

'Hi! Up early!' The tall woman with the neck as long as a giraffe waved as they passed crossing the double width of Seventy-second Street. 'It's Nadia, upstairs. I'm off to class. Teaching. Ballet.' She did a quick little balletic movement and was gone.

Iris hurried to the safety of the sidewalk as the lights, a green man walking, changed to a green man running and then to a red man, static. Out here on the street, full-length, you didn't need to be told Nadia was a dancer.

Added to her note, 'Gone to Nate 'n Eds join me if you wake up, love Eye x,' he had written, 'Call you later,

P x.' And fifty dollars. Poor P x. It must be a woman. But, why ask her to come and then avoid her? So. Nine o'clock here, two in London.

'Yes, Mrs Wimbourne, you have three messages. Bobby called – having a wonderful time glad you are there, Mrs Bucklebury called – suggest meeting on September 22nd, Flower Bowers called – need to talk to you concerning availability of snowdrops. Mrs Wimbourne, hope you don't mind me interposing here, but I am a gardener myself and snowdrops in September, no, my dear, no.'

'I don't mind. Thank you.' Mind your own bloody business. Silly cow. No, sweet really. They were looking for plastic snowdrops for a pre-ski ball. It would be wonderful if they couldn't find them. Vivienne Bucklebury, what did she want? Never mind, the door had been kept open. She must have called this morning. Don't show too keen, call her tomorrow. But what did it mean? Meet, about what? Last time, as usual with clients, they discussed everything on the telephone before meeting.

How long did Peter expect her to sit here and wait for his call? Later. How much later? Did the money mean, look after yourself, I won't be around? Well, get on with things first: make bed, clean bath. It was beginning to get warm, open the windows. Lovely. If she lived here, eating out, just sitting out on this terrace would be perfect. Nadia hadn't watered this morning, she would do that and weed those tubs. The scent wasn't as pronounced yet, it had faded in the cooler night.

Pulling out little tufts of grass and tiny weeds, some hardly rooted, she sniffed. There was something else. There, facing the sun in the corner, was jasmine twining itself round the trellis.

She stood and stretched, pushing her arms up and straightening her fingers. How strange, all this was so pleasing; separate from what had happened in that flat on a Friday twelve years ago, but it was the jasmine here that had recalled it. And it was jasmine that reminded her of Floris in Jermyn Street, and a kitchen with a bath in it in Piccadilly.

The *New York Times* was full of things to do. She sat on a towel in the sun and planned her day. Walk across the park at Seventy-ninth Street to the Metropolitan Art Museum, only look at two painters, about an hour and a half, or she'd get museumitis and feel faint. She could go again another day. Matisse, Nick liked him, all bright colours and patterns. And someone called Sassetta, there had been a book with him at the Albany, not as jolly as Matisse. Perhaps Nick's old painter friend might be in a gallery here. Why not? If the English bought French paintings and the French bought American – why wouldn't Americans buy English? Then walk down Madison Avenue, look at the shops, price the clothes. Bus back, change. Either for dinner with Peter or go to the theatre. A jazz-club was the thing to do here but she'd tried that in London. The jazz was all right but the people – with their air of being in on something far out

– no. Perhaps a sad woman singing sophisticated songs at a piano in a bar, something like that. Nadia would know. Or Paolo at the cleaners.

OK. It was six. On the dot. She'd left the terrace doors as well as the front door open to hear the phone when she went up to see Nadia at about four. So 'later' couldn't be any later than this.

'Hello, may I speak to Mr Wimbourne . . . Mr Wimbourne-Smith, please.'

'Who may I say is calling?'

'It's his wife.' Silly, but she was nervous.

'Hello.'

'It's Iris . . . you said you would call . . . sorry to bother you.'

'That's OK.' It obviously wasn't. She knew it was him, but he could be speaking to a customer.

'So, Peter, what I thought I would do is, go to the theatre, and then have supper.'

'Not here, we're fully booked.' Very anxious, that was.

'That's splendid. No, Nadia, the girl upstairs, suggested a place in the theatre district. Forty-fifth Street . . .'

'Yes.' Oh, anxious first, *now* he was impatient.

'. . . Where we can eat and there's a great singer and a sort of cabaret, political satire. And Paolo, you know, on the corner, where you left the key? He might join us.'

'Good idea.' And now – relief!

'Just one thing, Peter. I didn't come here to go out with a ballet teacher and a dry-cleaner.'

Nothing. No reply. She hung up.

'There is bad, there is good. Al Capone and Fiorello La Guardia. Mostly there is neither. Franco Stambello. He was with one of the families but much in the background. Clever. Eased away when it was useful for him. Just a guess. To understand, Iris, and be understanding with your husband is correct. To ask no questions is to be told no lies.'

'Bullshit.' Nadia took some black olives, popping them in her mouth as she ate the pasta. 'He is making his way for you and your children,' he continued.

'Why do you eat the olives *with* your pasta, Nadia?'

'I need the salt. All dancers do. We sweat. I sweat in class.'

The pasta was good, thick spaghetti with Matriciana sauce – tomatoes, pancetta and chili.

'Does it affect the club, Paolo?'

'No, no, Iris. He is Frank Stamp now, he leave all that behind.'

Nadia took more olives and a chunk of bread which she sprinkled with the grated pecorino left on the table. 'Sure, but everybody's involved somewhere even if they don't know it.'

'Does the Mafia control your ballet shoes?'

Nadia laughed. 'Who knows?'

'It is not so serious. So much fuss. These days it is not so bad. Who notices if they have control of . . .' He shrugged. 'Garbage, laundry, some foods.'

'Olive oil?' She meant it as a joke.

'Naturally.'

In the back room the show was wonderful, rude and sharp. Very funny. Like the revues Bobby used to do in the little theatre off Leicester Square. They mixed everything; rock and roll and politics, fashion and religion. The Beatles had been a big success at the huge Shea stadium, and not only did the cast do them really well but they turned them into Indian and Pakistani people and it was all sad and funny and taught her more than the newspapers about the war. Best of all was President Kennedy and Albert Schweitzer as fallen saints. Nadia and Paolo were quite impressed that she'd been in a night-club with the Beatles and that Ringo had actually said 'Sorry, love' when he bumped into her while dancing.

They walked home, having lemon tea on the way at a little old-fashioned all-night diner on Third Avenue. There were piles of garbage bags stacked around lamp-posts and at every corner. Where the bags were torn and spilling their contents, rats moved, unafraid, foraging for the leftovers from over-filled plates.

'The Mafia hasn't been round yet I see, probably too busy with the laundry.'

Three young men lounging in a doorway watched, sad with envy, when Paolo pulled Iris's hair as she followed Nadia along the street copying her dance steps. The sun was just coming up when they turned the corner into Seventy-first Street.

This was happiness. She loved New York, and she was looking forward to being home too. And both feelings sat comfortably together.

It was Peter's turn to pretend sleep. He didn't move when she slid carefully into bed. He was facing the wall, his body uncurved, permitting of no accidental touch.

The bed was empty when she woke up. At last, some truth between them. She really had been asleep when he left. Today there was no need to bother about 'Call you later', he didn't leave a note. And it was just as well, there would be no time to hang around.

At Nate 'n Eds the atmosphere was calmer, the pace slower. Two hours made quite a difference. Young middle-class women, having given their children over to somebody else for the day, sat together over tea and coffee chatting. Elderly women, hunched and slow with osteoporosis or detached from reality with vacant eyes, were being cared for by black or Hispanic maids and nurses. Two or three men in late middle age were purposefully reading the *Wall Street Journal* while eating their eggs, trying to give the impression that they still had offices to go to.

'You're late, honey. Or is this your day off?'

'Yes, day off. So, I'd like a bagel, cream cheese and lox, please.'

'Coming up.'

*

At the airline office the woman was worried. 'It generally has to be a death in the family or at the very least a fatal illness.'

Iris sighed and shook her head. 'It isn't that, though God knows, I'd like to kill him.'

The woman played with the ticket and passport, examining and shuffling them. 'Oh my, Mrs Wimbourne, as bad as that.'

As she leaned across the counter Iris could see her name tag, CARMEN-MARIE STATZ. Spanish, French, German. Very American.

'You are very peaky under that tan,' she said in a Brooklyn accent which had absorbed all traces of her European antecedents.

Iris leaned forward to meet Carmen-Marie Statz across the counter.

'What's he done?'

'My husband is having an affair,' Iris whispered mournfully.

'Here?'

She nodded.

'On vacation?' she hissed.

Iris nodded again.

'The bastard. All men are bastards, I tell you. I found my husband in bed with my stepdaughter.'

Iris straightened, shocked. '*His* daughter!'

'No. *My* stepdaughter. From another husband.'

'I can't believe it. You don't look old enough to have a stepdaughter.'

'You're sweet. Look, wait here, OK?'

The place was full. The buzz of conversation was like

a geography lesson: Acapulco, Cuernavaca; London; Bath; Toronto; Helsinki; London; Stratford-upon-Avon. Venice. Palm Springs.

Mrs Statz returned. 'Right. I've fixed it. Your mother is threatening to commit suicide, OK?'

'Oh, that's very kind of you. Thank you very much.'

The sunlight penetrated the shutters and the thick pink and white curtains. It was a quarter to seven. She eased out of bed and tiptoed to the bathroom. Her teeth brushed, hair combed and tied back, she put on shorts and a T-shirt, too hot for underwear, and knotted a sweatshirt round her waist for the cool interior of Nate 'n Eds. The front door had two locks and a chain; she undid them and closed the door with an avoidable bang.

He gasped seeing her lean against the door. 'Christ, Iris, you startled me, I could have had a heart attack.'

'If you've got a heart.'

He had pulled yesterday's crumpled clothes on in the bedroom and unwashed and unshaved he looked seedy. 'What . . . what's all this about?' he said lamely.

'I had a lovely birthday – I didn't mind at all being thirty.'

'Oh, sorry.'

'What is it? Darling Peter. Whatever it is it will be all right. You will, I will, or we will. But if you don't tell me . . . well, you can't avoid me until I go home. Something is frightening you and you haven't got the nerve to tell me. Honestly, love, you're a fool. It's very ugly what you're doing. I am all right. But you're lucky that I am.'

'You're very brave,' he said quietly.

'Shall I begin for you?' Iris said. She had always changed types during the course of a day; in the morning, now, his wife was a keen, looking-forward-to-the-day, skinny kid. Then would come the stages of shiny-faced serious cook, a teenage raver dancing to the radio with pigtail flying, ending as a made-up woman of the world.

'OK if I open the French windows?' she said, reaching for the key.

'You can't, they're stuck.'

'I can.' A soft gust of sweet and sour warm air filled the apartment. 'So you have actually been here before?'

'What do you mean?'

'You tried to open the windows and couldn't.'

'I've been here,' he said.

'Not long enough to find the key. You're too old to live like this, Peter. Shall we sit down?' She stood between the glass doors, straight-backed, straight hair, short white shorts, T-shirt and tennis shoes, a scarlet sweater round her neck.

'New sweater?'

'Of course. I spent all the money on clothes, the theatre, museums, eating – on me.'

'Good.'

'I saw the Martha Graham dancers last night, that was my birthday treat.'

He had the same tense little smile. 'Good,' he said again.

'Right,' she said, 'this is what I've figured out. You are having an affair. A very important one. You got me over here to look me over, make sure you were doing the right thing. And if so, telling me in person would be kinder. Ho ho ho. But in between our last talk on the phone and me getting here something else happened. Right?'

The silence in the apartment was punctuated by the squeals and yelps of lap-dogs being led to the park on extended leads, by one person, ten dogs at a time.

'I can't do any more. If you aren't going to speak . . . I'm leaving tomorrow, they were very kind about changing my ticket. I told them you were having an affair and my mum wanted to kill herself. Not connected.'

He sighed, guilty and defensive. 'It happened before you came over. Franco found out – about me and her. Didn't like it. You know the Italians, big family people.'

'Catholics usually do have big families.'

He had been turned away from her, addressing her profile, reflected in a tin-framed Mexican mirror. The little joke surprised him into facing her. 'It was Franco. He told me to get you over. Pronto.'

'Why didn't you tell him to get stuffed? He would have got used to it. Or did he object to her?'

'He doesn't know who it is.'

'Introduce them.'

'They've met.'

She started laughing. 'Wait a minute, wait a minute – how does Franco know?'

'He, well, he heard me on the phone – he bugs them sometimes.'

'Bloody cheek.'

'It's his background,' Peter said apologetically.

'And why didn't he know it was "her"?'

'The bug only picked up outgoing.'

It was pretty nasty all this, he felt bloody stupid. Treating her, his wife, as if she had the pox, and here she was, gentle, figuring it out. By rights, a kick in the bollocks wouldn't have been out of line.

'I think I've got it,' she stepped back on to the terrace holding out her hands. 'Come out here, it's lovely, look at all the geraniums, smell the jasmine.'

He let himself be led into the bright city garden, automatically checking the contents of the pots, tubs and baskets for weeds and blight.

'You would enjoy taking care of this, Peter. You're good at gardening.'

He crouched to feel the earth.

'She works, or helps out – does something – at the club, that's why it wasn't good to have me there. Let me be seen my first day so he knows you've been a good boy, then give me the old heave-ho.'

'Don't put it like that, Iris, I still love you, you know.'

'Yeah, yeah, and my guess is he knows her *very* well. It's his daughter.'

It was a bit sick-making, his silly guilty smile.

'So, let's say, you love me, but face it, Peter, it's for old time's sake.'

'What about you, Iris?'

'Sure. I love you, even if only because you bought a grubby half-blind old woman a Guinness in a pub.'

'Years ago.'

'Exactly. But you are *in* love with her. Well?'

'All right, yes.'

'I'll go and see him today, Franco. Tell him I give you my blessing. We have been drifting apart, etcetera, etcetera. I got on with him fine when we met in London. But – I won't say I know who it is. You want to protect her name – deeply in love – very precious to you – want to take care of her, all that sort of stuff. And you want to marry her.'

He followed her back inside the shaded living-room.

'You do want to marry her?'

'Well, actually, I really ought to. She's pregnant.'

'Has she got morning sickness?'

Surprised, he nodded. 'Yes, pretty badly.'

'Right. There had to be a reason for leaving the marital bed so early. You'd better nip over there then, sharpish, hadn't you? Don't look so pathetic. He'll probably give you the laundry franchise as a wedding present.'

Standing in the queue at the airport, waiting to check in, rubbing her aching shoulder, she decided not having a porter was a false economy. Dragging one heavy suitcase, her shoulder weighed down with an equally heavy one full of her new purchases, could put her out of action for stirring sauces, beating eggs, whipping cream or chopping onions. As the line moved forward a woman in an airline uniform, whose official cute hat perched over one eye made her look like a drunk sergeant-major, appeared examining a clipboard. She moved down the line without taking her eyes off the board, asking everybody, man or woman, 'Are you Mrs Wimbourne?'

'I'm Mrs Wimbourne,' Iris said, holding out her ticket and passport and taking off her dark glasses.

The woman looked at her with grim suspicion. Iris tried to imitate the timid grin of her passport photograph.

'Follow me, please.' She signalled to a porter, who hoisted the suitcases with ease, and flanked by the two of them Iris walked the length of the check-in counters. Where were they going? Had they been tipped off that in her luggage was a bottle of olive oil from the private cellar of a one-time member of one of the East Coast's most feared 'families'? Or had they found out that her mother was never going to commit suicide?

Sitting in the wide comfortable seat by the window, her legs stretched out, her hand picked up first a caviare canapé and then a glass of champagne, Dom Perignon. *The Times*, the *New York Times* and *Harper's Bazaar* were on the unoccupied seat next to her, *Vogue* was on her lap. The only pity was that first class didn't get there any quicker. It must have been Franco. The only other people who knew she was on the plane, going home early, were Bobby, no way he could spring it, and Nadia and Paolo, but they couldn't get you an upgrade on a Greyhound bus. She hadn't told Peter which flight, no weepy goodbyes and guilt, and then relief when she'd gone. Nadia had loved the rope ladder. 'Use it to get down to the terrace, enjoy it, don't just water it. My husband – ex to be – won't be here very much and the lease has at least another six months. I might come back!'

Nothing would make Paolo smile but then there wasn't much emotion he showed between a face of tragedy or laughing like a clown. Short and thin, he was an entirely different type to Franco's box-like hulk. Of course it was Franco who had fixed this, quite bloody right too. Everything had been sorted out by him. Might have known Peter wasn't putting one past him. Of course he knew it was his daughter.

'You didn't know? He didn't tell you? *I* will tell you. It is Graziella, my daughter. You should have come with him, a wife goes with her husband.' Oh, it's all my fault now. Very sentimental but practical too. 'My little girl, my Graziella. She has been married before, poor baby.'

'Divorced?'

'No.' He was offended. 'She is a widow, my little one.'

'Oh, I'm so sorry.'

'He died . . . he died in . . .' Big sad sigh.

'In Italy?'

'No, in prison.'

'Oh, oh, poor thing.'

'My Graziella, my bambina, she won't let another man slip through her fingers.'

Child bride? Teenage widow? 'How old is she, Franco?'

'Thirty-eight.'

Aaah, get the bambino in before it's too late.

'He is good, you know, Iris, at his work, he makes a difference here.'

'Yes, he's always been a hard worker. Ambitious too.'

'That is good. And you, Iris.' He was looking at her, like a generous uncle. 'If harm comes to you – it would be taken care of.' Lovely. At last she'd got a godfather. If she went to China would the Warlords look after her too?

'So. Iris. That is it. All done. Si? I have much respect for you.'

A divorce would be arranged – pronto!

The first class cabin steward moved her newspapers and sat down.

'Sorry to disturb, dear, just wanted to say you're being very, very brave. Putting a very brave face on it. But I can see the pain behind the mask, I've been through the mill myself. I've been dumped on more times than a sailor's toilet.'

She gave him a sympathetic little smile, maybe he had, but then he was as queer as Dick's hat band.

'Don't worry. Mum's the word. I was told to look after you by you know who.'

The 'who' pursed his mouth into a shape ready for a kiss or a clarinet.

She echoed it. 'Who?'

'Carmen-Marie Statz, of course!'

A sliver of canapé went down the wrong way.

'Oh, I've upset you. Shouldn't have mentioned it.'

'No, no,' she choked. 'But if you could get me some water, please.'

'Would you like me to stay the night? You've taken it very well, Iris, but it might hit you when you are alone in your bed, here, where you lived and worked with the man you were married to for twelve years who has left you for a younger woman.'

'Thanks, Bobby, that's really cheered me up. And, by the way, she's an older woman – thirty-eight.'

'Fascinating. Richer too if she's the daughter.'

'Tell you what.' She looked around the immaculate kitchen. 'It would be smashing if you would stay till I went to bed. And thank you for keeping it all so clean and tidy. I'll unpack, tell you all about it and give you your present.'

In the bedroom she shut the wardrobe door on Peter's clothes.

'Is that why you didn't want to go, did you suspect?'

'No. I wanted to leave everything as it was. A pause. Wait and see. No decisions, let it ride.' She shivered. 'It's freezing after New York. Here, this is for you.'

She tossed him a Bergdorf-Goodman box, beautifully wrapped.

'Bobby, do you know what Steve really died of? Don't know why but I was frightened when he died. What would the others do? It was only him who kept an eye out for me. Me and mine.'

'I'm unwrapping this slowly to make the most of it, like undressing sloowly before a – Oh, fabulous! Too much.'

'It's fun, isn't it?'

'Gorgeous softest cashmere, but made like a sweat-shirt. Give me a hug, girl, I love it.' He lay back on the bed holding the soft sweater to his cheek. 'The word about Steve is that Artie killed him.'

'Artie? He adored Steve.'

'Who knows, but Artie is the only Brown who's straight. What if he saw him up to something, Steve wasn't always too careful. And those three goons with Artie aren't there to protect him, they're there to stop him. That's what's said. And he was the one who found him.' He jumped to his feet. 'A drink, darling? Little sandwich?'

'Only a small glass, I drank quite a lot on the plane.'

He handed her a small glass of champagne. 'Welcome home. You know, all the brothers were grateful for you looking after their mother. All the brothers respected you.'

She wasn't too sure how much she valued all this respect; theirs or Franco's. 'Next time you go to Morocco, I think I'll come with you. I miss Nick.'

The three days stolen from New York enabled her to tidy up and divorce herself from her husband's clothes. A new figure in her life, Barney Klein, an American lawyer, was effecting the divorce from the man himself. On transatlantic telephone calls, it was all arranged. No, she would *not* be the guilty party. But in exchange for that she would *not* be asking for any alimony. She would keep the flat and take over the mortgage. Apart from that she didn't give a toss where the divorce happened. A few things she sent to him, quite a lot was taken to the charity shop and the rest was thrown away. The big things had been easy but the bits and pieces were a reminder of the daily loss of his presence: a comb with a few hairs, an old wallet, a broken pen. Chucking those felt like an act of aggression. Every day she did something, like in New York. At a small gallery in Bruton Street she saw a Matisse alone in the window. Only a drawing but she liked it.

'Madam, may I help?' Dignified and discreet, an elderly man approached her.

'I would like to see the Matisse.' She pointed to the window.

'Are you interested in it?'

'I couldn't afford to buy it but I would like to see it.'

A bit of nerve went a long way.

He took it out of the window, set it up on an easel and talked about it. Like a nice little lesson.

Bobby took her dancing again, and she even had breakfast out, at Fortnum and Masons. Not as good as Nate 'n Eds. Maybe she would open a diner, Sam 'n Iris.

Then she called Michael Upton. She hadn't opened the little parcel immediately, addressed to Mrs Peter Wimbourne, c/o Full Course; she presumed it was to do with business and put it aside. It was a pair of gloves, a woman's version of his, cream suede lined with cashmere. 'DON'T SCRATCH. DR UPTON.'

His answering service picked up.

'No, no, no message. When do you expect him back?'

Around the twenty-second of September, when she was meeting – Vivienne Bucklebury. Had he been there, staying with his sister?

Sunday was lunch with Sam. He had finally moved the barge up near Warwick Avenue, Little Venice. And he'd got a new job. He was silent when she told him about the divorce, then just gave her the directions how to get there, adding, 'Take care.'

There were three barges in the stretch of canal he'd described. None brown and none called *The Barge*. From the bridge she sized them up – which would be his? Two were red and green, typical bargee's colours. MAID MARY OF TEDDINGTON painted with many a flourish and a curlicue. Another one red and green, but faded old paint, wooden flower-boxes, not much in them and a child's tricycle tied to the roof. FAIR MAID OF FAREHAM. The third wasn't the traditional colours. Blue and white, decorated with large bright red tulips. Tubs on the roof were full of tulips too, they must have been plastic. MAID AVAIL PADDINGTON. It could be any of them. She remembered the barge's brief existence as MAID OF WOOD. So, *not* MAID AVAIL, too jokey, drew attention, he'd learnt that. Got it. FAIR MAID OF FAREHAM. Who would bring a barge all the way from there, near Portsmouth, and how, even if there was a canal there, which she doubted. The tricycle was a nice touch.

Annie was there doing the lunch. 'Roast pork and three veg,' she said proudly. Over her long pink muslin dress she was wearing one of Sam's old sweaters, her curly red hair bouncing as she moved. Confident, she gave Iris a blissful smile.

'Tell her about your job.'

'Yes, go on, what is it?'

'I'm running a small transport caff outside Paddington Station.'

'Walking distance from here,' Annie added.

'You can't cook.'

'Neither could you till you met Peter and started the business.'

'True. What do you do? What's on the menu?'

'Well, the usual rolls and sandwiches, ham, egg, sardine. And everything hot I fry. I only cook stuff that can be fried. So I put it on, eggs, sausages, black pudding, bacon, kidneys, bread, and I fry it till it's done.'

Annie was gazing at him as if he was Escoffier.

'How do you know when it's done?' Iris laughed.

'Someone shouts, "I don't want a burnt offering" – and I take it off and serve it. You can laugh, it's all right, it's a useful skill. I can do it anywhere. What with that and the barge we're free, see, move around when we want to. Travel.'

After lunch they walked on the towpath round the canal into Regent's Park, near the zoo. Annie went ahead, throwing stale bread into the water, leading a flotilla of ducks, mallards, grebes and two beautiful but aggressive swans.

'I only need to know that you're all right, Iris. You look . . . you *are* all right, aren't you? I can tell. Put on a bit of weight and a nice bit of colour. It was out of line, him and that photo . . . I should've taken your side.' It was an apology. Not easy for him.

'Everything is fine, Sam, it's sorted itself out. The way he did it in New York was unkind, but so what, it makes it easier. And I still had a good time there. And I still care about him. But that life in the club, dancing attendance, that's not the job for me. I don't want to be beholden any more, to the likes of Steve and Franco.'

Annie crouched at the edge of the water surrounded by the water fowl backing and advancing to the bread in her outstretched hands.

'Isn't she lovely?'

'Yes, well, we're not getting married.'

'Of course not, love.'

'Right, remember that,' he said firmly.

'She's too young.'

'Oh, do you think so? She's mature for her age.'

'Mum thinks so.'

'When did she say that?' He was angry. 'She never said it to me.'

'I saw them after Peter left before I went to New York. Didn't do any good, that move to Ruislip.'

'There are money-lenders everywhere, Iris, wherever anyone's short of a bob or two.'

'Do you know, the tube even goes to Chancery Lane? Direct! Dad and I walked round the corner to get the paper and some fags, that's when I gave him a few quid, as we passed the station, I said, "That's handy, does it go to Chancery Lane?" Joke, that's all. He said, quick as a flash, "Eighteen stops."'

'We're too old, Iris, to worry about them any more.'

'No. Marvellous, isn't it? They never change. I gave her some cash secretly in the kitchen and she was going on about "next door" being noisy. "Which side?" I said. "One side has the telly on too loud and the other side has six kids." She doesn't even know their names!'

Annie stood suddenly, backing away from the swan who was menacing her, his wings stretched like a wall of feathers. Sam sprinted to her side, putting his short boxy body between the swan and the girl. Iris laughed as he shooed the bird back into the canal.

'Get off, bastard, leave her alone!'

Not getting married?

Chapter Fourteen

'It's Vivienne.' That was all she said. Like those people who said 'It's me' on the telephone. How did she know that there weren't more Viviennes in her life? Vivienne Clark? Vivienne Burton? Vivienne Evans? There weren't but she didn't know that.

It was tea this time, at the Hyde Park Hotel. The usual reason for a meeting, unspoken, was to make sure she looked passable. Clean. Not an embarrassment if stumbled on in the kitchen by a guest. And then under the influence of a drink and the warmth of a temporary friendship she might be persuaded to reduce the price. Strictly speaking this meeting wasn't necessary. Vivienne was aware of her cleanliness and resistance to lowering the price.

The table was in a corner, partly shielded by a large palm tree. She wasn't alone. Through the fronds of the palm she could see another woman.

'Hello, Iris, this is my friend Judy. She is staying here.'

Vivienne's friend was a carefully made-up woman, with rather a sweet face, little turned-up nose and softly waved brown hair. After the greetings and 'How are yous' and 'Isn't autumn a wonderful time of year' and 'New York must be having an Indian summer', they admired her skin, 'Golden brown not that walnut look, not grilling yourself like a crème brulée.' Little laughs, pouring of the tea, one Ceylon, one Earl Grey, one Lapsang Souchong. Waving away the cake and sandwiches with thin white hands, third fingers on the left hands wearing simple wedding rings guarded by engagement rings: one a square cut diamond, the other an oblong blue sapphire. That was the preliminaries done. Now, what did she want? Or they. It might be something complicated or bigger than she was used to. A charity do with a 'royal'? They would use a lot of pressure about the cost for that, comparing estimates. 'Oh, the opportunity,' they would say, 'some would pay *us* for the chance.'

'Did you see that article in *The Times*, or maybe it was the *Telegraph*: Today's Women?' Vivienne said. 'Everybody talks and writes about our freedom. The pill. Sex without guilt, sex without responsibility. I feel sorry for young girls today, really young I mean. We are still young, not as young as you, Iris, but not forty thank God.'

Was all this chat going to lead up to business? Was this part of what ladies up from the country did? Buy themselves inappropriate clothes from Biba, something short and revealing, and something much more suitable from Hardy Amies. See the latest play at the Royal Court, perhaps only half of it, and leave in the interval. Dine at a reasonable hour at a posh trattoria where they pretend to be pleased with the effusive welcome from demonstrative waiters. Have a massage and facial at Countess Von Ripoff's the next day and be conned into buying face creams that would delay – if not halt – the effects of age.

'How do girls say no these days? It must be frightfully difficult for prostitutes, men can get anything they want for nothing. They don't even treat ladies like ladies.'

Judy gave a flat humourless laugh, but after a tut-tut and a shake of the head there was a surprisingly hearty laugh from Vivienne.

'It is easy for us to be amused, but I don't suppose you . . .'

The laugh had stopped, replaced by a sympathetic smile.

'. . . Well, you might not find it quite as funny.'

Judy's little white hand reached for the delicate white and gold cup. Vivienne stretched towards Iris, making a soothing gesture. Why wouldn't she like a bit of a laugh?

'I know it's a long time ago, but you must have gone through absolute hell.'

She shrank from the hand, hovering, waiting to land somewhere. On her shoulder? Her arm? Maybe the little white hand would come to rest on her wide, strong, brown hand.

'Hell?' To avoid any sympathetic pat, she herself poured more tea and settled back in the chair holding the cup and saucer. She wasn't going to help. They knew something but it might not be *it*.

'You were a child, only seventeen I think.'

How did she know? Had she said something at the party, 'It's my thirtieth coming up'? And then, would

Vivienne remember the date of the Pilsherd wedding? And did she know it happened the day before? No, ridiculous, it must be something else. The other woman, Judy's, face was tilted to one side avoiding them.

'Extraordinary to think of what men are capable of.'

That was it then. She knew.

'Animals,' Judy shuddered.

But what did they want? A bit of gossip over the tea table? Who had told her? Not Michael.

'Beastly trick with the window. Five? Or was it six men?'

She closed her eyes and forgetting the cup on her lap covered her mouth. The little cup and saucer fell on the carpeted floor, the saucer was intact, the cup broken in two. Iris ignored it.

Vivienne picked them up. 'Shall I get you another?'

'No. Please don't. I would like to go.'

'No.' Judy stood abruptly. 'Let's go to my room.'

'I don't think so,' Iris said. 'I don't want to.' Bloody cheek. I'm not seventeen now, I'm a successful person in business.

Now they sat, sympathy gone, two practical women, talking to somebody who could do something for them. Cook a dinner? Sure. Give evidence in a divorce case? Fine. Judy Pilsherd was unhappily married, as who would not, being married to Johnnie Pilsherd. Both of them wanted a divorce, both had evidence of adultery. At stake were money, children and houses. Money? Lady Pilsherd's father had that. Children? She was bound to get them, women always did. But house? Pilsherd House and the position it conveyed was what she wanted. And so did Johnnie. Raping a seventeen-year-old the day before marriage, the day before he plighted his troth? That should certainly make her the aggrieved party regardless of her own adultery.

'You want me to give evidence in court. I couldn't. It's my past. No. I can't.' It would affect everything. It would be in the newspapers. Photographs. Victim of a gang-bang. 'I know I couldn't go through with it. Not in front of law people asking questions, and judges. And his lawyers, saying I was lying, they would ask, you know, details. No.'

They were looking at her all cold and calculating, she knew what they were thinking. She asked for it, little scrubber. Oh God. Let them not take away her lovely life.

'How do you know, please?' She hated herself for the shaky voice and the 'please'.

'My brother told me, after all, he *was* there wasn't he? Little beast.'

So it was Richard, you wouldn't refer to Michael like that. Did they look alike this family? Richard with the more obvious good looks, sleepy sexy eyes, disarranged thick hair, though the looks weren't so apparent in a drunken stupor. Vivienne was attractive too, especially with the sharp blonde bob, and Michael, leaner, more lined, but . . .

'I'm sorry, I have to go.'

'Oh dear, you are a stubborn little thing, isn't she, Vivi?' Judy Pilsherd spoke briskly. 'You don't have to worry about the cross-examination, you will be briefed. We will have solicitors, a barrister, all that sort of thing.

You will be taken through everything they might say, all the accusations. They will probably say you were paid for it, that you were willing . . .'

'Judy, honestly, hardly the way . . .'

'. . . But you just stick to your story and everything . . .'

'It isn't a *story*, Lady Pilsherd,' Iris said. 'I was raped by five men. I was seventeen and I was a virgin.'

'A rare commodity. Do you know that joke, Vivi? If you could put every virgin in London in a telephone box I wouldn't be at all surprised.'

Neither Iris nor Vivienne laughed.

'Did I miss a bit out?'

'Don't you see, it would be like a second rape, another rape, and, oh, this isn't maybe as bad but people would know. It could affect me getting work.'

'Why?' Vivienne was surprised. 'You're a cook. Nobody knows who you are or what you look like. You work in a kitchen.'

'Yes, that's right,' Judy joined in. 'And we could help you get work.'

'No. It's not possible.' She stood up feeling a little faint.

'Sit down.' A sharp tug at her sleeve pulled her back down to the chair. 'You don't understand, Iris, you have no choice; either you give your evidence voluntarily or I will have you served with a subpoena – do you know what that means?'

This was easier, more straightforward. There had been a threat lying around through the whole talk and this was it.

'I do, Judy. Not much point in being thirty if you haven't learnt anything.' And no point in being tearful and shaky, she could take that home and be frightened in private. Before she told her how she knew what a subpoena was it was worth trying something else. 'Are you sure that *you* want all this in the newspapers?'

'Nine days' wonder, less, I should think. Five pathetic drunk young men, on a spree, a stag night.'

'Ah, but Judy, under cross-examination I would be pressured to tell what Johnnie said about you. How he had been after me for months – all through your courtship.'

Judy shrugged dismissing it.

'Then there's his affair with that model girl – all through your courtship. What he said about how he'd shut his eyes and think of Yvonne de Carlo, after you were married.'

She was only a bit peeved, nothing to put her off. She probably shut her eyes too when they were doing it and thought of Jack Palance. Vivienne was enjoying it, the jibes, a nasty little sneery smile was crinkling her eyes.

It was time to use her ace in the hole. This once and never again.

'A subpoena.' Iris sat up primly, her hands folded in her lap, she addressed the two women as if giving a lecture. 'It is a writ issued by a court to a reluctant witness ordering their presence, with a penalty for failure to appear. The reason I know this is . . .'

She was interrupted by Judy. 'I am not particularly interested. It means you would be treated as a hostile witness and the questioning could be very unpleasant from both barristers.'

Very cold all this. No care for her, but no care for the children or families of the other men, either, and the divorce would happen anyway.

'You see, unlike you and Vivienne, I have friends in low places. Here. And in New York. And those friends have friends . . .'

'It sounds very dramatic.' Vivienne was amused. 'What could these friends do?'

'They don't like anybody shitting on their mates.'

She felt a little icicle stab of fear as she remembered the odd phrases over the years. 'You can call on us brothers any time, for anything.' 'You'd never know, Iris, who done it.' 'A little fire, a broken arm.' 'Anything you need, Iris, bella, we take care of it.' 'If I get to hear of you being done wrong by anyone I would arrange to have them taken care of.' 'It's a long-term contract, Iris, it lasts for ever.'

'And if anybody does, they sort them out. Violently. And I wouldn't even need to ask. You would be advertising the fact. And I wouldn't be able to stop them. I couldn't do anything about it.'

It should have been necessary to raise her voice to be heard above the sounds of the rush hour, but Michael bent his head towards her and she continued in the same anxious low tone. 'They bear grudges even unto the fourth generation. That's what Steve said to me once. They're all stark raving mad, of course.'

He took her hand. 'Thank goodness I saw you, I'm glad you didn't take a taxi or I would have missed you.'

'I wasn't about to tip the doorman, just for opening the door. I too am glad, Michael.'

The second she had heard him call her name she had jumped off the bus, dodging the slow-moving traffic, and ran to meet him.

'Look, I won't go on and on about it – Oh, did you notice that's the first time I've called you by your name – I only talked of me and me and me last time, but I don't understand why, after all these years, he told her.'

'It was my fault.'

'No, when Vivienne said her brother had told her, it could have been her big brother, you, but I knew it wasn't.' She squeezed his hand, smiling up at him. It was charming, her undisguised affection, but not without problems.

'I wanted to do something for you, "stand up for you" as you said nobody had. I drove out to see Richard a couple of days after we met. I don't know what I had in mind. He was there at home in his study, smoking a cigar, drinking whisky. Miranda was somewhere in the house with the children, I could hear voices. He can't be much older than you, five years? But he is a middle-aged, paunchy, smug stockbroker. We don't meet except on family occasions so he was surprised at my arrival. Off his guard. There wasn't time to speak to him . . . I was enraged at the thought of it all . . . this disgusting man . . . not only that he raped you, a little of that, maybe, I could understand, you are beautiful and he wanted you, and drunk . . . but trapping you and letting others . . . and watching . . .' He released her hand, afraid of hurting it in his grasp. 'I hit him, without saying anything, he fell, knocking over a chair and a lamp, the drink and cigar still in his hands. He was astonished, didn't even try to get up. I left, passing Miranda in the hall running to the study. I called him the next day and told him why. But I didn't say why it had taken thirteen years.'

They had been walking away from the Ritz across Green Park towards Buckingham Palace.

'I wouldn't mind sitting down, my feet are killing me.' The heels of her shoes weren't very high but the toes were narrow and pointed.

'Are those stiletto toes as opposed to heels?'

'Well, I thought I was going out to tea, didn't I, not for a walk.'

All the benches in the park were empty, it was too late and too cold for them to be occupied by the usual old men reading the paper, old women feeding the pigeons, tourists reading their maps.

'This one?' He guided her to a bench flanked by a rubbish bin and a street-lamp. 'It's cold, that's why I'm putting my arm round you.'

'If you say so.'

The few people in the park were walking purposefully, going home, crossing paths, heading for Queen's Walk, the Mall, Constitution Hill. In the yellowy fog-coloured lamplight her face was like a drawing of bones before the addition of muscles and flesh tones. He drew his finger along the clean cut jawline. She frowned.

'What? What is it?'

He took his hand away.

'It must be so much easier to get married or have an affair,' she said, 'if you all grew up knowing about the same things and people. For both high and low I mean.'

'Did you, Iris?'

'No. I married a stranger. Did you?'

He tightened his embrace, pulling her a little closer. 'Yes. She lived a few miles away. We were invited to the same dinners and parties, we danced at the same night-clubs in London. Had it not been for the war I would have been up at Oxford with her brother.'

'What did you talk about? The war?'

'Friends. What they were doing, in the war, for the war effort, what would happen after the war.'

'Go on,' she urged.

'Do you want the story of my life?'

'It's a bit cold for the whole forty-five years, but you could fill me in with a few high spots – oh, I'm sorry, what a thing to say.' She wriggled away and stood. 'Sorry, I'm so clumsy, just when you're remembering.'

It was difficult, she was right. Alone in his flat, isolated out here, with her wounds to talk about and his sibling's part in the act, there was a mutual memory, but . . . 'I'll do five years now and save the other forty for another time.' He lowered his head to her face and laughed.

'What?'

'I was going to kiss you but in the light from the lamp your mouth has vanished.'

'Oh, my lips always pop inside or shrink or something when they're cold.'

From Parliament Square they heard the chimes of Big Ben.

'Nine o'clock.'

'Have you turned into a pumpkin?'

'No. Into a cook. I've got a party tomorrow evening. Lots of preparation. If we walk over to Grosvenor Place I can get a taxi down the Kings Road home.'

He adjusted his stride to her geisha-like hobble. 'Feet OK?'

'Just.'

'We married after the war. Neither of us had met anybody else. It was fine. Two children, my work, the house. Friends. Then after a few years it wasn't enough. The relationship had been based on lust and affection. When only affection was left we started living discreet separate lives. When she was ill we both lived in London. That was for her treatment and where her boyfriend lived.'

'All sad.'

'Not all. And that was then.'

They were opposite St George's Hospital where they crossed the road. Had his wife been here? More likely the one in Brompton Road.

'Let's have a quick drink, rest your feet, and then I'll put you in a taxi. There's a pub round the corner in Halkin Street.'

'Yes.' Her face brightened. 'Lovely.'

The pub was busy and noisy. They stood near the bar drinking warm gin, the request for ice being considered bizarre, and the tonic forgotten.

'Whereabouts do you suppose swinging London is?'

'Ah, well, it's where I am cooking tomorrow evening. Dinner for a rock group and beautiful blondes.'

'Will you be all right alone this evening, after the horror of Judy and Vivienne?'

'As long as I know we have a date.'

'Very American. The day after tomorrow?'

He spoke to the driver when she was settled in the back of the taxi and gave him some money. A note. Going down Kings Road she checked the window of Mary Quant's shop, Bazaar. Maybe she was a bit old now for those clothes but being slim she might risk another couple of years. Outside the flat the driver turned to speak to her. 'He give me too much, miss, even with a handsome tip.'

'No, that's fine. You keep it. Goodnight.'

The kitchen table and every surface was stacked with used plates and dishes, the sink was full of pots and pans and the dirty glasses were soaking in two bowls of soapy water. The problem of having only the two of them meant no clearing away could be done during the meal. They had all trooped upstairs after dinner, four musicians and girlfriends, two other men and girlfriends. Two large trays with coffee and tea were ready to take up. On another tray was a long plate of home-made petits fours and in a shallow bowl were pieces of hash brownies also home-made, but not at her home.

'We can't join in, Bobby, honestly, we're not going to add much.'

'Maybe they'd like us to watch.'

Iris laughed. 'Me? All shiny, fingernails stuck with marzipan, and I'd have to wear my glasses. And you? A poof?'

'I wouldn't mind seeing *him*, that's a lovely bum and he's known for having the cock of death.'

'I don't think they mean that, I think they mean would we like to join them for coffee after – that is, if they are actually having an orgy.'

'Well, he said they'd like coffee now. It's all the rage, Iris, alternative charity dos, Excuse me orgies, Old Tyme Night, only the missionary position, Fancy Dress Fucks.'

It was all very businesslike. They were sitting around watching a film made for their latest album, and although the music was really wonderful and great for dancing nobody moved. It could have been a board meeting of bankers, Iris thought; serious discussions, arguments, criticism and compromise.

Down in the kitchen, finishing the clearing up, they could hear the music. 'Just as loud as upstairs, wonderful! It must be piped all over the house.'

'Please don't groove, Iris, or bop, or jive, you'll drop the mousse or break a dish.'

She danced around the long table, wrapping food and stacking plates. 'I'm only doing this till the music stops. Then we're going home and eating the leftovers and drinking nice wine.' She shuffled across the floor imitating Chuck Berry.

'Why are you in such a good mood, girl? No answer?

I am going to voice my suspicions – don't – don't – breathing on glasses is unhygienic.'

'Only if you are unhygienic yourself.'

'Anyway, *you* have met someone. Don't deny it, my name isn't Brighton for nothing. Bright by name, bright by nature.'

'I'm not denying it. Here, catch.'

He caught the tart, wrapped thank God, that she'd spun at him like a discus.

'I see a bed sore and I want it painted black,' she sang as he put the bread in a basket.

'Who is it then? Did you meet him in New York? What does he do?'

'Right, that's it, the music has stopped. Let's go. One: he's an English gentleman. Two: no. Three: translates pop lyrics into Urdu. Exports hats to Mexico for people to dance on. Are you ready?'

'Yes.'

'Open the door for me, please, I'm loaded up.'

'So it isn't serious?'

'No. I'm hoping it's going to be jolly. I don't want to get married.'

In the van, driving along the nearly empty Embankment before turning into Lots Road past the power station, she was quiet.

'Why don't you want to marry him?'

'He isn't suitable, Bobby, he comes from a very bad family. I don't even want to live with him, so you're not to be jealous, we'll still go dancing.'

'Good.' He gave her a quick peck on the cheek. 'What do you like about him, then?'

'Oh, the usual. Plenty of hot water and he changes his shirt every day.'

It was six o'clock. They were ready to go out. Michael was in a dark grey suit, white shirt and navy tie. She was wearing a black fine wool suit with a short skirt; a sheer black chiffon top showed in the vee neck of the jacket and a string of large obviously false pearls sat above that. The contrast of the sophisticated clothes with her long plait made her look like two people, as if a girl's head had been grafted on to an adult's body.

'What would you have done if it had been an orgy?' he asked, concerned.

'Washed up and gone home.'

They sat facing each other across the room, seated formally, addressing each other with undue attention, like first arrivals at a party.

'The sort of things I usually talk about are: shows and dancing with Bobby, we go to the theatre as well.' She spread her arms to indicate the breadth of her interests. 'Work mainly it was with Peter; food, ideas for menus, he was excellent at that sort of thing.' She stood but remained by the armchair. 'Then absolute codswallop with acquaintances, "Where were you when Kennedy died," "Why do you cook foreign muck," "The Beatles have degraded the honours list." Clothes and men with June LeSage. Mum, I discuss with Dad. Dad, I discuss with Mum. And I go down memory lane with my brother Sam.'

She was using her best accent, he noticed. 'What about Nick Wytham? Did you have another compartment for him?' Was that what she wanted now that he was gone, living in Morocco? Would he replace Nick as a friendly safe escort?

'Oh, yes. All sorts of stuff. Sex and crime, and politics and books, heraldry and the Commonwealth and he was so bloody rude. I've walked out on him many times.' She eased her feet out of her shoes. 'I got out of the car on a lonely country lane once after he gave me a terrible bollocking. He whizzed off. Past midnight. No street lighting. I was terrified.'

'But he came back?' He watched her unbutton her jacket.

'No.'

'My God, what a shit!'

'No, he wasn't.'

Sweet of her to defend him, and foolish to feel jealous of her interest in an ageing homosexual.

'He had meant to circle round and come back up the lane behind me where he knew I would flag down any car for a lift. Then he would tell me off for taking a lift from a stranger. But he got lost, and by the time he sorted it out, I *had* taken a lift from a stranger.'

Michael frowned. 'Not a good idea.'

'Would you believe it?' she went on, removing her jacket and draping it on the back of the armchair. 'It was a nice young couple, very pretty, both of them, all flower-power and long hair, both of them. Love-is-all-you-need types and the car reeking of marijuana.'

The sheer chiffon disclosed the fact that she wasn't wearing anything underneath it. 'And *they* told me off for accepting a lift from strangers.'

She reached round the back of her skirt, undid the zip and stepped neatly out of it, placing it over the jacket.

'What are you doing?'

She held out her hand. 'I'm seducing you. I hope. I thought it would be better to make love before dinner, I don't want you kissing me for the first time with spinach in my teeth.'

She lay sprawled across him, sighing.

'What is it, sweetheart?'

'Darling, Michael,' she whispered in his ear. 'I'm hungry. Have you got anything in your fridge?'

'Something, yes. Eggs, cheese, butter. Things like that.'

She was up and gone. He woke to the sound of running water.

'What are you doing?'

She was sitting in the bath, her plait anchored to the top of her head by a skewer and a fork. A plate was sitting on the bath rack in front of her. 'I'm peeling mushrooms. I'm beginning to see the point of having a bath in the kitchen.'

Wearing the white shirt he had taken off last night under her black jacket removed the evening look of her clothes and compensated for the strappy high heels.

'Good morning, Mrs Wimbourne.'

'Good morning.'

It was a different porter, how did he know her name?

'Do you need a taxi?'

'No, I'm walking, thank you.' It might have been a different porter since last night but they all colluded, sharing information and gossip. What would this man say to the other porter when they changed shifts?

'That young lady-friend of Mr Upton's left early this morning.' It would be an unimportant detail, part of twelve hours coming and going. The Albany was occupied by people so grand and important that she was only a tadpole in a pond.

In Piccadilly she crossed over at the Ritz and in Green Park sat on a bench to change her shoes, substituting the tennis shoes in her handbag for the high heels. The sky was pale grey, with rain just beginning to fall. The loose change and crumpled notes he had left on a chest of drawers with a comb and his keys she had left untouched. She could afford a taxi anyway. To walk back to Fulham was a choice. Outside the tube station she bought a *Manchester Guardian*. He read the *Telegraph*. As she fished the pennies from her purse, she smiled and said, 'We are not really suited.'

'Miss?' The newspaper seller wasn't surprised.

'Thank you.' She took the newspaper, folded it and tucked it under her jacket. It was raining quite hard.